Pra

"Great start of a new series featuring rival ranching families."

—*Fresh Fiction* on *Dark Side of the River*

"Daniels always nails it with her well-developed plot."

—*A Midlife Wife* on *River Justice*

"Daniels is a perennial favorite, and I might go as far as to label her the cowboy whisperer."

—*BookPage*

"Another ingenious plot from a grand author who deftly takes us along for the ride."

—*Fresh Fiction* on *Under a Killer Moon*

"I highly recommend this novel to readers who enjoy contemporary romantic suspense with great characters."

—*One Book More* on *Out of the Storm*

"Super read by an excellent writer. Recommended!"

—Linda Lael Miller, #1 *New York Times* bestselling author, on *Renegade's Pride*

"Will keep readers on the edge of their chairs from beginning to end."

—*Booklist* on *Forsaken*

RIVER LEGACY

Also by B.J. Daniels

Powder River

Dark Side of the River
River Strong
River Justice
River Wild

Buckhorn, Montana

Out of the Storm
From the Shadows
At the Crossroads
Before Buckhorn
Under a Killer Moon
When Justice Rides
Out of the Blue
Before Memories Fade

Harlequin Intrigue

A Colt Brothers Investigation

Murder Gone Cold
Sticking to Her Guns

For additional books by B.J. Daniels,
visit her website, bjdaniels.com.

BJ DANIELS

RIVER LEGACY

CANARY STREET PRESS

CANARY STREET PRESS™

Recycling programs
for this product may
not exist in your area.

ISBN-13: 978-1-335-50817-1

River Legacy

Canary Street Press
22 Adelaide St. West, 41st Floor
Toronto, Ontario M5H 4E3, Canada
CanaryStPress.com

Printed in U.S.A.

I dedicate this final book of the Powder River series to my agent, Lisa Erbach Vance, for believing in this story. Thanks for helping make my dreams come true. You're the best!

RIVER LEGACY

PROLOGUE

THE EXPLOSIVE DEVICE fit in his jacket pocket securely as he walked toward the hangar where he would find the Gulfstream G550 waiting. Still, he unconsciously walked more carefully knowing it was in his pocket. Would hate to trip and fall.

Not that it would be a huge explosion. The nice thing about an airplane, even an expensive private jet owned by one of the richest men in the country, was that it didn't take much to bring the bird down. It was all about knowing where to place the bomb—and when to detonate it.

Inside the hangar, he quickly secured the bomb in place. He'd helped work on this particular jet before, since along with his side job, he was one damned good airplane mechanic as well as a pilot. Not that his boss seemed to appreciate the fact. Hell, he'd wanted to kill him the moment he met the man.

When he finished, he set the timer on his phone. All it would take was pushing the button after the plane was airborne and over an isolated part of Montana on the return flight.

He'd already located where outside of Billings

would be the best spot for the plane to explode. There was a roadless mountainous area directly to the southeast. It would be hard for the FAA investigators to reach it and recover any evidence. No need for any rescue operations. No one would survive the blast, let alone the crash.

The dangerous part was that he would be onboard the plane with the bomb from Dallas to Billings. But as long as he didn't push the button, he told himself, he'd be fine.

No one wanted Forester dead more than he did. Then again, maybe there were a dozen others who would love to kill the man, he thought, looking around the unlocked, empty hangar. Except, he'd bet most of them didn't know how to make a bomb, let alone where to place it on an airplane for the most destruction. He'd be doing them all a favor.

Phone in his pocket, now all he had to do was wait for when the Gulfstream left Billings, Montana, for the return flight to Dallas—the flight he wouldn't be on.

CHAPTER ONE

RYDER STAFFORD TUGGED down the brim of his Stetson, keeping his head lowered, as he wound through the crowd at the Billings Logan International Airport. The name made it sound much more impressive than it was. For the largest city in Montana, the airport was small compared to others in the state.

Normally, it also wasn't this busy, but apparently some politician was flying in for a rally later tonight. Usually, the only time the state saw big-name politicians was when one of them was running for president.

Traffic would be terrible until Ryder got out of the city, he thought with regret. But he planned long before any rally began to be miles from here before that. He couldn't wait to get back to the Powder River basin where there was so little traffic it was laughable.

Working his way to a window overlooking the tarmac, he worried he might have missed the plane's arrival. But his timing seemed to be perfect, he thought as the Gulfstream G550 touched down against a blinding blue cloudless sky. If his intel was right, the man he'd come to confront would be on that plane.

Tycoon Wendell Forester made it impossible to get to him personally. Even as Ryder thought it, he noticed two of the airport security standing nearby as the plane began to taxi toward the south end of the terminal where the private hangars were. Ryder knew this might be a fool's errand. He very well might have trouble even getting close enough to the man to tell him what he needed to. Not that a couple of airport cops could dissuade him, he thought. Not at this point.

A cell phone rang next to him with a tune that caught his attention. "He just landed," said a young female voice after he hurriedly answered the call, cutting off the ringtone. "No, I haven't talked to him since he texted his ultimatum. He seriously can't think he's going to force me to marry his latest handpicked yes-man."

Ryder glanced over at her, curiosity getting the better of him. The woman on the phone looked to be close to his age, with curly red hair that looked natural given her fair skin and jade-green eyes that rivaled his own. Her hair was pulled up into a loose ponytail. Strands of copper had escaped to frame her face, accentuating high cheekbones that made her eyes all the more vivid. She was a stunner, and he had a pretty good idea that she knew it.

As if feeling his gaze, she looked at him, their eyes locking as a smile broke out on her lovely face. "I wonder what Daddy would say if I found myself a cowboy instead." She winked at Ryder before go-

ing back to her phone conversation. "You know my
father. He buys a ranch in Montana, and all of a sudden he thinks he's a Dutton. Why shouldn't I give
him more than he asked for? Besides . . . I've never
kissed a cowboy."

Ryder quickly dropped his gaze, turning away.
He knew trouble when he saw it, and he had enough
problems without adding a new one to his list. He
headed for the closest exit that would take him to
where the Gulfstream was now taxiing to a stop.

"Wait," the now-familiar female voice called after him as he pushed out of the terminal. He heard
her footfalls behind him, but concentrated on reaching the plane and Wendell Forester, determined
to have a word with him since according to his
daughter, he was indeed on that plane. The man had
avoided him so far, but not this time.

The redhead had to almost run to keep up as she
fell into step beside him. "I'll give you a thousand
dollars to pretend to be my fiancé for the weekend."

He didn't even bother to look at her. "Sorry. Wrong
cowboy."

"Five thousand," she said, having difficulty
keeping up with his long-legged stride. "Please,
help me out here. Look, I'm desperate. I can't
even imagine who my father might have brought
to Montana, determined to make him my future
husband. It's just for this weekend. With luck, by
dinner tonight I will have made my point, and we
can break up," she said, latching on to his arm as
she smiled up at him.

She did have a great smile and she smelled wonderful. But he was here on ranch business. "Trust me, I'm not the answer to your problem."

"You could be. Ten thousand dollars," she whispered urgently, sounding more desperate as the two of them headed for the private jet. The airport security guards Ryder had been concerned might try to stop him barely gave him a second look with this woman on his arm.

As they approached, the door on the jet opened, and steps dropped down. A couple of serious-looking men in suits embarked quickly and took positions at the front and rear of the plane. Both, he realized, were armed. Bodyguards?

"Ten thousand and an evening you'll never forget."

He shot her a look to see if she was actually serious an instant before she called "Daddy!" and, grabbing Ryder's arm, drew him forward with her. An older man carrying a large briefcase in one hand and a coat thrown over his other arm began to descend the plane's stairs.

Her daddy, like the other two men who had already exited the jet, wore a suit, only his fit as if it had been made for his contours alone. Ryder didn't doubt that it had been handstitched as he recognized Wendell Forester from the many news stories he'd read. Just this year that face had been on the cover of *Forbes* where he'd been referred to as one of the wealthiest men in the country. Another more left-wing publication had called him the richest and greediest tycoon in boots and a Stetson, listing properties from his latest "shopping" spree around the country—including Montana.

"Victoria." Forester strode down the stairs to his daughter and gave her an awkward embrace without putting down the large briefcase or changing arms for his coat. "I wasn't sure you'd be meeting my plane."

"Your text didn't give me much choice," she said as she stepped back. "But here I am!"

"Good," he said distractedly and turned to motion behind him. "You remember Claude Duvall." He indicated the thirtysomething man also in a suit who'd come halfway down the stairs behind him.

Ryder heard her whisper "Oh no" as her hand on his arm tensed at the sight of the man.

"I thought the two of you needed more time together," her father continued. "And with business in Montana this weekend—"

"There's someone I want you to meet, Daddy," Victoria interrupted him as she pulled Ryder closer to her. She squeezed his arm as she said, "He's a cowboy."

"A cowboy?" Forester repeated, then settled his gaze on Ryder. "I'm sorry, but if this is about a job on one of my ranches, you need to talk to Personnel."

Ryder noticed that the two bodyguards were now watching him closely.

"Daddy, he's my *fiancé*," Victoria Forester cried with a laugh as her fingers gripped Ryder even tighter and she looked from her father to her pretend fiancé pointedly, then back. "He already has a *job*." Ryder started to speak, but didn't get a chance as she rushed on. "You said yourself it was time for me to settle down. Who better than with a cowboy, since you're buying up ranches all over Montana?"

"Your *fiancé*?" her father repeated, eyes narrowing as he took in Ryder.

"Ryder *Stafford*," Ryder said and stuck out this free right hand, even as he told himself he should clear up this nonsense before it went any further.

Wendell shook his hand slowly. Ryder had seen his gaze widen as the name registered. "Stafford, from the Stafford Ranch over on the Powder River?"

"That's the one," Ryder said, ready to add *The one you've been trying to buy by throwing money and veiled threats at me, even though I've told your people repeatedly that the ranch isn't for sale.*

One of the suited bodyguards interrupted to announce that their car had arrived to take them to the hotel.

"You heard the man," Forester said, his booming voice sounding more cheerful than he looked. "Why don't we move this to the Northern Hotel where we can have more privacy to discuss these matters. Where are you staying, Mr. Stafford? I am most anxious to talk to you."

He hadn't been anxious to talk to Ryder in the months before. That was why Ryder had come to the airport today planning to ambush him and finally make a few things clear to the man. He figured the confrontation would be short before Forester had his heavies run him off.

Which would have been fine as long as Ryder got to tell the man what he thought of him. Then he planned to climb into his pickup and get out of Billings, putting this problem behind him.

What he hadn't anticipated was for his plan to go so awry, he thought as he looked over at Victoria, still holding his arm as if she never intended to let it go. He'd figured before this moment that the best he was going to get was a few minutes to tell Forester off. This was more than he could have hoped for. He couldn't leave here until this man realized he'd better back off. Stafford Ranch wasn't for sale.

But now Victoria, for whatever her reasoning, had gotten him a sit-down with the man he'd come to straighten out Montana-style. Ryder had to admit he was getting a lot more than he would have on his own with so much security around. The two bodyguards would have escorted him off the premises before he'd gotten a word out. So he told himself he should be grateful for her ridiculous ruse.

"I also stay at the Northern when I'm in town," Ryder said. Which was true. He just hardly ever came to Billings, much preferring the ranch. "I look forward to sitting down with you."

"Then, we'll see you there," Forester said. "Unless you need a ride."

"Thanks, but I drove my own rig."

The man nodded, seeming to take this in stride. Something told Ryder that Forester would be having a word with his daughter on the way to the hotel, though.

As if on cue, Victoria said, "I'll ride with my fiancé."

"Ride with us, sweetheart," Forester said, his insistent tone making it clear that it wasn't a request. "I hardly ever get to spend any time with you. I'm sure you're with your . . . cowboy all the time, and Claude came all this way to see you."

Ryder could see how badly Victoria wanted to get him alone to try to dig him in deeper with this scheme of hers. "See you soon, then," she said to him and gave him a quick kiss on the cheek before whispering, "You won't regret this."

He wasn't so sure about that. But *she* would, he thought as he watched her walk reluctantly toward the waiting large SUV that would take her, her father, his two bodyguards and Claude Duvall, the man Wendell Forester was apparently trying to set her up with, all to the hotel.

Even from a distance, he could see that Claude was furious. Clearly, he'd thought he would be leaving here this weekend engaged to his boss's daughter. From Victoria Forester's reaction to the man, Ryder doubted that was going to happen now.

Ryder figured the ride to the hotel would be especially uncomfortable for her. What had she been thinking? *What had he?* He should have spoken up, straightened this out at once. Her impromptu deception might have inadvertently gotten him what he'd wanted—a chance to have Wendell Forester's undivided attention—but he couldn't let it go on.

As he walked to his Stafford Ranch pickup, he

pulled out his phone and thumbed in the name Victoria Forester into his search bar. The first article that came up read *Princess to a Fortune. Ultra-rich daddy demands handpicked best for only daughter. Insiders say Daddy's rushing wild child "Victoria" toward the altar.*

The story was accompanied by a photograph of her holding up a hand in front of her face as photographers caught her coming out of a New York City nightclub. Looking more than a little tipsy, she wore a silver dress that hugged her body like a glove. Everything about her said *spoiled-rotten* and *wealthy*. The cutline read *Is there anyone special enough for Daddy's princess, Victoria?*

He turned off his phone, having seen more than enough. Well, at least her fear of being forced into a marriage with a man chosen by her father appeared to be true and explained her apparent desperation, Ryder thought as he pocketed his phone and walked the rest of the way to his pickup. He remembered something she'd said back at the airport. He'd just bet she'd never come close enough to kiss a cowboy. She'd only picked him because she knew it would upset her father. Well, this cowboy knew trouble when he saw it. He wanted nothing to do with the woman even before he'd known who she was. Now that he did, he planned to clear this up as quickly as possible and be on his way. He wasn't going to let her pull him into her problems. He was only here to solve his own.

Sliding behind the wheel, he took a moment to

catch his breath. He hadn't expected this turn of events. But he would handle it. He would straighten it out at the hotel. Then he would hopefully get his business with Forester settled and go home.

Ryder was no fool. While he wanted Forester to know who he was dealing with, Ryder also knew who *he* was dealing with—a rich and powerful man who believed he could buy anything he wanted because money was no object. He thought about the man's daughter and chuckled. They seemed to be cut from the same cloth.

With Forester determined to have the Stafford Ranch at any cost, the man was dangerous. The question was, how far would the tycoon go to get it?

And how far would Ryder go to stop him?

He worried he'd already gone too far as he started his pickup and drove along the top of the rock cliffs that rimmed the city before dropping into downtown on his way to the Northern Hotel.

ONCE IN THE two middle seats of the hotel's large SUV, Victoria had expected her father to immediately demand answers from her. Or at the very least reprimand her. Instead, he was busy looking at his phone. She leaned toward him a little to see what was so interesting on his screen.

With a shock, she saw that he'd called up information about Ryder Stafford and the Stafford Ranch. She hadn't even known the cowboy's name until he'd introduced himself to her father. From what she could see online, the Stafford Ranch was beautiful and huge and exactly the kind of property her father would want to snatch up.

She groaned inwardly as she saw her father's expression. He was pleased with whatever he'd been reading. She hurriedly looked out her window, glad he was satisfied with even her pretend choice of fiancé and at the same time sorry she'd put Ryder and his ranch in jeopardy. Once her father saw something he liked, he went after it.

Was he actually taking her engagement seriously? He couldn't really think that the cowboy was her fiancé, could he? Clearly, he didn't know her at all. Which had already been established. *He'd picked Claude Duvall for her!*

She realized that all of this was about to blow up in her face. Once they reached the hotel, Ryder Stafford would out her. She hoped it wasn't in front of Claude. He would enjoy her embarrassment way too much.

If only she could have ridden in the cowboy's pickup with him. She was sure she could have talked him into playing the fiancé role at least for the weekend. It would only postpone the problem because her father wasn't going to change his mind about her getting married. But this pretend engagement would maybe finally send the message to Claude that she wasn't interested. She thought they had settled this the last time they'd been thrown together.

Claude was exactly the kind of man her father would choose for her, she thought, watching him talk to the valet. Not bad-looking, but dull as dirt. Not to mention he was one of her father's yes-men.

Clearly, her father wanted her to marry a man he could handle. She gagged at the thought of Claude as her husband. Never going to happen no matter what her father offered her—or threatened her with.

Not that she could imagine the cowboy as husband material either, she thought with a silent chuckle. Ryder Stafford *was* drop-dead handsome in a rough-around-the-edges sort of way and certainly more interesting than Claude, even if she had been in the market for a husband.

But if her father believed she was engaged, at least for the duration of this weekend, he might send Claude back to Dallas on his private plane. If she could get Ryder to play along, this pretend engagement could be beneficial for both of them. She didn't doubt if she could get him alone she could talk him into it. She was her father's daughter. All she had to do was find his price.

She smiled to herself at what her father had thought when she'd first introduced Ryder. A handsome cowboy dressed in Western shirt, jeans and boots, a gray Stetson shoved down over his curly blond hair who was nothing like the men she'd ever even consider dating.

At first, she'd been joking around—until he'd met her gaze. A frisson of something close to electricity had raced through her at those jade-green eyes—so like her own. What were the chances that their children wouldn't inherit them?

Victoria chuckled at the thought. She could never live in Montana. It was too remote. She'd thought

Dallas was dull before she and her father had moved there from New York City after her mother's death. She'd been raised in the big city where things were happening, and that was where she needed to be.

She also liked her men in three-piece suits smelling like the latest men's cologne—not boot leather and cow manure. Yet she had to admit that Ryder in those butt-hugging jeans and that Western shirt stretched across his broad muscled back might just change her mind. But as her father knew, she was always up for an adventure, and Ryder Stafford just might be it.

The more she thought about Ryder, she realized that it wasn't even the cowboy's looks or the way he was dressed that had made her notice him. It was his confidence. She found that very attractive. He was his own man—nothing like Claude. She smiled to herself at the thought of Ryder Stafford. He was definitely the kind of guy she could be serious about—if he wasn't a cowboy. No thanks, she thought even as she worried how long she'd have before everyone who mattered knew Ryder wasn't her fiancé.

Her only hope was to get him alone at the hotel before he spilled the beans, as her grandmother would have said. But convincing him to stay through the weekend wouldn't be easy. She'd pay anything, something she'd learned from her father. As Wendell Forester always said, *Everyone has a price.* You just had to find it.

Ryder Stafford might be the exception, though. So, what would it take to keep him from telling everyone the truth and leaving?

"Here we are." Her father put away his phone and smiled at her. He was always working. Most of the time, Victoria thought that he forgot he had a daughter. It had gotten worse after her mother had died. She'd feared the reason he seemed to ignore her was because she looked so much like his deceased wife.

Now lately, instead of ignoring her, he was trying to marry her off. Same thing. He was just passing her off to another man to take care of her.

As the hotel came into view, he said, "Let's see what your fiancé has to say for himself, shall we?"

She returned his smile even as she knew that once Ryder Stafford arrived at the hotel, he was going to blow her cover. As if the multibillionaire developer wasn't already suspicious.

That was why he was grinning, wasn't it?

CLAUDE DUVALL HAD never been this furious in his life. He'd been humiliated at the airport. How dare Victoria snub him, let alone pretend she preferred some cowboy over him.

Being forced to hide his fury only made it worse. No one would think the cowboy was the better candidate for that spoiled brat's hand. Just as no one treated him like this, he'd told himself as he'd ignored her and her father riding in the back. Not that Victoria Forester even noticed him ignoring her. Or if she did, she was enjoying it.

She'd been playing hard to get from the first time they'd met. She seemed to think that being rude to him was going to send him packing. Ha! He wanted to tell her that he only considered her rudeness foreplay. But wait until they got to the real event. She was in for a surprise.

The thought made him want to laugh, since he wasn't worried about this cowboy she'd dug up to try to fool them. She'd thought that she'd one-upped her father and put Claude in his place. But no way was Wen Forester going to let his only daughter marry that saddle tramp.

Claude was looking forward to how fast Wen would get rid of this one. There'd been a long line of inappropriate boyfriends. None of them had even lasted through a meal. Those poor suckers never knew what hit them as they found themselves thrown out into the street.

He bet that the cowboy wouldn't last long enough to check in to the hotel—let alone stay the weekend. Wen would see to that.

Claude chuckled to himself as the driver pulled up to the valet entrance and finished telling him the history of the hotel. "When built in 1902, it was to be the most modern hotel in Montana. After burning to the ground in 1940, it was rebuilt and in 2009 brought back to be one of the most modern and luxurious hotels in the state."

"I can't wait to see it," Claude said, acting more interested than he was. At least interacting with the valet had passed the time and kept his mind off how angry he was. "Only the best for Wendell Forester," he said under his breath. But wasn't that what Claude was doing here? Wasn't that why Wen had invited him? He'd been handpicked for Victoria, he reminded himself as he climbed out of the SUV. There was no reason to feel as if he'd come in second best, because the best definitely wasn't some Montana cowboy. He should be embarrassed for Ryder Stafford. He wasn't even worthy competition.

Not that Claude expected there would be a competition. He'd gotten the impression the minute Wen invited him on the trip that when the weekend was over they would be announcing their engagement. Claude had already been her date once before. It hadn't ended quite as he'd hoped, but he knew Wen was giving him another chance.

Everyone who had Wi-Fi had heard that one of the richest men in the country was looking for the perfect son-in-law. Honored, Claude told himself that he would make a hell of a son-in-law. Just the thought of the wealth and power that came with the position made him giddy.

All he had to do was stay in his boss's good graces and put up with the man's awful daughter long enough to get what he wanted: married into the Forester family.

But after today at the airport, he planned to make Victoria Forester's life miserable until she cried "Daddy" and Wen agreed to a huge payoff to get rid of him and keep him from going to the media with stories about the infamous Victoria Forester. Then Claude would never have to see her or her father again.

CHAPTER TWO

WHEN RYDER WALKED into the lobby of the Northern Hotel, he wasn't surprised to see Forester waiting for him. He figured the man wanted to get this over with as quickly as possible. Lucky for Wendell Forester, Ryder wanted the same thing. He couldn't believe he was finally going to get to tell the man face-to-face what he thought of him before he threatened him if he ever came near his ranch.

"Mr. Stafford," Forester said in greeting, a smile on his face.

"Mr. Forester," Ryder said and touched the brim of his Stetson. He was ready for the brush-off, but he wasn't leaving until he had his say, he thought, even as Forester said, "Please, call me Wen." He motioned to one of his bodyguards standing a few yards away in the large lobby. The man stepped forward quickly as if ready to throw Ryder out of the lobby. But to Ryder's surprise, the bodyguard handed Forester several packets of room keys.

"My treat," he said as he handed Ryder one of the packets. "This way, we'll all be on the tenth floor overlooking the city and the rock cliffs that border it. Locals called the rock formation the rims. It's beautiful at night as I'm sure you already know. No wonder they call Billings the Magic City."

Ryder wouldn't have taken the free room key under normal circumstances. He would have informed the man that he was more than capable of purchasing his own room for the night. Nor did he have any desire to stay on the same floor as the tycoon, let alone his daughter.

But since he had no intention of staying long enough that he would need a hotel room, he didn't cause a fuss. He'd be headed back to the ranch as soon as he accomplished what he came here for. "Wen—"

"Let's have a drink," the man said, not giving him a chance to say more. Forester put a big paw on his shoulder as he motioned toward the bar with his other hand. "It's early enough we should have the place to ourselves so just the two of us can talk. You have any luggage you need taken up to your room?"

Ryder shook his head. "I was planning to go back to the ranch tonight."

Forester raised an eyebrow. "And that was all right with my daughter?"

"About your daughter—"

The man held up a hand to stop him. "Victoria is best discussed with a drink in our hands," Forester said with a chuckle and led the way to the bar. Ryder went along, determined to end this charade, once the man gave him a chance.

Just before entering the bar, Ryder saw Claude Duvall talking to one of the bodyguards that he heard him call JJ. His expression looked menacing as he mumbled something under his breath to the man before grabbing a key package and storming off toward the elevator.

Forester led Ryder to a table in a back corner. A waiter appeared at once, and the tycoon ordered bourbon neat. Ryder ordered a beer, determined to keep this as civil as possible—until it wasn't.

"There are a few things I need to clear up," Ryder said the moment the waiter left to fill their orders. So far Forester had been calling the shots. "My ranch is not for sale," Ryder said as plainly as he could. "I met your plane today to tell you that I don't want to see another one of your . . . *associates* on my property trying to strong-arm me into selling, making veiled threats or throwing money at me. I haven't shot one of your people yet, but I've come damned close. I'll be running the next one off with a double-barreled shotgun loaded with buckshot. But I have plenty of real ammo if needed. Trespassing in Montana is a shooting offense—at least in my part of the state."

Forester leaned back with exaggerated shock, then began to laugh heartily as he looked at Ryder as if just now seeing him.

"You find something funny about that?" Ryder demanded.

"You are nothing like I expected. My daughter normally has the worst taste in men. I say that with love, since she knows how I feel. But you . . . I actually think you might be the man to handle her."

He was still smiling and shaking his head as their drinks arrived. He grabbed his and held it up as if about to make a toast.

"Let me stop you right there," Ryder said. "Your daughter—"

"What about his daughter?" Victoria said as she put an arm around Ryder's shoulder and gently, but determinedly, shoved him over to sit on his side of the circular booth. Leaning toward him, she whispered in his ear, "Name your price," just before she kissed him on the check.

"Victoria, you're interrupting an important discussion between myself and Mr. Stafford," her father said.

"Daddy, don't you think you should call my fiancé by his first name? It's Ryder." She turned to smile at him, but only for an instant before she turned back to her father. "I was so bored in my room I had to come down." The waiter appeared, and she ordered a margarita.

Ryder figured this was good, they could end the duplicity together. But before he could speak, she said, "Now, tell me what you two been talking about."

"You, of course," Forester said as he looked from her to Ryder. "We were just about to talk about your future."

VICTORIA HAD GOTTEN downstairs as quickly as possible. Knowing her father, she'd figured she could find him in the nearest bar. As she walked in, she wouldn't have been surprised to see her cowboy long gone and Claude sitting next to his boss, leering at her.

The fact that her father and Ryder were still talking at all came as a shock. Maybe more unlikely, her father was smiling. Had Ryder already told him that he wasn't her fiancé? What else could have put her father in such a jovial mood?

"My future?" She shot a suspicious look at Ryder. Maybe he had already told her father the truth. In that case, Wen must be relieved. She tried to see Ryder through her father's eyes. Another handsome man after her money? Or, after seeing the Stafford Ranch online, had her father now looked past Ryder's collar-length curly blond hair that her fingers itched to run through . . . straight to the ranch?

Ryder was a man who either didn't have time to worry about a haircut or he didn't care. Both things her father would normally have found lacking. This cowboy was nothing like Claude Duvall, thank heavens, but that probably wouldn't be a plus according to Wendell Forester. Ryder didn't sit behind a desk. Anyone could see that, from his tanned rugged looks to the way his shirt fit those shoulders and his jeans hugged his behind perfectly before running down the length of his long legs to a pair of worn but clean boots.

She suspected Ryder also wasn't the kind to say *yes* to her father.

Ryder started to speak as her father's cell phone chirped. After a quick look at the screen, her father was on his feet, saying, "Sorry, I'm going to leave you lovebirds to enjoy your drinks without me." He drained his bourbon and put down his glass. "I have some calls to make." He looked at Ryder, smiled and with a tip of his head said, "I'll see you both at dinner. Six sharp." With that he was gone.

Victoria turned to make sure her father had left the bar before she looked at Ryder and demanded, "What was that about? Did you tell him about us?"

RYDER SWORE UNDER his breath. The man hadn't given him a chance before Victoria had interrupted them. "There is no *us*," he reminded her as he picked up his untouched beer and took a single gulp before putting it down. He had a long drive ahead of him.

"Then, what was that I just witnessed between the two of you?"

He sighed. "The reason I was at the airport today was because I had business with your father. That business is completed." He pulled the packet of keys that Forester had given him from his shirt pocket and dropped them on the table. "Please give those to your father and tell him *thanks, but no thanks*. Now, if you will kindly move and let me out of this booth, I'm going back to the ranch."

"Can we discuss this first?" From her determined expression, he decided not to make her move. Instead, he slid around the booth until he was across from her and about to stand up and leave when she reached across and grabbed his arm. "Wait, you can't just leave. Please, stay the weekend as my fiancé. That's all I ask. You'll be saving my life. You met Claude Duvall. You can't leave me here with him and my father to gang up on me. I mean it," she said and lowered her voice to a whisper as she leaned toward him. "I'll pay anything."

Ryder jerked his arm free with a shake of his head and leaned across the table toward her, keeping his voice down. "That's the problem with you Foresters. You think you can buy anything you want. Sorry, but neither of you can buy me."

In a matter of seconds, he would have been gone, headed home after he'd said what he had to say to the wealthy developer—and his daughter.

But as he started to rise, he saw Claude snatch Victoria's drink off the server's tray and make a beeline for them. Something about the cocky way the man approached warned Ryder things were about to get ugly fast.

"Leaving so soon?" he said to Ryder with a sneer. He turned to Victoria. "I figured you'd need this after your father broke your so-called engagement to this cowboy," Claude said as he set down the margarita in front of her. "Another boyfriend sent down the road. So embarrassing. Aren't you getting tired of dragging losers home for your father to reject?"

"You have no idea," Victoria said and took a sip of her drink as she shot Ryder a look he could easily decipher. *Please help me.*

The man was an arrogant jerk, no doubt about it, but Ryder wasn't going to get into it with him. This wasn't his rodeo, and this wasn't his bull. He rose, planning not to say a word, just leave, but Claude stepped in front of him.

"I knew it wouldn't take long, but this time Wen broke all of his earlier records getting rid of the worst of the ones his daughter had dragged home like the alley cat she is," Claude said. "Wish I hadn't missed it. Bet it was *nasty.*" He laughed. "Wendell Forester would never let his precious daughter marry a cowboy, especially one like you who can't afford a haircut or a new pair of boots."

Thinking the man had run out of sarcastic remarks, Ryder again tried to step past him because Claude was looking for a fight and he wasn't going to oblige him. Unfortunately, Claude refused to move, and Victoria had slipped from the booth, shooting to her feet to confront the man. They were attracting an audience from the bar.

"You owe my fiancé an apology," Victoria demanded, shooting fire from those green eyes as she looked from Claude to Ryder. Claude got the icy stare, Ryder got the and-you-would-leave-me-with-this-jackass? look.

Before he could move, she'd turned back to her father's handpicked son-in-law, grabbed her drink and thrown the contents in Claude's face.

Ryder swore under his breath, resigned that he wasn't getting out of here without a fight. He had really wanted to leave without slugging Claude and having to spend the night in jail. He could feel the other patrons all looking in their direction as well as the waitstaff. Everyone seemed to tense as if waiting with alarm to see what happened next.

Claude was sputtering furiously and trying to save his expensive suit with the bar napkin Wendell had left on the table as he now stood between Ryder and Victoria, still blocking the rancher's exit. "You're no more her fiancé than I am," Claude said raising his voice. "Count yourself lucky that you're not really marrying this bit—"

Victoria slapped Claude with a roundhouse smack that reverberated through the bar. The man looked ready to hit her back until tears filled her eyes and she covered her face with her hands, her body racking with silent sobs.

Still determined that this wasn't going to turn into a knock-down, drag-out bar brawl, Ryder realized Victoria was right. He couldn't just walk away now and leave her with this man. "Vicky, I think it's time to get out of here," he said and reached around Claude for her hand. As she grabbed his, she pulled him away from Claude, who looked furious. "Tell your boss thanks for the dinner invitation and the room, but I'm going to pass. I'm sure he'll understand."

Moving past him, the two of them headed for the nearest exit. Neither said anything until they were outside on the sidewalk. The moment the doors closed behind them, Victoria burst into laughter, making him realize that she hadn't been crying at all. "That was wonderful. Did you see Claude's face?"

Ryder had already been mentally kicking himself.

He'd let that arrogant fool get to him—just as he'd let this woman catch him up in her drama. He couldn't keep doing this, not even to piss off Claude.

Nor did Victoria need saving, he realized as he looked at her. She'd handled things just fine back in the bar. It was time for him to go back to the ranch and put this all behind him. "Look, Victoria—"

"*Vicky*," she said, grinning at him. "I like it. It's more . . . intimate."

"You and I aren't . . . intimate. We're total strangers. That back there—" He waved toward the bar and shook his head, unable to even explain what that had been or why he'd done what he had. If it had happened in the bar in Powder Crossing, he would have put Claude on his ass and everyone would have cheered as they threw him out in the street.

"This whole thing has gotten out of hand," Ryder said, surprised how much he still wanted to punch Claude. He'd known that if he'd had to spend another second with the man talking about this woman like that . . . But he couldn't leave her in there with him. Which made him question how he could leave her to face both her father and Claude now.

He saw her look back toward the hotel bar. She had a determined expression on her face that he recognized even from the short period of time their paths had crossed. "Don't try to talk me into staying here," he said with a shake of his head. "I don't understand you or your father. Earlier I told him off, and he invited me to dinner. Neither of you seem to understand the word *no*."

"You're right. I shouldn't have put you in this situation. I'm sorry. I was desperate, but you can see why."

He sighed. "As it turned out, you made it possible for me to talk to your father face-to-face. I appreciate that. But this game has to end now." She nodded. "I need to get back to the ranch where, as crazy as things often are, they seem normal right now."

"I can't go back into the bar or the hotel." She shook her head, chin tilting up. "Can you imagine how delighted Claude would be to find out that you and I aren't engaged?"

"We *aren't* engaged."

"Worse, can you imagine how embarrassing it would be to admit that while you came to my rescue in the bar like a scene out of a movie, you then left me out here on the street without my cell phone or my purse. It appears I left them both in the bar."

"I see what you're doing."

She grinned. "Sorry, but I can't give Claude that satisfaction—or my father, for that matter. All I'm asking for is a ride to the airport. I'll get Daddy's pilot to take me home in the jet. Without my phone, I can't even call an Uber, let alone pay for one."

With a curse, he knew she was right. He couldn't just leave her out here on the street. If he did, he wouldn't be any better than Claude. Also, if he was being honest with himself, he couldn't stand giving Claude the satisfaction either. But if he stayed, he'd end up in worse trouble. He might punch Claude and Forester too while he was at it. He hadn't come to Billings to get thrown behind bars.

"Won't the pilot call your father?" he asked.

She chewed at her lip for a moment. "You're right . . . Here's a thought."

Ryder knew that before she said a word, he wasn't going to like it.

She looked up at him all doe-eyed and said, "You could take me to the ranch with you—just for the rest of the weekend. I can call my bank and have them send me some funds so I can get home after I know my father and Claude are gone. After that I shouldn't have any more trouble with either of them."

He held up both hands and took a step back, but she rushed on, talking over his *not happening* reaction. "Just for the weekend," she repeated. "I've never been to a real Montana ranch. I promise not to be any trouble, and after the weekend you'll never have to see me again. I promise."

Ryder swore under his breath, wondering how he'd gotten involved in all this. He should never have gone along with the pretense, but once he had, he had only managed to get in deeper and deeper. His own fault. "Here's a thought," he said. "Maybe it's time you were honest with your father about how you feel."

She stared at him aghast. "You saw what he's like. He seems to listen, but then he does whatever he wants. So you really told him off? Why?"

"It's a long story, but now my business with him is done, and I need—"

"To get back to the ranch." She met his gaze and grinned. "Do you think we could stop on the way to the ranch at a fast-food restaurant? I'm starving." She practically batted her eyelashes. "I'd offer to pay, but I wouldn't want to insult you since you can't be bought. Also, as you might recall, I don't have my purse."

Ryder groaned. "Did anyone ever tell you that you're a lot like your father?"

"Not to my face. Nor has anyone dared call me Vicky."

He chuckled at that, realizing it was probably true. Everyone probably handled her with kid gloves because of who her father was. "Look, it's a long way to the ranch and a boring drive."

"I love long, boring drives."

Ryder could see how this was going to end. He couldn't abandon her, and she knew it. It was only for two days, maybe less. Also it *was* a long boring drive, and she was better company than picking up a hitchhiker who wouldn't smell half as good as she did.

Mostly, he figured she wouldn't last even the weekend at the ranch, especially if he showed her a real ranch and a real cowboy—not the romantic version she was probably expecting.

After that . . . well, then she was on her own. How she'd get home from his ranch, though, was another story. The big-city girl wouldn't be able to hop on a subway, call an Uber or hire a limo and charge it to her daddy. Once the shine wore off her idea of ranching, her best bet would be to hitchhike back to Billings—if someone was going that way.

He told himself it wasn't his problem. She could probably hire a helicopter to come pick her up. He didn't doubt that one phone call, like she said, and she'd have all the money she needed at her disposal.

"Speaking of your father, shouldn't you at least let him know where you're going?"

"I'll call him after I eat. I can't do it on an empty stomach," she said and flashed him a smile.

I'm putty in her hands, Ryder thought and mentally kicked himself. "Come on, my pickup's parked over here." Usually, he valeted it, but he'd figured he might want a fast getaway if things went the way he had expected with Forester, so he'd parked on the street. "Don't you have to get your luggage?"

She shook her head. "I can charge whatever I need to my father."

Not in Powder Crossing, he thought with a chuckle. This woman had no idea where they were going. The Powder River basin in southeastern Montana was another world. She was about to get a rude awakening, but maybe a little reality as to how working farm and ranch people lived would be good for her. Well, she'd asked for it, he thought as they headed for his pickup.

CHAPTER THREE

ENRAGED, CLAUDE MARCHED up to his room, showered and changed, before sending his suit out to be cleaned compliments of his boss. He wanted to kill that cowboy, but it was nothing like what he would do to Victoria Forester if she was ever his bride. Which was probably never going to happen after the things he'd said in anger.

He tried not to think about that. Wen couldn't possibly be on board with this cowboy. Anything either of them told her father about his behavior Claude would deny. When they got back to Dallas, he would get Victoria alone. Maybe they could make a deal. A short marriage in name only and a cash reward at the end to keep her father from marrying her off to someone worse.

What angered him the most was that this weekend wasn't supposed to go this way. He already had Wen's blessing. Surely, he could make his boss see that Victoria needed a strong hand and a whole lot of discipline.

But first he had to get her away from that arrogant cowboy who'd talked to him as if Claude was an errand boy. *Tell Wen thanks for the dinner invitation and the room keys, but I'm going to pass. I'm sure he'll understand.* Had the cowboy really expected him to run to his boss with a *message*?

Maybe more unbelievable was that Ryder Stafford was even considering blowing off Wen's dinner invitation. No one did that. Wen would go ballistic when Stafford didn't show, let alone if Victoria didn't either.

So let her amuse herself with the cowboy, he thought. She'd be back. Especially after tonight. Wen demanded punctuality and abhorred people who made him wait even a minute.

Claude smiled to himself. No way was he passing on the cowboy's message. He could wait to see how Wen liked it when his daughter and her so-called fiancé didn't show up at precisely six o'clock for dinner.

Yes, tonight just might finally make his boss see what needed to be done about his precious Victoria. Wen had been threatening to cut off her allowance if she didn't do what he wanted. This would be the last straw. Then they'd see how long it would take Victoria to come around to reason without her daddy's money. No way could she live on any money she made at that nonprofit organization where she taught underprivileged kids art classes.

Claude laughed, suddenly feeling much better about his chances at getting what he wanted. The more the thought about it, the more assured he was that Victoria Forester wasn't engaged to that saddle tramp. This was just another of her stunts. When he met Wen for dinner, he would pretend he knew nothing about Victoria and her fake fiancé.

He could see it now. He and Wen would be seated downstairs in the restaurant before six. They'd have a drink. When six rolled around, no Victoria, no cowboy. Wen would wonder where his daughter and her fiancé were. Claude would play dumb. He'd seen his boss fire employees who were five minutes late to a meeting.

It would get later. Victoria or Ryder wouldn't show up. Nor would they send an explanation, expecting Claude to deliver Ryder's message—something he would deny having heard. And if that wasn't the end of the cowboy and Victoria wasn't brought into line, then Claude would do whatever was required to help things along.

Seeing the time, he smiled and went down to the restaurant ten minutes early. Wen was always punctual. Which was why Claude was always at least ten minutes early. He was sitting at the bar when his boss walked in. He saw him look around for Victoria and Ryder before letting the waiter show them to a table reserved for four.

Wen ordered a drink. Claude brought his from the bar. He'd already warned himself to go easy on the booze. He had to play this just right, reminding himself that he was perfect son-in-law material and needed to act like it. Wen looked toward the entrance of the hotel. No sign of his dinner guests. Claude made a point of looking at his expensive watch but said nothing, careful to keep his expression neutral.

When five minutes had gone by, Wen called his daughter and left a message that they were waiting. A few more drinks and an appetizer later, Wen called her hotel room. Still no answer. Then he tried Ryder's room and was told that the cowboy hadn't checked in. Claude had pocketed the packet of keys Ryder had left.

"Let's go ahead and order," his boss said tightly and picked up his menu. "She knows how I feel about being forced to wait on anyone. She's probably doing this to get back at me."

"She should know better, but I'm really surprised her fiancé is late too," Claude said from behind his menu. "I would think he would go out of his way to make a good impression on you."

Wen put down his menu with a sigh. "You don't like Ryder, do you?"

He felt the atmosphere change and warned himself to be careful. "I wouldn't say that."

"You think my daughter has made a bad choice."

Claude couldn't believe how quickly this had gone wrong. "I . . . I wouldn't presume to—"

"Ryder Stafford and his family own one of the largest ranches in eastern Montana. I've been trying to buy it for some time now, but he's refused to even consider selling." Wen picked up his drink and took a sip. "Earlier he told me that he would start shooting anyone I sent with another offer."

"I had no idea—"

"Exactly," his boss said as he motioned the waiter over to take their orders. "You had no idea." Wen turned to the waiter. "I want the biggest beef steak you have. So rare it still moos. I'm celebrating tonight."

Claude glanced at his menu, his heart pounding. What was going on? This wasn't going the way he'd thought it would at all. He started to order a steak, but quickly changed his mind. He knew how his boss felt about anyone who ordered a steak well-done—the only way Claude could eat it.

He hurriedly ordered baked chicken and another drink. "Make it a double. It seems we're celebrating tonight." He waited until their drinks came before he had to ask. "I'm trying to understand why you're happy about this."

"About my daughter threatening to marry into a family that owns a ranch I want? What's not to understand?"

Claude frowned. "You really think they're engaged?"

Wen laughed and shook his head. "I should get so lucky."

"TELL ME ABOUT the ranch," Victoria said after he'd pulled through the first fast-food drive-through he'd spotted on the way out of Billings. Two burgers, two orders of fries, two chocolate milkshakes and two apple pies later, they were headed east to the Stafford Ranch.

"Remember, you were going to call your father,"

Ryder reminded her as she finished her meal, stuffing the packaging into the bag the food had come in.

"Daddy will be at dinner. With Claude. That alone would have put him in a bad mood—not to mention you and me not showing up. And I don't have my phone." She mugged a sad face.

"You never planned to call him, did you?" he said with a groan.

She smiled and added, "I suppose it wouldn't hurt to email him. Later. After he's eaten his dinner and had a few drinks, the pain of spending time with Claude might mean he'll be numbed some by then."

Ryder had to laugh. She was enjoying this. He couldn't blame her. He was glad he hadn't had to sit through a dinner with her father and Claude, and maybe a little happy that he'd saved Victoria from the same fate. Not that she couldn't have held her own. But he hated the thought that her father and Claude would have tried to gang up on her. He couldn't imagine her marrying Claude under any circumstances, but who knew what her father would do to get what he wanted? Look how relentless he'd been about purchasing the Stafford Ranch.

Victoria Forester was way too much like her father and far from being Ryder's type, but he still wouldn't have wanted to make her spend an insufferable weekend with either her father or Claude, never mind both.

Though, he had to question what the hell he was doing taking her home with him—not to mention what her father might do when he realized where she'd gone. She was probably expecting this weekend to be like going to a dude ranch, though he doubted she'd ever even been to one. He hoped to make her time on the ranch as unlike anything she'd ever experienced, he thought, smiling to himself.

He pulled out his phone and handed it to her. "Text your father. I don't want him thinking I kidnapped you."

"*Kidnapped*. I like the sound of that." She grinned until she saw his expression. "I'll tell him I'm having a lovely weekend with my fiancé at his ranch." She glanced at him, attempting to look innocent. He was way beyond believing that.

She thought for a moment, then said, "How about *Talked Ryder into taking me to his ranch for the weekend to avoid Claude. BTW we aren't engaged. I'd never laid eyes on him before earlier at the airport. Stop trying to set me up. I'm not ready for marriage. Your loving daughter*."

"Sounds good to me," he said.

She laughed. "If I sent that, he'd know I'd been kidnapped." She tapped the keys for moment, then hit Send before handing back his phone. He worried about what she'd sent. Maybe, if she made her father angry enough, he'd send a chopper for her sooner rather than later.

Ryder had no desire to see the man again—especially on his ranch. Yet if truth be told, he was enjoying the drive back to Powder River. Victoria was clearly more intelligent than he'd first thought, and she could be quite amusing. She was nothing like he'd expected after what he'd seen online. She was much more down-to-earth and quite charming. He figured Wendell Forester was proud of her. No wonder he wanted someone special for her. Too bad he thought Claude was that man.

She picked up his Stetson on the seat between them and put it on.

He thought of that old cowboy superstition. *Never let a woman wear your hat unless you're planning to take her home.*

"Come on, tell me about the ranch," she said as she settled into the seat, looking full and relaxed with her bare feet on his dash.

"Not much to tell," he said as he drove east to Hardin, then took 212 toward Broadus where he would eventually turn south. "We raise cattle."

"Do you have horses?"

"We do."

"You said *we*," she pointed out. "I never even asked if you had a woman in your life."

He shot her a look. "What if I did?"

"Oops. Daddy would be so upset," she teased.

Ryder shook his head. "It's a family ranch. My mother is the matriarch, though she's on an extended vacation right now. My brother Brand and I work the place. Our sister Oakley's married to a ranch hand from the McKenna spread. Our older sister, Tilly, is married to Cooper McKenna. They both live on McKenna land next door."

"Is it really right next door?"

"Not in the city sense. You have to cross a creek

and a wide patch of country to go from door-to-door. Holden McKenna's made that trip a few times. My mother too." He instantly regretted opening that door. He could feel her gaze on him.

"Why do I sense there's a story there?"

He chuckled. "It's a tragic love story between the Stafford matriarch and the McKenna patriarch. I'm sure you wouldn't be interested."

"Tell me more," she said excitedly.

He wondered if it was possible she already knew the story. Knew more about him and his ranch than he'd thought. Was it possible that she'd recognized him at the airport and this whole thing had been her father's idea? He shook his head at how paranoid he felt when it came to Wendell Forester and the billionaire developer's determination to buy his family's ranch.

He reminded himself that Wen, as Claude called him, hadn't even known Ryder was going to Billings to confront him. This couldn't have been a setup, right? He mentally shook his head. It was this Forester family, he thought. They made him question everything.

"Your mother and the rancher next door?" Her eyes widened with delight. "Come on, how does it end?"

He sighed as he drove. It was a story that he'd lived with growing up so he knew it only too well. "My mother, Charlotte Stafford, fell in love with Holden McKenna when they were teenagers, maybe even before then knowing my mother. He married someone else and broke my mother's heart, and the two families have been at war ever since. It's a love-hate relationship. They've been rivals for years. With my mother gone from the ranch right now, we aren't sure how her and Holden's story ends. People in town I'm sure have taken bets on if they will ever resolve their differences and find their way back together, because we all know they still love each other."

Ryder knew that was way too much information. He looked over at Victoria to find that she'd dozed off. He chuckled to himself. "You think the story bores you? You should have lived it."

WEN HAD BEEN in an odd mood all through dinner, something that had given Claude heartburn. By dessert, he'd expected Victoria and Ryder to show up. He hadn't realized that the Stafford Ranch was the one his boss had been trying to buy. Wen bought whatever he wanted. If the man had mentioned problems acquiring a certain ranch in Montana, Claude didn't recall.

When neither Victoria nor Ryder appeared, even after dinner, he said, as if merely curious, "I wonder where they are."

His boss seemed to give that some thought. "It would be just like her to elope. But not with that cowboy—even if Victoria was telling the truth and he was her fiancé." He smiled broadly. "I know my daughter. She's just playing chicken with me right now."

"You're taking all of this awfully well," Claude noted irritably. This night hadn't gone anything like he'd hoped. He'd expected Wen to blow his top and send his bodyguards out to find her—and that damned cowboy.

"The best thing that could happen is for her to fall for Ryder, marry into the Stafford family, and I'd have the ranch I've been trying to buy and the husband my daughter needs."

Claude blinked at him in shock. "You couldn't wish that cowboy on your daughter—even if you do want the ranch. He's . . . he's all wrong for her." He shook his head. "She wouldn't really marry him and live on a ranch anyway. The celebrity rags would have a field day with it. How embarrassing for the both of you." His boss hated what social media wrote about him and his daughter.

To his surprise, Wen laughed.

It annoyed the hell out of him. "You aren't worried that the cowboy might actually want to marry her for your money?" Claude demanded, knowing that his boss valued his money more than anything else.

Wen shook his head as he threw down his napkin and rose to leave. "Ryder Stafford knew what I'm worth long before today, and I really doubt he was impressed. I'm not worried about *Ryder Stafford* marrying Victoria for my money."

The way he said it made Claude's face heat. He instantly wanted to deny that his interest in the man's daughter had anything to do with money. Fortunately, Wen didn't give him a chance.

"If she eloped with the cowboy," his boss continued as they left the restaurant for the elevator to go to their rooms, "she would have saved me a bundle in the cost of a huge wedding—not to mention what I was offering for the ranch." The man looked too pleased with himself. "Any man worth his salt would be crazy not to marry my Victoria."

Claude gritted his teeth. "So what am I still doing here?" he demanded, realizing that he'd had more to drink than he should have. "I thought I was your choice for a son-in-law. If you knew your daughter had no intention of marrying me, why did you bring me on this trip?" The booze had loosened his tongue dangerously, but right now he didn't care. He'd care in the morning when he was out of a job. But tonight, he was sick of trying to contain his fury.

"You're right, Claude. What *are* you still doing here?" Wen said, slapping him hard on the back as they took the elevator up to the tenth floor. "Truthfully, you, Claude, are what is known as a perfect catalyst. That's why I brought you to Montana with me and strong-armed Victoria into meeting us. I thought it would force her into realizing that I'm serious about her finding a good man to marry. I knew it would force her to take action."

"I don't understand," Claude said, worried that the alcohol was making it hard for him to follow.

Wen was looking at his phone. "I just got an email from my daughter via Ryder Stafford's cell. If I'm right, she talked him into taking her to his ranch because she'd do anything to get away from the two of us, especially you. I wanted her to know how bad it could get if *I* picked her husband. See, you were the catalyst that now has her on her way to the Stafford Ranch. It couldn't have worked out better if I'd planned it."

Wen laughed so hard that Claude thought he might have to slap him to bring him out of his frenzy—which he would have gladly done. He stared at his boss, feeling heat rush to his face. "You don't think I've been humiliated enough today?" he demanded.

"Oh, come on, Claude. I'm sure it's not the first time. I suggest you get used to it. I see a lot of humiliation in your future."

Clearly, his boss had drunk his share of alcohol tonight too. Claude had never seen him like this. "I don't have to put up with this. I quit."

They'd reached the tenth floor. The elevator door slid slowly open. "You can't quit," Wen said, unruffled as he followed him out. "You have a contract with my organization. You've known me long enough to realize that I would bankrupt you and see you behind bars before I'd let you break that contract. So go to bed and sleep on it," he said as he dug for his room key. "We'll meet for breakfast at seven downstairs in the café to discuss your future in the business and your trip to the Stafford Ranch where you will try to win back Victoria."

Claude stared at him. "What? Why would I do that?"

"Other than you're contracted to do pretty much

anything I ask, you mean? I thought I made myself clear. If anyone can get her to actually become engaged to Ryder Stafford, it will be you showing up at the ranch. Just seeing you there will remind her that I'm not giving up on finding her a husband of my choosing."

"Do you realize how insulting that is?" Claude said wearily.

Wen looked him in the eye. "There are two options here as I see it. Victoria is going to marry someone. If I have my way, and I usually do, it will be to someone I want her to marry. She thinks I couldn't possibly approve of Ryder Stafford. That's why she came up with this so-called engagement to him. True, he definitely won't make the son-in-law I'd hoped for. He would fight me at every turn. You, on the other hand, will do whatever I say, which makes you my perfect choice for a son-in-law. So that is why I know she'll choose the cowboy."

Claude was dumbfounded. He hung on to the only part he'd wanted to hear. Wen just said he would make the perfect choice for a son-in-law. With that, he couldn't agree more because he hadn't given up.

But Wen didn't know his daughter. There was no way Victoria would marry the cowboy and give up her flush lifestyle with her friends in Dallas and New York City. Trade her penthouse apartments for a dusty ranch? Not a chance, and not even Claude showing up was going to make her rush into the cowboy's arms.

His boss stopped in front of his hotel room a few doors down the hallway and turned back. "The problem, Claude, is that I'm not sure you can handle my daughter. You did let her take off with that cowboy. So consider this your chance to prove yourself."

He groaned. He didn't need to prove himself to anyone, especially Wen's spoiled-rotten daughter. "You can't play with people's lives like this."

"Really? You didn't say *no* when I invited you to Montana for the weekend. What did you think I had in mind?"

"I thought you were trying to hook me up with your daughter," he snapped.

Wen smiled. "That was my intention, which Victoria had also figured out, which is why she came up with her own plan. I can't help but admire that quality in her."

Claude could now see why the man needed two bodyguards, because right now he certainly wanted to kill the bastard. But one of the bodyguards was standing at the end of the hallway, and he figured the other one wasn't far away.

"You can force me to go to the Stafford Ranch, but nothing in my contract says I have to make a play for your daughter," he said indignantly.

Wen seemed to consider that for a moment. "I'll make you a deal, Claude. You steal her from that cowboy, as you call him, and I'll tear up your contract and throw you and Victoria the biggest wedding you've ever seen."

"You're only saying that because you don't think I have a chance," he said sullenly.

His boss shrugged. "Let's see what you've got in you. Who knows? After some time at that ranch, my daughter might be so grateful that you came to save her that she'll throw herself into your arms. Haven't you always dreamed of being my son-in-law?"

Claude thought of Victoria and the chance to make her life a living hell. "Yes, I have," he said.

CHAPTER FOUR

VICTORIA WOKE WITH a start, surprised to see daylight streaming through the windows. She hurriedly looked next to her in the big bed. Empty. For a moment, she had no idea where she was or how she'd gotten there. A breeze stirred the curtains, billowing them in and back out again.

She felt as if she'd gone deaf. She heard nothing. No traffic, no honking or sirens, no music drifting through the open window. Instead, she heard birds singing and smelled . . . freshly mowed grass?

Frowning, she sat up. Through a crack in the curtains, she saw a giant stand of trees she didn't recognize and caught a whiff of something pleasant even though she couldn't put her finger on what it was. The day, from what she could see, was beautiful, all brilliant blue sky and sunshine, not a cloud in sight over the mountains. Mountains? She smiled as she remembered where she was, even though she couldn't remember getting here. She vaguely remembered Ryder carrying her upstairs to bed.

But clearly he hadn't shared the bed with her. Such a gentleman, she thought, smiling as she stretched before lying back on the pillow. So this was the Stafford Ranch?

She really wished she had grabbed her cell phone before leaving the hotel bar. She would have loved to put this place up on her social media. Her friends would get such a kick out of it. After spending her life in huge city penthouses, she enjoyed the quiet— for a moment. She told herself that it would get to her before very long, but she could handle it for a weekend, if she stayed that long.

Last night, she'd been half asleep so hadn't noticed the room Ryder had given her. She did recall him saying something about it being his older sister Tilly's before she married a cowboy from the next ranch.

Now she took in the room from the wonderfully large, comfortable bed and its intricate patchwork quilt to the pale shade of rose on the walls and the white trim. It was definitely female decor including the chair by the window with the rose-colored cushions and the light green-and-white-leafed wallpaper in the bathroom. It was lovely. Ryder's sister Tilly had good taste.

After showering, she considered the clothing she'd been wearing before opening the closet. Hadn't Ryder mentioned that she could borrow some clothes from the closet? She and Tilly seemed to be about the same size, she noted. The jeans fit perfectly, the boots were a little large and the Western shirt was a little tight across the bust, but she doubted anyone would care. She thought of Ryder, knowing that she would make a play for him before the weekend was over. Her friends would expect details. She certainly couldn't go home without something tantalizing to tell them about a real-life Montana cowboy.

She tried not to think about what would happen after this weekend as she went looking for him. Her father would be upset and would probably cut her off financially. He'd been threatening to for some time. She told herself that she'd cross that bridge when she came to it, since she really didn't think he'd do it.

Whatever he did, she wouldn't marry anyone she didn't love. If push came to shove, she'd be forced to get a better-paying job. She loved teaching art to her young students at the nonprofit community arts center. It was why her father had never taken her career seriously.

With a sigh, she knew it was time to do what Ryder had suggested. She needed to be honest with her father and make him listen for once. Otherwise, he might abduct her and force her to the altar with someone like Claude. She shuddered at the thought.

But for now, she felt safe. She planned to enjoy herself, knowing that her father would be having a fit and Claude would be beside himself—if they were still in Billings. They could have taken the jet and left. She wondered if she'd even hear from either of them or if her father's attorney would be contacting her instead to give her Wendell Forester's latest ultimatum.

As she left the room she realized that she had no idea where she was going. Tilly's room was on the second floor so Ryder had carried her upstairs last night. But then where had he gone? Apparently to another part of the house.

"This room has a great view of the cottonwoods along the Powder River, a view I've always loved," she recalled him saying.

Anything else he might have said she couldn't remember. She had curled up in the big bed and fallen back to sleep. But she remembered the look on his face before she'd closed her eyes. He wanted her to like the place—temporarily, of course. Then she would be gone. She had the feeling that would be the last he'd ever want to hear from her—or her father. Not that she could blame him.

"LET ME GET this straight," Brand said at the kitchen table. "You told Wendell Forester off and then kidnapped his daughter?" Brand and his wife, Birdie, were still living in a private wing of the house until their home on the ranch was completed. Birdie had gone shopping in Billings for the weekend, but Ryder was sure Brand would fill her in when she returned. He could see that his brother was enjoying this way too much.

"I didn't kidnap her," Ryder said. "I just brought her here for the weekend. I didn't know what else to do, under the circumstances."

His brother stared at him. "Something tells me it wasn't with Wendell Forester's blessing."

Ryder shook his head, picked up his coffee mug and took a sip before answering. "Things got out of hand." Brand lifted a brow. "Not like *that*. She just needed a place to hide out for the weekend."

"Hide out?"

"Her father's intent on marrying her off to a man of his choosing. This weekend's lucky winner was a real loser. I was her escape hatch."

Brand chuckled. "Sounds like the two of you got pretty close for her to agree to come with you."

"Believe me, she would have taken off with anyone to get away from the obnoxious Claude Duvall."

"Okay, but what happens after the weekend?"

Ryder shrugged. "We didn't get that far."

"Aren't you worried what Forester will do?"

"I'm not worried about Forester. I made it clear to him that if he sent anymore of his associates to try to strong-arm me into selling the ranch, I would shoot them."

"Uh-huh," Brand said. "And then he invited you to dinner. Doesn't sound like he was shaking in his boots. After that, why not invite his daughter to the ranch?"

"It was Victoria's idea to come to the ranch for the weekend." Ryder raked his fingers through his hair. He knew how it must sound. Like his trip to Billings to confront Forester had been a waste of time. It certainly hadn't turned out like he'd planned it, that was for sure.

His brother lifted a brow. "And this is going to

solve the problem with her father trying to buy our ranch how exactly?"

With a sigh, Ryder said, "Look, I told Forester to leave us alone. Short of shooting the man, that was the best I could do. I think I made my point."

His brother looked skeptical. "Yet you ended up with his daughter."

"Do I smell bacon?"

They both turned to see Victoria and quickly got to their feet. She'd borrowed some of the clothing Tilly had left behind in her room, Ryder saw. She now wore a pair of worn jeans, a Western shirt and a pair of Tilly's scuffed up cowboy boots. The jeans seemed to fit quite well, the shirt stretched a little tight over her breasts, and the boots might have been a little big. He realized that he hadn't paid much attention to her body, or he would have realized she was taller that Tilly and more . . . endowed. Now he couldn't help but notice.

"Come join us," he said, his voice sounding strange even to him. "This is my brother Brand. Brand, this is Victoria Forester."

"It's nice to meet you, Brand," she said as she flipped a strand of her curly copper hair back from her face. "Just call me Vicky." She smiled at Ryder. "Ryder does."

"Nice to meet you, Vicky."

Ryder groaned inwardly as he pulled out a chair for her. All the while, he tried to ignore his brother, who was grinning from ear to ear—no doubt seeing how flustered he was and enjoying every moment of it.

As he sat back down, he kicked his brother under the table. "Coffee?" he asked Victoria. At her nod, he said, "How about bacon, eggs, hash browns with a side of flapjacks?"

Her green eyes widened, her lips turning up. She looked from Ryder to Brand and back. "Seriously? You don't really have that for breakfast."

"We have a long day of work ahead of us. Gotta eat," Brand said.

She smiled. "All right, but only if you let me help with your work today."

"Why not?" Brand said and excused himself to go turn her order in with the cook. "You were planning to put her to work, weren't you, bro?" he said over his shoulder.

Clearly, Victoria Forester knew nothing about ranching. Ryder doubted she'd ever had a job of any kind. More than likely she'd been waited on her whole life. So what was it he found so appealing about her this morning? Then it dawned on him like a bolt of lightning. She looked as if she could fit in here, he thought and mentally shook himself.

"How'd you sleep?" he asked her as his grinning brother disappeared down the hallway. Bringing her here had been a huge mistake—even if she hadn't been Wendell Forester's daughter. *Only* daughter. He obviously hadn't thought it through, which wasn't like him.

"That is the best I've slept in I can't remember when," she was saying, sounding surprised. "It's so . . . quiet here."

"It can give you the willies if you're used to traffic and noise other than nature." He wished he couldn't smell the scent of the girly shampoo in her still-damp hair. Her face, free of makeup, seemed to glow this morning, making him aware of how pretty she was without makeup and how different she looked from yesterday. She seemed like a completely different young woman.

"You're sure your sister won't mind me borrowing some of her clothing?"

"Not at all. You look great in them," he said and wished he hadn't as his brother joined them and quickly agreed that she looked great.

"So this work we're going to be doing. What is it?" she asked, looking almost excited at the prospect.

If Ryder had taken the time to imagine how this was going to go, he would have thought she would just want to hang out. He'd never imagined that she would want to help. He and his brother exchanged a look. Ryder figured she would be more of a hindrance than a help and hated that his brother was enjoying this so much.

"We have some stalls that need to be shoveled out," Brand said. "You don't have anything against manure, do you? We also have some barbed wire to string on a fence, but it's out in a far pasture," Brand said. "You don't ride, do you?"

"It's not that hard to ride a horse, right?" she asked, looking from one to the other of them.

"Ryder's a great teacher," Brand said as the cook brought out her breakfast. "And there's the mare that's about due," his brother said, clearly trying hard not to laugh. "Might have to pull the foal. Vicky could help with that."

As she dove into her breakfast, Ryder shot his brother a warning look. He could see how this weekend was going to go—unless he could quickly convince Victoria that ranch life wasn't for her and send her packing.

CLAUDE FELT LIKE CRAP. He hadn't slept well last night. About three in the morning, he'd decided he would quit his job, to hell with the contract he'd signed. By five, he'd changed his mind. Wen had him over a barrel. He had no choice but to go after the man's overindulged princess. But winning her?

He'd rather swallow rat poison. He despised Victoria Forester, he thought, remembering the drink she'd thrown in his face. And that slap! Some men liked a fiery woman: not him. He wanted an obedient wife and couldn't imagine how any man could rein in Victoria.

This morning, he'd looked online for a town called Powder Crossing, Montana, wondering how he was supposed to find this ranch where Victoria had presumably gone with the cowboy. Wen apparently didn't seem to mind sending him on a wild-goose chase. For all they knew, she hadn't gone with Ryder Stafford.

He'd thought about calling to see if she was even there. She and the cowboy could have parted company outside the bar last night. She could have used Ryder's phone to text Wen to say she was spending the weekend on Stafford Ranch with the cowboy. She could still be in Billings, planning to take the private jet home. That sounded more like the woman he knew.

He still had her purse with her phone inside. He'd picked it up after she and Ryder had left the bar. He'd been planning to give it to her at dinner. When she hadn't shown up, he'd thought she would come looking for it. He liked the idea of her having to come to him to get it. But so far she hadn't appeared. That wasn't like her. She couldn't bear not having her phone.

How could she have stayed in Billings last night without her purse and money and credit cards, let alone her phone? She couldn't. Maybe she really had gone with the cowboy.

He retrieved her handbag now from where he'd tossed it in his hotel room bureau. He figured she'd want it when he found her. He called her room, just in case she'd sneaked back to it last night. No answer.

Maybe Wen was right. If she had gone to the ranch, she might already be more than happy to leave by the time he showed up. If nothing else, she'd be excited to get her purse—that is if he gave it to her right away.

Maybe he would just hang on to it so her only option was letting him take her to Billings. He liked the idea of her being dependent on only him. It would be the first time he'd be in charge of her since he'd met her. He was starting to feel a whole lot better about this latest job his boss wanted him to do.

At ten to six, he was downstairs in the café, a cup of coffee in front of him waiting for Wen. One of the bodyguards, JJ Gibson, was at the counter eating his breakfast. Claude didn't fraternize with the hired help, but he was aware that JJ wasn't a fan of Wen either. Claude suspected that a lot of people who worked for his boss didn't like him. The man had made enemies: Why else did he feel the need to have two bodyguards traveling with him all the time recently? Was Wen worried that someone would try to kill him?

That thought made Claude feel even better as Wendell Forester swept into the café, the second bodyguard, Brice Schultz, right behind him. Brice dropped back to sit at the counter next to JJ while their boss made his way to Claude's table.

"Given any more thought to my offer?" Wen asked as he sat down. His boss had said, "Sleep on it." Like Claude was expected to get sleep after being humiliated. And his *offer*? His ultimatum? To make matters worse, Claude suspected that Ryder Stafford would have told Wen to shove it where the sun didn't shine rather than be bullied by this man.

"I'm going to the Stafford Ranch to see Victoria,

if she is indeed still there," Claude said. "For all we know, she could have already left."

"You think it's a waste of your time," Wen said without looking at him. Claude heard the reprimand in the older man's tone. "You could call and ask for her, I suppose, but then she'd know you're headed that way. She probably wouldn't be surprised to see you, anyway. Your decision." He pulled out his phone. "I'm sending you the ranch number."

Wen turned then to the waitress who had appeared. "I'll take the chicken fried steak, eggs over easy and a short stack on the side." He glanced at Claude. "You already ate?"

He shook his head. "I'll have the biscuits and gravy, eggs scrambled." He heard his phone whoosh as Wen put his cell away. He didn't have to look to know that his boss had sent him the phone number at Stafford Ranch. One phone call and he might not have to go, if Victoria wasn't there. Or his call could make her leave so she didn't have to see him again. He groaned inwardly at the thought.

Wen was waiting for him to make the call. The man thought he knew his daughter so well. Claude would love to prove him wrong, but was hesitant to make the call because he feared that Wen did know Victoria—probably because they were so much alike.

"Or you could just go to the ranch, pretending you weren't looking for my daughter at all," his boss said as if nothing had interrupted their conversation. "I'm sure you can come up with an excuse for being there other than Victoria, since Ryder Stafford knows I want the ranch and that you work for me."

"And get myself shot?" Claude had heard about the others Wen had sent and how they'd been run off. He sipped his coffee, hoping the food came soon. He'd had all he could take of Wendell Forester. He would drive to the ranch and take his sweet time about it. Anything was better than hanging out here with this man since Wendell was his ride home. He couldn't bear the thought of flying coach. That would be the ultimate humiliation after everything else he'd had to endure.

Anyway, he liked the idea of Victoria trapped in the middle of nowhere without money or a phone or even a credit card to pay for a ride out of there.

She was too much like her father to call him to rescue her. Why not let her stay there long enough to appreciate not just her privileged life but maybe Claude Duvall?

As they waited for their breakfast orders to be served, Wen spent the time on his phone. Claude found himself watching the two bodyguards. They both looked miserable, as if they hated their jobs as much as he did. It made him wonder why they didn't quit. Wen must be paying them a whole lot, given that they were both pilots as well as trained bodyguards. One of them even worked on Wen's private plane as a jet mechanic. The boss liked to cover his bets in case his usual pilot fell ill.

Why put up with Wendell Forester? There had to be more money working as pilots or even jet mechanics. Or was it the allure of flying around the world, staying in the best hotels and eating on the billionaire's dime that was the draw? Claude realized that he had been doing just that and enjoying it. At one time, he'd thought it wasn't such a bad gig.

The difference was he wasn't expected to risk his life to save Wen should someone try to kill him. Which was good, he thought with a hidden smile. He'd never risk *his* neck for the man.

He wondered absently who'd been sending the death threats he knew his boss had been getting. Wen liked to act like they didn't bother him, but Claude had seen him after one arrived. But why just threaten? Do it and get it over with, he thought.

Then again, Claude was looking for anything that would save him from being forced to go to the Stafford Ranch after the evil Forester princess.

BRAND SUGGESTED HIS brother show Victoria around the ranch. "I can handle the work that needs to be done today," he said, letting Ryder know he would owe him big-time. "Saddle up Susie for her and go for a ride."

"Susie?" she asked as they finished breakfast and got ready for the day ahead. "She sounds sweet. I'd love to ride her."

"Thanks for suggesting that, Brand," Ryder said, knowing he was never going to live this down. Nor was he ever going to forget how much his brother was enjoying his discomfort.

Since Victoria was dressed for riding, they headed

out to the stable where he saddled Susie and his own horse. Taking the reins, he walked Victoria through the basics of horseback riding even as he told himself this was a terrible idea. If he got her killed, Wendell Forester would end up owning this ranch.

"I think I've got the knack of it," she said after his instruction. With that, she stepped to the horse, swung up into the saddle and reached for the reins he was holding.

"You've done this before," he said, nodding to himself.

She grinned. "I learned to ride at the boarding school I attended."

"Of course you did. Do you have any other surprises for me?"

Her grin broadened. "I should hope so." She took the reins he handed her and gave him a look that told him he was in for a long weekend. This was a game to her, something she could tell her friends about when she went back to her real life. He told himself that he could get through the weekend. At least he hoped so, but only if she quit flirting with him. That was what she was doing, wasn't it?

Ryder swore under his breath. He wasn't good at games, especially with the opposite sex. He knew horses better than women. Worse, he'd never met one like Victoria Forester.

They rode out across the ranch. The feel of the horse beneath him, the sunshine and the smell of summer in the Powder River basin made him forget everything as he rode. His earlier annoyance with

Victoria quickly evaporated too as he noticed what a good rider she was.

He pointed out things that might interest her as they went. His mood got better as she showed an appreciation for the country from the river bottom to the mountains and the badlands in between.

It was one of those Montana summer days that made people fall in the love with the state. Puffy white clouds floated in a sea of deep blue above the treetops. The air smelled fresh and clean, just cool enough this beautiful morning to make the ride even more enjoyable. He loved mornings like this.

But today he couldn't help being distracted by the woman with him. She seemed so different here, her face flushed, her eyes bright. He had to keep reminding himself that she was the same woman he'd seen in the photograph of her coming out of a nightclub after clubbing with friends.

He also had to remind himself that she was Wendell Forester's daughter. The man's princess. He watched her take in the view for a few moments before he asked, "Why does your father want to buy my ranch so badly?"

Vicky seemed surprised by the question. "I have no idea. But when he sees something he wants, he buys it."

"There are a lot of ranches in Montana, a lot of them larger and considered much prettier, with rivers more famous than the Powder. What is it about this ranch that makes a man like him want it so badly when he can afford to buy anything?" It was a question he'd asked himself many times as Forester had become more relentless in his attempts to purchase the Stafford Ranch.

"I honestly don't know," she said. "There must be something about this place in particular that makes it worth owning. He doesn't just collect things unless they have a financial value to him."

"Such as?"

"He recently bought several ranches in North Dakota because they had oil on them."

"We have coalbed methane."

"Did he send a geologist out here?"

"Not that I know of." It dawned on him that a man like Forester didn't have to send anyone. "We have a local geologist, Alfred "Tick" Whitaker, who works for the gas company. He has already surveyed the ranch when my brother CJ hired the CH_4 company to drill for methane. Tick would know what is here."

"There you have it," Victoria said. "The geologist must have found something that would be of interest to my father." She seemed entranced by the wide-open spaces. "I love the way the river winds through the valley," she said as they stopped on a hill to admire the view.

"That's the Powder River. It begins in Wyoming and travels more than a hundred and fifty miles to empty into the Yellowstone River to the north of here. We'll go along the river on the way back."

"I'd like that," she said and tucked a lock of that copper hair behind her ear as she had this morning.

He found himself mesmerized by the simplest things this woman did. There was such a confidence in her. How many women would proposition him in the Billings airport, let alone make some enticing offers just to get him to pretend to be her fiancé? Most women wouldn't come to the ranch for the weekend either—not having a clue what she was getting into.

That she was brave to the point of being reckless hadn't escaped him. No wonder her father wanted to get her married off so he didn't have to worry about her.

As they rode toward the river, she asked about the area's history, if his family had been one of the first to settle the land and what it was like to have those kinds of roots.

"I can't imagine the first settlers who came here to homestead the land," she said as she looked out across it. "Such strong, brave women and men. I've never had roots like you do—never mind family living all around me."

He told her about his two sisters, Tilly and Oakley, and their husbands Cooper and Pickett. "Once you meet my sisters, you might change your mind about wishing you had family close by."

"Pickett. I love that name." She asked about Tilly and when she was due to have her baby. "Another generation on this land. I can't imagine what that's like for you. What a sense of pride you must feel to be part of it."

He'd never thought of the ranch quite that way, but seeing it through her eyes he did feel it. "It's just what we do. Ranching and living out here are all I know."

"You've lived here your whole life," she said as if in awe. "I've never lived in a place long enough to feel like it was home. My father's always on the move. I think he was better at staying put when my mother was alive, but I don't remember it. She died when I was twelve."

The trees seemed to open up before them, and there was the Powder River. The moment Victoria spotted the clear water that flowed through the rocks, she was off her horse and kicking off her boots. He laughed as he watched her peel off her socks and roll up her jeans to wade out into the shallow water to a large flat rock at the river's center.

He was tempted to take a photograph of her in the middle of the Powder River and send it to her father. He pulled out his phone and took the photo, but changed his mind about sending it to her father as he quickly dismounted and, removing his boots and socks, waded out to join her.

"The river isn't what I expected," she said with a laugh. "But I like it. It's . . . gentle but determinedly steady." Her gaze went to him. "Reminds me of you."

He chuckled at that. She thought she knew him after such a short time together? He couldn't say the same. This woman was still a mystery to him. Every time he thought he had her number, she surprised him.

"The Powder is said to be a mile wide, an inch

deep and runs uphill," he told her. "The joke was always that it was too thick to drink and too thin to plow."

"Why *Powder* River?" she asked.

"Captain Clark of the Lewis and Clark expedition named it Redstone River. But the Native Americans called it Powder River because the black shores reminded them of gunpowder, and that stuck."

She leaned back against the warm rock. She looked content. He suspected it was the breakfast that she'd put away like one of the ranch hands.

"I have to ask," he said. "Your father's bodyguards. Are they just for show?"

She glanced over at him. "I can see why you would ask that. You didn't threaten to kill my father, did you?"

Ryder shook his head. "If he's been trying to strong-arm other Montana ranchers, though, then I would imagine one of them could have threatened him. But the bodyguards are something new?"

She nodded. "He pretends it's nothing, but he's been getting death threats. Says he took on extra security for me and will keep them until he can get me married off so he knows my husband will keep me safe." She rolled her eyes. "I have a feeling he's more worried than he lets on, because I haven't seen him without the guards since he received the first threat a few weeks ago."

"Threat, like a real death threat?" he asked, remembering that he'd told Forester that he'd shoot the next person the man sent to buy his ranch.

Turning her head to look at him, she said, "Most people who meet my father want to kill him. Seriously, I know he's made enemies. I wouldn't be surprised if Claude doesn't hate him. My father seems to be getting worse, as if he can't buy enough. I don't think it makes him happy. He just likes to win. What will you do if he makes another run at your ranch?"

"I already threatened to shoot the next person he sends with an offer," Ryder said, smiling to let her know he was kidding, kind of. "I doubt he'll come himself, so he should be safe."

"I wouldn't put it past him to show up here. Best keep your gun loaded," she said and chuckled, but he wasn't sure she was joking.

CHAPTER FIVE

CLAUDE HAD NEVER seen Montana except from the air or out a hotel room window. He realized that he should treat this unappetizing job his boss was sending him on as a paid vacation. The plan had come to him after grousing for a while about the situation Wen and his daughter had put him in.

Right now, Victoria wouldn't be desperate enough to get away from the cowboy and ranch life. She'd be treating it like an adventure, a story of her wild impulsive behavior she could share with her rich city friends. Why not give her more time on a working ranch with her cowboy before Claude rode in to save her?

He just hoped the cowboy gave Victoria a real taste of ranch living. Claude knew her. She would get bored stiff in no time, out in the middle of nowhere. She'd be expecting her father to come after her. Or to send someone after her. Someone like him.

The sour taste in his mouth made him curse. He knew he was dragging his feet about going after her. He was stalling for time to come up with a plan that didn't require him to grovel.

Since there were no flights anywhere near the

town of Powder Crossing, he rented a luxury SUV on Wen's dime. But in no hurry to get to the ranch, he looked on a map and decided to drive down to Yellowstone Park and treat himself to a much-needed vacation.

He recalled with a smile that Victoria didn't have her phone or any money. She also didn't have her clothes or her makeup, things he knew she couldn't live without. He highly doubted that in Powder Crossing she would be able to find the expensive, hard-to-find brands that she only wore. So no social media, no shopping, nothing but cowboys like Ryder with manure on their boots?

His smile broadened. Maybe there was a chance that she might actually be glad to see him when he finally showed up, he thought. He wasn't worried about her falling for the cowboy. Like Wen had said, it was only a ploy. By now, she could already be missing the big city and her so-called friends, those hangers-on who loved the attention of being seen with Wendell Forester's high-rolling daughter. By the time he showed up to rescue her, she could be begging him to take her away.

And if she wasn't happy to see him when he arrived at the ranch?

He ground his teeth at the thought of her still being that snooty brat he'd have to deal with. Victoria needed something to bring her to her senses, he told himself as he drove south to Red Lodge and the Cooke City entrance to the park. When the plan came to him, he immediately rejected it. Too dangerous.

Except that the more he thought about it, the more it appealed to him. If he couldn't win her away from the cowboy, then he really didn't have any other choice.

But first he was going to see Yellowstone Park.

AFTER THAT WADE in the river, Ryder and Victoria rode their horses back the long way, stopping on a rise that overlooked both the badlands in the distance and a long stretch of the river.

"There's so much . . . sky here," she said in a kind of awe. "It's so . . . blue."

"Is this your first time in Montana?" Ryder asked as he watched her wide-eyed wonder at the huge expanse of sky and open land.

She nodded. "I couldn't understand what my father had found to be so enamored over about the state." She laughed. "He said there were more cows than people out here."

"There are."

"But he never said how breathtaking it was." She huffed. "He probably didn't notice." She was looking out across the ranch again. The look of astonishment on her face when he told her how many acres they ran made him smile. He'd thought she would hate this country and be bored by now. Maybe she wasn't as shallow as he'd thought she was and felt a pinch of guilt. He'd expected her to be the princess the media wrote about in less than glowing terms. A pretty, spoiled-rotten young woman looking for her next party.

She glanced over at him as if feeling his intent gaze. "What?"

"You. I thought you'd hate this," he said. "I got the impression you only liked glitz and glamour, cared only about what to wear to your next party and who to be seen with on social media."

"Ouch! I like to think there's more to me than how I'm portrayed in the tabloids and social media," she said. "After all, I have my MBA from Harvard and graduated with honors from Sarah Lawrence."

He couldn't help his shocked expression.

"I'm not sure how to take your surprise," she said with a chuckle. "And no, my father didn't build them a new library to make that happen, although he had thought he was going to have to." She snickered. "Like a lot of men, he underestimated me. My father never mentions my degrees because he thinks it intimidates the kind of man I need to marry."

Ryder laughed, not about to touch that. "Business administration, huh?"

"Business and art," she said. "Admittedly, the business part was my father's idea, but I actually enjoyed it. I have ideas for starting a variety of small businesses to help other women achieve their dreams."

Ryder found himself trying to reconcile the different images he'd had of Victoria Forester. The young woman at the airport offering him money to be her fiancé, the party girl online and this young woman next to him on the back of a horse beside the Powder River who wanted to help other women start their own businesses.

"I would think that your father wanted you to major in business so you could work with him, but that doesn't explain why he would try to marry you off," he said.

"Doesn't it?" she said. "He wants to keep me close and married to one of his clones so he can control me and yet not worry about me. For my father, everything is about money and business. If he wants this ranch, it's just to take its treasures."

Ryder knew she was probably right. Montana had a history of men like Wendell Forester coming in and mining the riches and leaving a mess behind them. Now called Big Sky Country, Montana had originally been known as the Treasure State.

"So your property runs to the mountains in all directions?" she asked as if wanting to change the subject as much as he did.

"Not quite. As I said, we border the McKenna Ranch. The two ranches, though, run from mountain to mountain and beyond. You need a lot of land to raise cattle here. The only thing that divides the two ranches is a creek and section of the river."

"Where your mother used to rendezvous with the handsome rancher next door," she said as she grinned and shifted to meet his gaze, her arm brushing his. He felt an electrical current arc between them.

"So you were listening last night," he said. They were so close, he could see tiny gold flakes in her green eyes. The scents of summer seemed to fill the air, mixing with a hint of something sweet. His gaze went to her lips, and he felt a pull that had him leaning toward her for a kiss—even as his common sense warned him against it.

IT HAD SEEMED like the most natural thing she'd ever done. The summer sun warm on her skin, the cloudless blue sky overhead, the scents of pine and saddle leather in the air—all making the moment perfect as her body gravitated to Ryder's for the kiss. A warm breeze stirred the air between them. She could barely hear it rustling the cottonwood leaves over the pounding of her heart.

Only their lips touched softly. Breaths intermingled for what felt like a mere instant before he drew back. His surprised gaze locked with hers, and she saw that he had felt it too. Something almost magical had passed between them.

He cleared this throat and said, "We'd better get back."

She nodded, feeling like a girl after her first kiss. Only her real first kiss hadn't been anything like this. Her lips still tingled, or she would have thought she'd imagined it. She warned herself not to get too attached to this cowboy. She was having fun: that was all this was. When the weekend was over, she was going back to her old life, this place and this cowboy only a nice memory.

"I'm surprised we haven't heard from your father," Ryder said as if also thinking about how temporary this was. This adventure had an expiration date. Still, she wished he hadn't brought her father up.

"You just had to go and spoil this beautiful day," she joked. "Seriously, thank you for the horseback ride. I haven't enjoyed anything like it for a very long time."

He looked surprised by that and maybe not quite sure she was being truthful. He really didn't trust her, but who could blame him after the way they'd met? "I thought you'd be making plans to leave by the time you got up this morning. Not everyone appreciates the solitude, the silence, the absence of everything the city has to offer."

"I can understand why you'd think that," she said, although wondering why he was saying this. Because of the kiss? Because he hadn't expected to feel anything and wished he hadn't? He didn't need to tell her that this was short-term. She knew how he felt about her father—and her as well, given that he thought she wouldn't even last a night here.

They rode in silence for a few minutes. "I could have contacted my father by now if I had wanted to, you know. You have reminded me several times that the ranch has a landline, since I don't have my cell. All I'd have to do is call, and I'm sure my father would send someone to pick me up."

Ryder looked a little sheepish. "I wasn't suggesting that you should do that. I just wanted you to have that option." He sighed. "Knowing your father, I wouldn't be surprised to find a helicopter sitting in the front yard when we return to the house."

Men, she thought with a silent groan. That kiss must have really scared him. Why else would he keep reminding her of not just her father, but their so-called weekend arrangement?

Whatever his reason, she'd had enough. "Race you back?" She didn't wait for his answer as she spurred her horse and took off. Let him try to catch her.

WENDELL FORESTER FELT his chest squeeze his breath from his lungs as he looked at the latest death threat. It had been shoved under his hotel room door while he was in the shower. He'd gotten a variety of threatening letters over the years. Those hadn't bothered him. When you ran an empire like his, you made enemies. But these latest death threats had a ring of promise to them.

Someone didn't just want to scare him, they really wanted him dead.

Coming to Billings hadn't been only about trying to close a merger deal between Claude and his daughter. He'd desperately needed to get away to some place he'd thought would be safe. But the death threat that had been pushed under the door proved that his alleged killer not only knew he was in Billings, but had come here after him.

He thought about taking the note to the authorities, but knew it was useless. There wouldn't be fingerprints or any way to find the device the note had been printed on—just like the first one he'd taken to the FBI.

From the time he'd been knee-high to a grasshopper, raised dirt-poor, he'd been on his own. It was what made him so successful. He went after what he wanted, and he didn't give up. He picked up his phone and called Brice Schultz, the bodyguard who was supposed to be watching his room. No answer. Odd, he thought and tried JJ Gibson. Again, no answer.

Walking to his hotel room door, he opened it to find the hallway empty. Was it possible they'd both gone off somewhere? Not if they hoped to stay employed. He closed the door and looked around his hotel room. Anyone could have put the note under his door. It didn't take a room key to go to any of the rooms on the different floors. He'd brought his own security where he didn't have to worry about it.

He started to call Claude, but remembered he'd sent him off on a wild-goose chase. There was no way the man was going to get Victoria away from the cowboy. It was as he'd said: Claude was only a catalyst. If there was any chance that Victoria might be interested in Ryder Stafford, then Claude could push them together. It was a long shot. It wasn't as if he thought his daughter would do something drastic like marry Ryder Stafford to spite him.

No, he'd failed miserably in the Getting His Daughter Married department. It was time to fly back to Dallas where he would hire more security. All he had to do was get there alive. Even as he thought it, he knew that whoever was after him could still get to him. He thought of his daughter and worried that he'd put her in the line of fire as well by insisting she come to Montana this weekend.

Maybe worse, Ryder Stafford had her. What if he was the one who'd been sending the death threats? The moment he thought it, he realized he was wrong. He'd always been a pretty good judge of character. Stafford had been upfront with him. He wasn't sneaking around putting death threats under hotel room doors.

Also, he'd allegedly left town with Victoria. Maybe it was time Wendell found out if his daughter really was at the Stafford Ranch—and safe. After all, the text saying she was at the ranch with her fiancé had come from Ryder's phone.

He realized he should have called right away to find out if she really was there since he didn't believe she was Ryder Stafford's fiancée. If someone wanted to hurt him, a sure-fire way to do it would be to use his daughter. Which was another reason he wanted her married.

The woman who answered the phone at the Stafford Ranch hadn't known Victoria and said Ryder had gone out on a horseback ride. She could have him return the call. He'd declined and hung up.

There was only one way to find out if she was safe. He'd have to go to the ranch. Pulling out his phone, he called his pilot only to learn that there was no airport near the ranch that could accommodate the jet.

Swearing, he called a local rental agency to have a car delivered. As he hung up, there was a knock at his door that made him start. He turned to look at the door. He hadn't succeeded in life by being afraid of anyone or anything. But wasn't that the problem? He barreled his way through to get what he wanted, unconcerned by who got hurt in the process. Was it any wonder he was getting death threats?

"Mr. Forester?" a male voice he recognized called from the other side of the door.

He moved swiftly to the door and threw it open. "Where the hell have you been, JJ?" he demanded.

Wendell saw something in the man's eyes before JJ quickly masked it. Not even his security guards liked him.

"I was just down the hall."

"Really? Then, why didn't you see whoever shoved a death threat under my door?"

"I thought Brice—"

"Are you telling me you don't know where he is?"

JJ looked as if it was the last thing he wanted to tell his boss.

"Neither one of you got a description of the person who sent me a death threat. Is that what you're telling me?"

JJ's face tightened, his eyes narrowing slightly. "I'm afraid not, since I thought Brice was covering your door."

"You're both fired," Wendell said. "I'll leave your severance pay and commercial coach tickets for your flights back to Dallas at the main desk."

He slammed the door, shaking. He couldn't trust anyone, and he sure as hell didn't trust JJ Gibson. He recalled that JJ had come highly recommended, though he couldn't remember by whom.

The main desk called to say his rental had been delivered. He quickly packed, anxious to get on the road. It had been so long since he'd driven himself, he was actually looking forward to a trip alone.

Someone was trying to scare him. Or maybe really wanted him dead. He had no idea who, but plenty of people had good reason. As he got ready to leave Billings, he realized that he hadn't heard from Claude Duvall.

Or maybe he had, thinking of the death threat he now had tucked into his suitcase.

CHAPTER SIX

OAKLEY STAFFORD MCKENNA had just gotten off the phone with her brother Brand. She loved that Brand enjoyed relaying juicy news as much as she did.

Ryder had brought home a woman? That was shocking enough, but the woman was the daughter of the tycoon who'd been trying to buy the ranch?

"I'm going to pick up Tilly and go out to the ranch," she called to her husband who had come in for a break from the construction work still being done on their house. It was almost finished, and she adored everything about it.

"Before you leave, we need to talk about your brother," Pickett called back.

"Brand?" she asked in surprise as she walked into the kitchen still trying to get her earring on. Had her husband heard about Victoria Forester before she had and not mentioned it?

"Not Brand," he said almost irritably, "CJ."

"Oh." She got the earring in and turned to face him. She'd known Pickett would be furious when he heard that CJ had been not just released from jail, but that the charges had been dropped after one of the witnesses had left the country and another had retracted his testimony.

"CJ is an attempted murderer," her husband said with a curse. "You know your mother was behind getting him out. What was she thinking? CJ is dangerous, and now he's running free?"

"He isn't free. He's on probation," she said quickly. She would have loved to argue that her mother had nothing to do with getting rid of the two witnesses but saved her breath. Pickett knew Charlotte Stafford. CJ had always been her favorite offspring.

Pickett made a rude sound. "This has your mother's fingerprints all over it. But I can't believe she didn't warn you about what she was planning to do."

He wasn't wrong. Oakley's mother had come to her asking her to forgive and forget what CJ had done. He'd shot her, claiming it was an accident, and when Oakley had tried to stop the drilling of another methane well on the ranch, he'd hired two men to do whatever they had to, to stop Oakley from interfering once and for all.

She hadn't told Pickett, who would have gone through the roof at even the suggestion that she listen to her mother let alone forgive and forget. Nor did he know that Oakley had visited CJ in jail at her mother's request.

She recalled the day at the jail when she'd watched CJ come in on the other side of the plexiglass and pick up the phone handset. Oakley had hesitated to pick up hers on the partition that separated them. A lot more had separated them their entire lives. CJ had bullied his siblings, who eventually just made a point of staying clear of him—all except Oakley.

She'd always stood up to him, even when she got the worst of it. And suddenly she found herself in the middle. CJ behind bars and their mother wanting Oakley to forgive him when she'd almost died because of him.

CJ had looked nervous. He hadn't expected her to come visit him. From his expression, he'd thought she'd come to the jail to tell him what she thought of him.

They'd been at each other's throats since they were kids. True, he instigated it, but Oakley always held her own. She'd thought that sometimes he'd admired her for not being afraid of him when she should have been.

But then again, she was the reason he was locked up now.

"Mother asked me to come see you," she'd said, making it clear it hadn't been her idea.

"It's good to see you. I heard you got married."

Oakley had always been able to see right through his facade. Of course, that was why their mother had sent her to the jail. Charlotte Stafford wanted to believe CJ could change.

"What do you want me to say? I'm sorry for what I tried to do to you? *I am.*"

"Sorry I'm alive or sorry you got caught?"

"Sorry I've been such a shitty brother." He'd almost sounded truthful.

"Mother wants to believe that you've reached rock bottom and might now see the error of your ways," she'd said, glaring at him. "I think she's deluding herself. You're incapable of changing even if you seriously wanted to. Oh, you'd say anything to get out of this. But I know you, CJ. You're rotten to the core. If you get out of here, you'll go back to your old ways in a heartbeat. No one will be safe from you."

She'd seen that he was trying to keep his cool. She always could get under his skin.

"Then, why did you bother to come here?" he'd demanded.

"Because I had to look into your eyes to make sure."

"And now you're sure?" He'd held her gaze for a few moments before dragging it away. "You're right. I'd do anything to get out of here, let alone not go to prison for years. Why wouldn't I? But maybe I'm not all bad. Maybe there's hope for me. Don't you believe in second chances?"

He must have seen that she wasn't buying it, because he'd continued. "How's life with Pickett? I heard he's building a house for the two of you."

"You aren't really interested in my life."

"Heard Tilly's pregnant. Do we know if it's a boy or girl yet?"

"Stop it, CJ."

"You think I don't know that things have changed?" he'd demanded. "Tilly's married to a McKenna, and you're practically married to one too. Both of you will be living on the McKenna Ranch. Brand and Ryder have taken over the family ranch. Brand's now with the daughter of Dixon Malone, mother's murdered second husband? I hear about all of it. Isn't it possible that I wish I'd done things differently so I'm a part of it? It's like you've all written me off, forgotten about me as you all go on with your lives as if I never existed."

Oakley had smiled. "There's the CJ I know. Poor you. If you'd gotten your way, I would be dead right now. You would have kept the feud going between the two families. It's been a relief not having you around." Her voice had broken with emotion. "You're the family's bad seed. You will never change."

She'd seen the look on his face. He'd thought he was never getting out as she'd slammed down the phone and, without even a look back, walked out.

But her mother still wanted to believe that CJ could change, that being in jail all that time had put the fear of God in him.

"Your mother is delusional if she thinks CJ has changed," Pickett said now. "I'm worried about what he will do. CJ is dangerous when it comes to you. I shouldn't have to tell you that." He didn't. She knew her brother better than anyone. Anyone except her mother. Not to mention Pickett had been the one who'd saved her life that night when CJ's hired thugs had almost killed her.

Charlotte desperately wanted to believe that a person could change, because she had finally forgiven her former lover Holden McKenna. When they were both young, Holden had broken her heart. While Oakley believed that her mother probably had forgiven Holden, Charlotte seemed to have forgotten her decades-long vendetta against him—a battle she'd dragged her and Holden's families into.

"I know that look," Pickett said, drawing Oakley into his arms. "The *I want to believe CJ's changed and to forgive and forget* look."

She smiled. She wasn't about to do that. Nor did she trust that he'd changed—even though their mother apparently did. But then, CJ had always been her favorite.

"It doesn't matter how I feel about CJ. I'm married to a handsome cowboy," she said, snuggling up to him. "I'm living in this beautiful house you built for us and happier than I ever knew possible. I want to enjoy it. No conflict, no drama."

After her last miscarriage, the doctor had told her that she needed to relax. Getting upset wasn't helping. "Forget about conceiving for a while," he'd suggested. "Find something you enjoy doing and throw yourself into that."

She'd thrown herself into making her new house a home with the man she loved. The doctor had been right. It had taken the stress off in the bedroom. Instead of trying to conceive, she found she was enjoying the lovemaking more. She'd convinced herself that they would have a child someday even if they had to adopt. Pickett had assured her they would fill this new house with children even if he had to steal them from an orphanage.

"I don't think we have orphanages anymore. Maybe you can steal a few from a foster care program," she'd suggested, only partly joking.

He smiled at her now and gave her a kiss. "I just want to enjoy you too. But knowing that CJ's out . . . I can't help but worry about you."

"We don't have to see him. If our paths ever cross—"

"You'll play nice," he said as he let go of her. "And so will I. We want him to think that we're not a danger to him. Otherwise . . ."

"Maybe all this time in jail waiting for his trial has taught him something," she said, not believing a word of it.

Her husband scoffed at that.

She changed the subject. "I can't wait to see Ryder and this woman he brought back from Billings. She's the daughter of the developer who's been trying to buy the Stafford Ranch."

"That sounds suspiciously dangerous."

"I'm going to get Tilly to go over there with me to check her out." She didn't mention that she'd been avoiding her very pregnant sister out of jealousy and felt guilty about it.

"Are you sure that's a good idea to go to the Stafford Ranch right now?"

"It's a great idea. You know Ryder. All my brother has thought about is running the ranch with Brand while Mother is gone. This is so out of character for him. He hardly ever dates. Now he's brought a woman to the ranch. I have to find out what's going on."

He sighed. "Well, be careful if CJ is around. Or your mother for that matter."

"Neither CJ nor my mother are staying at the ranch. She's staying at the hotel in town. She got CJ an apartment in Miles City. Mother isn't letting him back on the ranch." At least for now.

"So you've talked to your mother about this." He gave her the side-eye. "She convinced you that CJ is no longer a danger to you."

"*Convinced* isn't exactly the right word. I'll never trust CJ ever. But I do want peace in the family. Families," she added. All the years with the McKennas and Staffords being at war seemed to be over. Pickett had worked on the McKenna Ranch since he was a teenager, so he was Mc-Kenna kin.

Her husband still looked worried as she left. But then again, he had been worried long before her miscarriages. Now they were both waiting, hoping the doctor was right and she could still conceive a child and carry it to term.

CLAUDE TRIED TO enjoy Yellowstone Park, but it smelled like rotten eggs and had a lot trees, way too much traffic and no bears—at least none that he saw. How many bubbling, boiling mud pots could a person look at before they'd had enough? He'd had enough quickly, mostly though because he couldn't get his mind off Victoria and her cowboy. When he wasn't thinking about them, he was thinking about how much he hated her and her father.

After fighting the summer traffic, he'd finally left the touristy part of the state for the wild, open spaces. He couldn't imagine what his boss thought was so appealing about this part of Montana. The farther east he drove, the more boring the country became with miles of nothing but prairie broken only by badlands and mountains. He yearned for some sign of civilization. How he would have loved to see a town, any town.

When his phone rang, he snatched it up, thankful for the break in the monotony of this drive. "Hello?" He instantly regretted not checking first to see who was calling.

"Where are you?" Wen demanded.

"I'm trying to find this ranch where your daughter may have run off to," he snapped back. "You didn't tell me it's in the middle of nowhere. Why do you ask?" He realized that his boss might be calling to tell him that Victoria had returned, and he could turn around and come back. That would have been the best news he'd heard in a long time.

"You should have already been there hours ago," Wen snapped.

"I decided to let her enjoy ranch life for a while." Silence. "I thought you told me to use my good judgment."

"Did I?"

Claude heard something in Wen's voice, also in

the background. "Is everything all right? It sounds like you're driving. Wen?" No answer. "Wen?" Maybe he was having a heart attack or—

"I'm being followed." His boss sounded scared, which was so not like Wendell Forester that it scared *him*.

"Do you want me to call the police or something?"

"I have to go." With that he disconnected.

Followed? What was Wen doing driving? Where were his bodyguards? Where was he?

Ahead, Claude saw a town appear on the horizon. It wasn't much of a town, but he'd take it. Unfortunately, it wasn't Powder Crossing. Well, it didn't matter. Tired, he'd had enough driving. A thought struck him. What would happen if the person who sent the death threats actually made good and took his boss out? What would that do to his contract with the bastard? Wouldn't it be null and void? Wouldn't he be free?

He found himself rooting for whoever was following Wen.

At the only motel sign in town, he pulled in and let himself breathe, suddenly a whole lot less tired. He paid for one night and drove down to his room to park right out front. The room had knotty pine walls and a cowboy bedspread, making him realize he was in another world, one he couldn't wait to get out of.

He reminded himself it was just for the night.

There was one other positive he realized. If whoever was following Wen did him in, he wouldn't have to go to Powder Crossing. He'd never have to see Victoria Forester or her father ever again. Except at the funeral. He probably should go to the funeral. He'd see how he felt.

Claude told himself that he would decide about his future in the morning. Maybe there would be something on the early-morning news. He fell into the lumpy bed and dropped off to sleep, hoping that come morning he would be free of Wendell Forester and his daughter.

TILLY STAFFORD MCKENNA waddled over to answer the door. Her ankles were swollen, although she could no longer see them. She'd gone from a cute baby bump to this giant watermelon pressing up against her lungs. She couldn't remember what it was like to get a good night's sleep. The only way she could breathe was by not lying down. The thought brought tears to her eyes since she craved sleep so badly. If she didn't have this baby soon . . .

She opened the door to find her sister standing there. "Oakley," she cried, never so glad to see anyone. Oakley had been avoiding her since her sister's last miscarriage. She'd missed her so much that she began to cry, both sad for the toil this pregnancy was having on her sister and joyous that Oakley was finally here. Tilly threw her arms around her, getting as close as possible in her condition.

"Not the waterworks again," Oakley said with a

groan. "Really, sis. I can't believe you haven't had this baby yet." That only made Tilly cry harder because it was exactly what she would have expected from her sister.

"That was a joke, you know," Oakley said, alarmed as Tilly sobbed. "It's a good thing I'm here. You desperately need to get your sense of humor back. You did have one, didn't you? It's been so long, I can't remember." Oakley pulled back to look at her sister. "Tell me what's wrong."

Tilly tried to quit crying. "I'm just so tired. I can't sleep, if I eat I get heartburn, I can barely walk, and I haven't been out of this house for weeks."

"That's all? Well, I can't do much about some of those problems, but I did come to get you out of the house." Tilly perked right up, blew her nose and quit crying. "Ryder went to Billings on Friday and brought back a woman."

Tilly wiped her eyes, sick also of feeling sorry for herself. This wasn't the way she'd pictured being married, pregnant and about to have her first child any day. Had she not fallen in love with Cooper McKenna, the son of her mother's worst enemy, she kept thinking things would have been different. Cooper assured that she wasn't cursed. Tilly wasn't so sure.

"I talked to Brand this morning," Oakley said after she'd helped her sister find her shoes and a jacket and had gotten her into the pickup cab and buckled up. "She's staying in your old room."

"Really?" Tilly said, trying to imagine the sort

of woman her brother might have brought home to the ranch.

"See, even Ryder is enjoying not having Mother and CJ living in the house, although I wonder how long that will last," Oakley said. "Have you seen CJ?"

Tilly shook her head. "I still can't believe Mother got him out of jail, let alone found a way to have the charges dropped. He almost killed us both." Tilly had been at the house the day her brother had realized the sheriff was looking for him. He grabbed her, forced her to go with him in the pickup and made a run for it. When he crashed the truck, he'd been injured. But Tilly had thought for sure she was going to die.

"You know Mother," Oakley said. "She would have pulled strings, paid off everyone she could and probably even promised to sleep with the judge."

"Honestly, Oakley!"

"He's an old judge, so it really was a nice favor."

"Stop it. You're going to make me pee my pants," Tilly begged.

"You're right. This is serious, Ryder bringing a woman back to the ranch. He's never done that before. Why would he do it now?"

"Because our mother isn't there?" Tilly suggested. "Who is this woman?" she asked, feeling like the protective older sister she was.

"That's the kicker. According to Brand, she is Victoria Forester, daughter of billionaire and real estate tycoon Wendell Forester. The same man who's been trying to buy the ranch. Pickett thinks it's dangerously suspicious. Don't you love it?"

"Why would Ryder bring her back to the ranch and put her in *my* room?"

Oakley laughed. "Apparently, she's rich and sexy and our brother was saving her from a fate worse than death. Her father was trying to marry her off to one of his handpicked flunkies, Brand said. So, we are going to stop by the ranch and check her out."

Tilly groaned. "Like we did when Brand had Birdie Malone out at the ranch."

"Exactly. The snoopy sisterhood is back. Hopefully, it will keep your mind off all that," she said waving a hand in front of Tilly's giant baby bump. "I hope you brought crackers. You aren't throwing up in my pickup, are you?"

RYDER AND VICTORIA returned to the ranch after their ride to find his sisters waiting for them. At once, he realized that they'd already gotten the lowdown from Brand. In fact, that must be why they were here, he realized. Brand had called Oakley to tell her about Victoria, and Oakley had dragged her very pregnant sister out to the ranch to check her out. He groaned, hating to think what all Brand had told them.

Inside the barn, Tilly was pacing the floor, holding her stomach and looking as if she could drop this baby at any moment. "Shouldn't you be on your way to the hospital?" he asked her. She waved a hand to silence him in answer. He turned to his younger sister, no doubt the ringleader of this little escapade.

Oakley gave him a Cheshire smile. "Tilly was

just dying to get out of the house, and I said, 'Let's go see Ryder, and see what he's up to.'"

"Brand called you, didn't he?" her brother said with a curse, hating to think how much Brand had enjoyed that as Oakley's gaze went to Victoria.

"I didn't realize you had company," his sister said innocently. There was nothing innocent about Oakley.

"Right," Ryder said and looked at Tilly. "Do you need to sit down?"

She shook her head. "Can't sit. Can't sleep. Can't do anything until this baby comes out."

He shook his head in commiseration and turned back to Oakley. "Victoria Forester, these are my sisters, Oakley Hanson and Tilly McKenna."

"It's nice to meet you," Victoria said. "Tilly? Thanks for the clothes and your room." Tilly waved it away as if it was nothing and speaking would make her even more miserable than she was.

"It's not like she'll ever need either again," Oakley said. "So, Victoria, are you really Wendell Forester's daughter?"

Ryder rolled his eyes. "I apologize for my sisters. They're very . . . protective and nosy. Oakley is the worst."

"I don't admit this to a lot of people, but yes, I am his daughter. I'm here for the weekend after your brother saved my life," Victoria said.

"Saved your life? How dramatic," Oakley said, shooting a look at Ryder. "My brother is just full of surprises. Is your father really trying to marry you off to some loser?"

"Oakley," Ryder protested, giving her his zip-it face.

She ignored the warning. "Just wondering if he's trying to marry her off to *you*, brother dear."

"Not to worry," Victoria said. "It's actually a funny story how we met. Are you sure you don't want to try to sit down, Tilly? No? Okay."

"Victoria, I really don't think they need to hear—"

"We were both at the Billings airport. I was on the phone with a friend when I saw your brother." To his horror, she proceeded to tell his sisters the story, not leaving out a single detail.

"Wow," Oakley said when she finished. "That's going to be an interesting one to tell your children."

"What's so funny is that I'd never kissed a cowboy." She looked over at him and grinned. Ryder felt heat rush to his face as she said, "But I have now."

Oakley's eyes widened before she shot a look at her sister. "I hope you're listening to all this, Tilly." She turned back to Victoria. "You should know you're the first woman my brother has ever brought to the ranch."

"Really?" Victoria grinned over at him, making him want to disappear underneath the floorboards. He would have gone to find something else to do, but he couldn't bear the thought of leaving his sisters with Victoria. He hated to think what could happen.

"Okay, we have work to do here," Ryder said through clenched teeth. "Maybe the two of you should go, since it looks as if Tilly is going to have this baby right here in the barn."

"Subtle," Oakley said, looking from Victoria to him as if making up her own mind about what was or wasn't going on. "Victoria, in case we don't see you before you leave at the end of the weekend, it's been a pleasure. But in case this *thing* lasts more than the weekend, maybe we'll be seeing you around here again."

Ryder took his sister's arm. "Why don't I walk you out to your truck."

Oakley laughed. "I can find my own truck, Ryder. Come on, sis." But he didn't take no for an answer. Oakley looked around as the three of them headed to where she'd parked earlier. "Isn't CJ getting out of jail today? I thought you might have already seen him."

"No. Fortunately, you're the only one who's stopped by," Ryder said. "And no, I don't want to talk about CJ or anything else," he said. "You also don't need to mention this to the rest of the family, especially Mother."

"You like her," Oakley said, grinning with glee. "Be careful, brother," she called after him as he walked away. "He likes her," she said as she helped her sister back into the pickup. "You really should just go ahead and have this baby, Tilly."

"Thank you for that wonderful advice."

"You ever find out what you're having?" Oakley asked as she climbed behind the wheel.

"A boy or a girl."

"You sure that's all that's in there? You might be having a whole team."

"Just drive," Tilly said. "Try hitting all the pot-holes in the road."

CHAPTER SEVEN

CJ STAFFORD HADN'T expected a brass band when he walked out of jail. But he had expected someone to pick him up. He stood just outside the gate, waiting. He hated waiting. Worse, he hated the feeling that he was no longer relevant.

He thought of his sister Oakley. When she'd come to visit him in jail that one and only time, she'd made it clear that he was no longer part of their lives. He was still surprised that their mother had gotten him freed—especially after what Oakley had probably told her about their conversation at the prison.

She'd made it clear that she didn't think he could ever change.

You're right. I'd do anything to get out of here, let alone not go to prison for years. Why wouldn't I? But maybe I'm not all bad. Maybe there's hope for me. Don't you believe in second chances?

Clearly, she hadn't when it came to him.

He hadn't bothered to ask her if she would ever forgive him for what he'd done to her. He was no fool. He knew his sister, and apparently she knew him. Or at least thought she did. Maybe he'd just show her that he could change. Maybe he'd show them all.

Isn't it possible that I wish I'd done things differently? he'd asked his sister that day in jail.

Oakley hadn't believed it, said it was a relief not having him around and that he could never change.

Maybe she was right, he thought now. Worse, it seemed she was right that life had gone on just fine without him since no one was here to pick him up. Hadn't she warned him that there was no place for him in any of their lives?

Grinding his teeth, he hated that it might be true. At least for a while. His mother thought he should be happy with the life she was offering him. An apartment in Miles City, miles from the Powder River basin where he'd grown up. Miles from the Stafford Ranch, the ranch he'd always promised himself would one day be his alone.

His brothers Brand and Ryder were now running the ranch. Oakley was married to Pickett Hanson, a McKenna ranch hand, and living next door. Same with his sister Tilly, who'd married Cooper McKenna. How cozy was that! The two fraternizing with the enemy.

The McKennas had been the enemies long before CJ was born. That bastard Holden McKenna had used their mother and then broken her heart when he married someone else—someone with more property to add to the McKenna Ranch. It was bad enough that their mother had never gotten over the rancher. But now CJ was expected to play nice? After all, he'd promised his mother he could.

But there was one thing he couldn't do no matter what promises he'd made her. If Charlotte Stafford even thought about getting together with Holden McKenna, all bets were off.

Just thinking about it brought back that blinding fury he'd felt that day long ago when he first went away and his sister Oakley had come to the jail. He remembered sitting there, the phone to his ear, wanting to make her pay for what she'd said. It had hurt a lot more than he'd thought it would, hearing how she felt about him. That he would never have the Stafford Ranch. That no one except their mother wanted him out from behind bars.

As he stood alone, waiting for a ride, he no longer wanted to even try to change. That hatred he'd felt most of his life now boiled up inside him. Like Oakley had said, his family didn't give a damn about him. He wanted to show them all, but they weren't going to like what they saw, he told himself.

Easy, he warned himself. He'd convinced his mother that he'd changed. That was the only reason she'd gotten the case against him thrown out. Any trouble, though, and he would be behind bars again. He didn't know how he was going to do it, but he was going to get even with all of them.

He spotted a car coming and felt both relief and embarrassment mix with his bubbling rage. Finally, he thought. He had expected his mother to be sitting here waiting for his release, since she'd fought so hard to get him out. But even she didn't seem all that excited now that he was free.

As he started for the car, he realized it wasn't his mother driving the large black SUV. It was her *lawyer*. He tried to hide his revulsion. He couldn't stand the sight of Ian Drake. Tall, gray and dressed like an undertaker, the man had a constant facial expression that foretold of doom and gloom.

CJ opened the passenger-side door and peered in. "Where's my mother?"

"She couldn't make it. She sent me. Get in."

He swore under his breath, but today he had to take what he could get.

"Welcome back, CJ Stafford," he said under his breath as he climbed in and looked out his side window. As the lawyer drove, CJ promised to rain down his wrath on the entire Powder River basin and everyone in it, especially his family that had deserted him.

VICTORIA FOUND RYDER'S embarrassment sweet and his sisters delightful, especially the obvious ringleader, Oakley.

"I'm so sorry about that," Ryder said after his sisters had driven away. "I'm going to throttle my brother for calling Oakley."

She laughed. "I loved Oakley. She reminds me of me. I do hope Tilly is all right, though, and doesn't have that baby in the pickup on the way to town. I can't wait to meet the rest of your family."

"Now you are scaring me," he said. "It would be

just like my mother and CJ to show up next. You really don't know what you're wishing for."

"Oh, they can't be that bad. After all, you've met my father. Maybe we can get your mother and my father together."

"They would be perfect for each other, but she's already taken. She's been in love with the same man, Holden McKenna, her whole life, and has made his life hell."

"She does sound perfect for my father. Now I really want to meet her."

He smiled and shook his head. "I think we need to get away from the ranch and any chance of crossing paths with more of my family. What do you think about going into town for dinner?"

She studied him. "Are you that worried they might show up?"

"I just thought you might want to see Powder Crossing. You say you don't miss the nightlife. We'd have to go in early before they roll up the sidewalks."

"I think you're just trying to get me away from here, but I'd love to see Powder Crossing." Behind him she saw his brother approaching.

"Glad you two are back," Brand said, ignoring Ryder's warning look. The two of them would have this out later. "It's time to feed. Thought Victoria could drive the truck and we could toss out the bales."

RYDER SAW WHAT his brother was up to, but the idea of getting his brother alone on the back of the flatbed full of hay appealed to him, since he had a few choice words to share with him. He wanted to kick his butt for calling Oakley.

"Fine," he told Brand and turned to Victoria. "You don't mind driving the truck, do you?" Then he saw her expression. "Let me guess. You can't drive a stick shift."

"I can't drive at all."

"*What?*" the brothers said almost in unison as they stared at her.

"I've lived in a large city my whole life. I had no reason to learn to drive."

Ryder looked at his brother. "I'll teach her how to drive the truck, and you can throw out the bales, Brand, since this was your idea." He thought Brand would know what was coming and try to get out of it.

But instead, he grinned and called Ryder's bluff. A novice behind the wheel of a big truck learning to drive a stick shift would be one hell of a bumpy ride, but Brand deserved it for siccing their sisters on him.

Once in the truck, with Victoria behind the wheel and Brand on the flatbed with the pile of hay bales, Ryder said, "It's easy. See those pedals? The left one is the clutch, the middle one is the break, and the far-right one is the gas." He put down his window and yelled back to Brand. "Better hang on!"

Victoria pushed in the clutch, started the truck and, at his instruction, gave the truck some gas as she eased up on the clutch. The truck jumped, and Brand let out a cry in the back.

"This is going to be a lot more fun than I thought," Ryder said after checking to make sure his brother hadn't been injured. "Try again," he said to Victoria. "A little gas and a little less clutch all at the same time."

CHARLOTTE STAFFORD HAD been waiting for the text from her lawyer. He'd picked up CJ who was now settled into the apartment she'd rented for him in Miles City. That was a relief, she thought, knowing that CJ would be upset that she hadn't picked him up herself. For years, he'd been her favorite child, the one she doted on, the one she knew she'd help ruin.

In the past, she would have been waiting for him outside the jail. She would have coddled him and assured him that she would take care of everything. But she was no longer that woman. What he did now was up to him, she told herself, her thoughts and worries elsewhere.

All morning, she'd had a feeling she couldn't shake that she needed to see Tilly. She wasn't looking forward to her daughter's reaction at seeing her again after the way she'd left things with her. She'd missed most of Tilly's pregnancy.

But now she was home. CJ wasn't the only reason she'd come home. She had fences to mend with all her children, especially Tilly and Oakley.

Her return had caused a stir. Just as her disappearance had. Charlotte knew there would be even more talk now that she was back and had gotten her oldest son out of not just jail but a prison sentence. Let them talk, she thought as she drove toward the McKenna Ranch. She saw the looks on the faces of people who saw her drive by. They were surprised she'd come back. Most thought she didn't have the courage to ever show her face here again. The rest thought she'd died.

Were they really that foolish that they thought they'd seen the last of her? She owned a huge ranch with her family next to the Powder River. And she wasn't the kind of woman who, even after being knocked down, wouldn't get up again.

If anything, she was surprised that she'd stayed away for so long. She'd lent her house to the McKennas after theirs had burned to the ground. She'd escaped a prison sentence herself before she'd left town without a word of explanation.

Rumors had run rampant. Her friend Elaine had kept her informed in the time she was gone. "She's sick," one wife of a rancher had been overhead saying at the general store. "Mayo Clinic, I heard. It's bad."

"I heard she checked herself into rehab for alcohol abuse," another said. "I would have been driven to drink too if I had son like CJ."

"With her kind of money, I'd bet if she checked herself in anywhere it would be a five-star hotel or a spa," another offered. "She'll be back looking so great that Holden McKenna won't be able to resist her. That's what she really wants. To ruin that man's life even more."

But another argued, "I doubt that woman even knows what she wants."

Charlotte would have found the conversations amusing except she did know what she wanted, what she had secretly always wanted. She just wasn't sure she could have it since she'd spent so many years denying it. She pushed thoughts of Holden McKenna away and thought of her children instead. Maybe later she would entertain the idea of again being with the man she loved. Right now, she was worried about Tilly, she thought as she turned into the McKenna Ranch where her oldest daughter lived.

She wasn't sure what kind of reception she would get—if her daughter even opened the door to her.

Not that she could blame Tilly.

Charlotte had played favorites with her children and was now paying the price. As her son CJ would have said, she'd bet on the wrong horse when she'd put so much of her love and hope into him.

She parked and hurried to the door, feeling a sense of urgency she couldn't explain. After ringing the bell twice, she began to worry that she was too late. Maybe Tilly had been taken to the hospital to deliver her baby already. Maybe she'd missed the pregnancy *and* the delivery.

Charlotte heard a sound inside the house. A moment later, Tilly opened the door, her hand going to her hugely protruding stomach as tears filled her eyes.

"You haven't had the baby yet," Charlotte said with relief. For a moment, the way her oldest daughter was looking at her, she thought Tilly would tell her to go away. When she didn't immediately, Charlotte held out hope that maybe the past could be forgotten. That Tilly could forgive her for missing so many of the important events in her life because of some overblown feud between her and Holden McKenna.

So many regrets rushed over her in that instant. She felt so foolish that she'd fought Tilly marrying Cooper McKenna. How could she explain how hard it was to see the man that she had loved all those years ago, Holden McKenna, walking her daughter down the aisle to marry his son? She hadn't been able to breathe, the pain threatening to kill her with jealousy. That should have been her and Holden up there at the altar all those years ago.

Now because of her foolishness, she'd almost missed the birth of her first grandchild. She would never have forgiven herself if she had. She could see in her daughter's green eyes, so like her own, that Tilly wouldn't forgive her either.

"What are you doing here?" Tilly said in a whisper, tears spilling from her eyes.

"I couldn't miss the birth of my grandchild," Charlotte said. Her throat had gone dry, her heart a cramping ache in her chest. "I'm sorry I wasn't here sooner. I'm so sorry about everything. I had this feeling that you were going to have the baby today. I had to tell you before—"

She stopped as her daughter's face crumbled, and took a step, falling into her mother's arms. Charlotte closed her arms around her child, something she hadn't done in years. Her body trembled with her own unshed tears as she rocked Tilly, letting her daughter weep.

Suddenly Tilly pulled back, her expression one of surprise. They both looked to the floor as the liquid that ran down her daughter's legs began to pool at her feet. Tilly began to cry harder in huge gasping sobs. "I'm finally having this baby."

"Where is Cooper?" Charlotte asked.

"I insisted he leave to take care of a bull that was coming in today on the train," Tilly answered, gasping the words out. "I had contractions, but I've had so many false alarms I thought I was never going to have this baby."

"Well, you are now, so let's get you out to my SUV and to the hospital."

A few minutes later, Charlotte had loaded her daughter and her suitcase into the SUV. Sliding behind the wheel, she started the engine as she called Cooper to meet them at the hospital. The hospital was ten miles away in Powder Crossing. "Don't worry, I'll get you there."

"I don't know what I would have done if you hadn't been here," Tilly said as she tried to compose herself.

"You would have been fine," she assured her. "You're the strongest and most capable woman I know."

Her daughter cried harder at that assertion. "I used to be. But . . ." she waved a hand over her stomach ". . . now I'm not so sure."

"Don't worry, you're going to make a great mother."

Sixty minutes later, Charlotte held the precious infant in her arms. Her granddaughter had been eager to get out into the world—once she got around to it. "Oh, Tilly, she is beautiful."

Eyes bright, her daughter nodded from the bed. "Thank you."

"I'm just glad I was here," Charlotte said. "I'm sorry I wasn't here sooner. Did you enjoy any part of the pregnancy?"

"Buying cute baby girl clothes in secret since we didn't tell anyone the sex. But the morning sickness and the rest . . ." She shook her head, looking exhausted.

"Well, you did great," she said as Cooper came rushing in, going first to his wife, then turning to her. *Thank you*, he mouthed, and Charlotte held out the baby to him. "Your daughter. Congratulations."

If he seemed surprised to see her, he hid it well as he took his daughter in his arms and moved over to the bed with Tilly.

Charlotte slipped out to call Holden to let him know he was a grandfather.

"I'M DOING IT!" Victoria cried excitedly as the truck moved forward without all the herky-jerky starts and stops she'd been struggling with. She couldn't believe that she'd finally gotten the hang of driving—let alone driving a stick shift.

She shot a look at Ryder. He was grinning, where earlier he'd been grimacing. "I knew you could do it," he said.

Victoria had to laugh at that. There was definitely a point where she hadn't been so sure about that. It hadn't come easy. All that clutch and brake and gas stuff, she thought and again wished she could share this with her friends.

But even as she thought it, she knew they wouldn't really appreciate what she was doing. Their lives were in the city with shopping, lunches, club-hopping and parties. It was about being seen. She'd certainly fallen into it as well, always worried about what she was going to wear because she had a reputation to uphold.

Now all that seemed . . . silly, she thought as she caught her reflection in the rearview mirror. Here she was wearing secondhand clothing that didn't quite fit like it should. And she could have cared less.

Brand pounded on the top of the cab, and she slowed up so he could throw off more hay.

"Nice," Ryder said as she pulled it off perfectly.

She couldn't help being touched by his encouragement. There'd been some tense moments and some hilarious ones, but she'd finally driven the truck. True, there had been a lot of stopping and going with Brand pounding on the roof and almost falling off the flatbed more times than he would want to remember. But he'd been able to toss out bales to the cattle, and once she'd figured it out, it was fun.

Brand pounded again, signaling that they were all finished, and it was time to drive back to the ranch. She couldn't help smiling all the way back as she drove.

"I might have to get my license when I get home," she said. "Bet I could talk my father into buying me a car. Or maybe a pickup."

"You did a great job," Ryder said.

She caught something in his tone and shot a look at him. She realized, her heart dropping, that she shouldn't have mentioned her father or home. They'd been having a good time, and she'd spoiled it. Both her father and the fact that she would be leaving soon had been an unwelcome reminder to them both. She'd done it earlier too, but both her father and this very short weekend were a fact, one neither of them should ignore.

Once she'd parked the truck and turned off the engine, she said, "If you still want to go into town for dinner, I'll go get cleaned up."

Ryder nodded. "I'll help Brand with a couple of things and get cleaned up myself. Meet downstairs at six?"

"Sounds good." She met his gaze. "Thank you so much for teaching me to drive the truck. I can't remember the last time I had this much fun." It was true, and that drove home how routine her life was in Dallas and New York too. She used to think she couldn't live without social media from the first thing in the morning until the last thing she checked at night.

It surprised her that she hadn't even missed her phone, let alone social media. She reminded herself that it had only been a day. She'd probably feel differently by the end of the weekend. She had to keep reminding herself that this was temporary.

She thought about how patient and kind Ryder had been, given his brother was cursing in the truck bed behind them. She could laugh now, but if it hadn't been for Ryder, she would have been too nervous and given up.

As she raced up the stairs and started to go into Tilly's room, she heard footsteps coming down the hallway behind her. She turned, expecting to see one of the household staff. But the moment she saw the man's face, she knew he had to be a Stafford. He was tall, blond, green-eyed and looked enough like Ryder and Brand that he had to be their brother CJ.

"Who are you?" he demanded as he gave her the once-over through hooded eyes. "And what are you doing in Tilly's bedroom?"

Victoria couldn't believe that she was actually face-to-face with the infamous CJ Stafford. But Ryder had said she wouldn't be seeing him because he was on parole and not allowed to come to the ranch. Apparently, CJ hadn't gotten the memo.

"I'm Victoria Forester," she said as she sized him up. "And you're CJ Stafford. I heard they let you out of the slammer."

He cocked his head at her. "You seem to know a lot about my business. Again, what are you doing going into my sister's bedroom?"

"I'm a guest of Ryder's."

"Really?" he asked, looking amused. "Good for Ryder. Apparently, everyone gets a run of this house but me. You his girlfriend?"

She couldn't help herself. "Fiancée, for the weekend."

His eyes widened. "You said *Forester*. Any relation to Wendell Forester?"

"He's my father."

"No kidding? I tried to contact him a while back about the ranch. I was curious what it was worth on the open market."

"That's probably how the Stafford Ranch came on his radar, then," Victoria said. "Your brother will be delighted to hear that. My father's been trying to buy the ranch ever since."

All the color had bled from CJ's face. "Buy it? Is Ryder thinking about selling it? The ranch isn't for sale, is it?" He sounded scared and upset.

"I would say definitely not." She saw the change in him immediately. He let out a breath, looking relieved.

"So you're Ryder's fiancée." He raised an eyebrow. "I guess I underestimated him. Your father must be very pleased."

She shook her head. "It's just for the weekend."

"Wise, since you look like someone who isn't cut out for ranch life." With that, he turned and headed back down the hallway to what she assumed was a back stairway before she could tell him otherwise. She could now drive a large truck with a stick shift, she wanted to call after him.

She watched him go, thinking about what he'd told her. Ryder would be furious and not just about CJ being on the ranch. After contacting her father, he'd put the ranch in jeopardy, since Wendell Forester always got what he wanted, one way or another.

Victoria shuddered at the thought, remembering that he wanted her married to the man of his choice. She was surprised, now that she thought about it, that she hadn't heard anything from him. That didn't bode well, but maybe more surprising she hadn't heard from Claude, she thought as she went into Tilly's room and locked the door, suddenly not feeling as safe as she had before meeting CJ.

Her father wasn't going to give up on the Stafford Ranch or marrying her off to Claude. She hated to think that the two men might be together plotting against her.

CHAPTER EIGHT

WENDELL FELT HIS blood run cold. There was no mistake, he was being followed. He sped up, took the next right down a side street, then took the next left. The driver of the vehicle stayed right with him. For a moment, he didn't know what to do.

His first instinct in the old days would have been to stop and storm back there and demand to know what was going on. But times had changed, he'd changed. He wasn't that cocky young man who had nothing to lose. He was Wendell Forester, a billionaire with a daughter and a whole hell of a lot to lose.

He had no idea where to find the police department or he might have headed there. Instead, he tried to stay where there was traffic and plenty of people. The last thing he needed was to get caught on a dead-end street away from everything.

His cell phone rang. He hoped it wasn't that fool Claude. It wasn't. All he saw was the name Stafford, and he quickly picked up, terrified that whoever was behind him wasn't working alone and that someone had his daughter.

Why had he insisted she meet him in Billings? He'd never thought he might put her in danger because he felt safe away from Dallas, away from the death threats. Yet one had been slipped under his door. Now he feared that whoever had threatened him had taken his daughter to get back at him.

He answered the call.

"Wendell Forester, right?" said a male voice on the line. "This is CJ Stafford. We spoke almost a year ago about my ranch."

CJ Stafford? How could he possibly forget? He'd never heard of the Stafford Ranch before that phone call. He wound his way through the city, the car still behind him. Right now all he could think about was Victoria. "Are you calling from the ranch?"

"Yes, why?" CJ said, sounding a little annoyed.

"Did you happen to see my daughter? Is that why you're calling me now?"

"Victoria? Yes, I ran into her going into my sister's bedroom. She told me that she is Ryder's fiancée."

"Is she all right?" He hated how his voice sounded, winded, weak, afraid. Too many strange things had been happening. Was CJ calling to say that he had her? That he was holding her for ransom?

"She's fine," CJ said impatiently. "I didn't call you to talk about your daughter. I called about the ranch. Are you still interested in buying it?"

He glanced back at the car behind him, trying to make sense of what was happening. This didn't have anything to do with Victoria? She was safe at the ranch. Now CJ Stafford was offering him the property? "Your brother says the land isn't for sale."

"That could change. Just tell me if you're still interested in buying it."

That could change? "Yes, but let me call you back at a better time. I'm in the middle of something right now." He disconnected, saw a yellow light ahead and pressed down on the gas. He knew he would get there before the light turned red. As he roared through the intersection, cars from the other direction were already pulling out.

Wendell just missed them as he sped through the light. Behind him, the car following him was forced to stop. He quickly hung a left, then a right, then another left. He looked behind him again.

He'd lost the tail.

But he was shaken. He wasn't sure who was after him, but someone was. After the call from CJ Stafford, he was more anxious than before to get to Powder Crossing and the Stafford Ranch. He needed to make sure that Victoria was all right. He'd love nothing better if she was engaged to Ryder Stafford, but he had his doubts, which was why he was interested in seeing what CJ Stafford was offering.

With a little luck, he would get the ranch. At least he would get something he'd come to Montana for.

Then he and his daughter would get on his private jet and go home, leaving Claude to take a commercial flight in coach.

VICTORIA TOOK HER time getting ready. She'd found a little blue number and a pair of knee-high boots in the back of the Tilly's closet. She'd wrangled her coppery hair into a clip and found some mascara in one of Tilly's drawers. She didn't need blush: the sun had put a glow in her cheeks.

Looking in the mirror, she liked what she saw and hoped Ryder did too. She looked so . . . alive. She couldn't help but wonder what her friends would have thought about this look. It was so different from how she would have looked on a date in Dallas or New York or Paris. That world seemed so far away, she thought, listening to the sound of the breeze in the cottonwoods along the river.

A date. That was what this was, wasn't it? She smiled to herself, excited about tonight, actually more excited than she'd been about a night out in a very long time. This was such a different world. She had no idea what they would do if the town was as small as Ryder had told her, but she couldn't wait to find out.

It isn't the Wild West that has you so excited. It's the cowboy.

She grinned at herself in the mirror. Nothing wrong with enjoying Ryder while she was here, right? Yet she felt she was playing with fire. This wasn't her life. It was one weekend in Montana. She warned herself to be careful.

Victoria glanced at the clock beside the bed and hurried downstairs. As she reached the bottom step, she saw Ryder and stopped. He stood staring at her as if he'd never seen her before. This was so different from when he'd seen her at the airport. This look warmed her toes up and made her tingle in all the right places. But it was the shocking current that arced between them that told her she was in dangerous territory.

She struck a pose and then laughed, wondering if he'd felt it too as he moved toward her, took her waist in his big suntanned hands and lifted her down from the last step to the floor.

"Aren't you that woman I saw driving a feed truck earlier?" he said jokingly, but she could tell that he liked this woman too. Her heart beat a little faster as he helped her put on the only jacket she'd found in Tilly's closet, a denim one. "You look great."

She smiled, feeling buoyant as she let him escort her out to his pickup. She told herself not to get too excited about tonight—or the town of Powder Crossing. But she couldn't help it. There was something in the air that made her feel more alive than she'd ever felt. She glanced over at Ryder. He was so handsome, so sure of himself, and he'd dressed up like it was a real date. He wore the Stetson he'd had in Billings, a green Western shirt that complemented his eyes, and new jeans—just like the boots.

So there, Claude, she thought. The man just hadn't been putting on the dog in Billings. He'd come there to confront her father, not impress him. She liked that, she realized.

"So how was your first day on the ranch?" he asked.

She heard it in his voice. He wanted her to like

the place, and she did. "I loved every second of it. That horseback ride was amazing."

He chuckled. "After you tricked me into thinking you didn't know the front end of a horse from the back."

She grinned over at him. "Sorry. I couldn't help myself. But I wasn't joking about never having driven a vehicle before."

He laughed. "Oh, after a few minutes with you behind the wheel, you had me convinced—and Brand too. We about lost him off the back more times than I want to remember."

Victoria smiled at the memory of finally getting the hang of it. "I loved meeting your sisters. I'm sure Oakley made your childhood fun."

"Ha! You have no idea. She's a spitfire, always has been."

"I almost forgot. I met your brother CJ earlier."

"What?" Ryder shot her a surprised—and worried—look. "Where?"

"Upstairs. I was just going into Tilly's room when he came down the hall."

Ryder let out a curse under his breath.

When he spoke, it was through gritted teeth. "He wasn't supposed to be on the ranch."

"He was very curious about me. When I told him who I was, he recognized the name. Apparently, he had called my father about selling the ranch months ago."

Ryder hit the brakes so hard and so fast that if she hadn't had her seat belt on, she might have gone through the windshield. "Sorry," he said quickly as he pulled to the side of the road. "Are you okay?" She nodded. "CJ told you he had contacted your father about the ranch?"

She nodded. She'd known he wasn't going to like hearing it, but she hadn't expected him to take it as badly as this.

"That explains how your father came into our lives. It was all CJ's doing." He cursed, then apologized as he got the pickup going again. "No wonder your father has been so persistent."

"But when you were in Billings you made it clear to him that the ranch wasn't for sale, right?"

He glanced over at her. "Have you forgotten that we're talking about your father?"

"Sorry, you're right. I shouldn't have brought it up." She really was sorry. She didn't want it to ruin their night. Honestly, sometimes she just needed to keep her mouth shut and wait for a better time. She just hadn't expected Ryder to take it so hard.

"No," he apologized. "I'm glad you told me about seeing him and about him contacting your father before he was locked up. I wondered how your father even knew about the Stafford Ranch."

"I'm sure that after talking to your brother, my father researched the ranch, the area, talked to a local geologist—"

"That's if my brother hadn't already told him about the methane gas on the property."

She reached over and touched his thigh. "I'm sorry. But if my father hadn't been trying to buy your ranch and hook me up with Claude, we would never have met."

He chuckled. "A silver lining, huh? For that I am grateful." She sure hoped he felt that way. She hated that she might have made things worse. He'd saved her from what was going to be a very ugly weekend with her father and Claude. He was right, though. She could have handled them both, but she feared what it would have done to her relationship with her father.

When Ryder looked over at her, she saw that he was enjoying her being here. It filled her with a strange kind of joy. She realized how much she'd wanted him to like her, because she really liked him. She thought about how patient he'd been with her driving lessons. Ryder Stafford was a good man.

"It's just that my brother worries me," he said. "CJ was always our mother's favorite. He could do no wrong. We all knew that he thought of the ranch as his own. I'm sure my mother thought that he would run the ranch one day, as the oldest. He certainly tried to run all of us off so he could have it to himself sooner. But I never thought he'd actually try to sell it."

"I saw on our horseback ride how much the ranch means to you."

"There are some things in life that don't have a price tag on them," he said as she spotted the lights of a town ahead.

She wished what Ryder had said was true but feared that wouldn't stop her father. She told herself that there was no way CJ could get his hands on the ranch and no way Ryder was ever going to sell it. But what worried her was what her father planned to do about that.

"Is that Powder Crossing?" she asked, hoping to lighten the mood that had filled the cab of the pickup. The last thing she had wanted to do was spoil their night together since it was all they had. But she'd known that Ryder needed to know about CJ and what she'd learned. After meeting CJ, she'd realized that her father wasn't the only one wanting to take the ranch away from him.

Ryder reached over and squeezed her hand. "Tonight is about having fun. Welcome to Powder Crossing."

She saw at once how small the town was. It almost looked like a Western movie set. A line of pickups was parked in front of the apparently only bar in town. A couple more were parked in front of the hotel and the café. The general store looked closed.

"Is this as lively as town gets?" she asked as he parked in a spot near the café. She could hear country music coming from the bar across the street.

"Saturday night in Powder Crossing," he said with a grin. "You are in for a treat." His cell phone rang. He checked it and declined the call. It rang again a few seconds later. He frowned.

"Take the call if you need to, it," Victoria suggested.

He shook his head and hit Decline. He was about

to shut off his phone when it rang yet again. With a sigh, he said, "This time it's Brand. I'd better take it. What's up?"

She watched him listen for a few seconds before he said, "We're on our way." Disconnecting, he said, "Tilly just had a baby girl."

"That's wonderful." Victoria couldn't believe how excited she was for Tilly. She had looked so miserable earlier.

"Mind if we make a quick stop by the hospital before dinner?"

"Not at all." She broke into a smile. "I'm so excited for her. A baby girl." She felt goose bumps, happy for Tilly, but also for the whole Stafford and McKenna family. That old ache for family felt like a punch in the gut. Ryder had no idea how lucky he was.

CHAPTER NINE

HOLDEN HAD ONLY seen Lottie once, as he'd always called Charlotte Stafford, since she'd returned to the Powder River basin. He'd ridden over to the creek where they used to meet and found her after so many months of missing her and worrying that she would never come back.

Just the sight of her standing there by the water had filled his heart to overflowing. Yet he hadn't been sure if her coming back had anything to do with him. He'd been worried with her gone so long. While he could never stop loving her, he wasn't so sure she felt the same way.

He'd dismounted, and as he'd moved toward her, she'd looked in his direction. There had been so many times when he'd found her here. A few times she'd been so angry and unforgiving that she'd gone for her bullwhip. Other times she'd threatened to go for her rifle.

But this time, her gaze had met his and he'd seen the tears were because she'd missed him maybe as much as he'd missed her. As he'd moved closer, she'd stepped to him and fell into his arms. He en-circled her as he'd pulled her to him. He'd felt the past slipping away, all the hurt and pain and animosity evaporating into the cool summer morning air.

They'd only held each other, not needing words. Since then, though, he'd been trying to give Lottie time, but he was growing impatient not just to see her, but also to start their future together. She hadn't said they had a future, yet he felt that they'd both mellowed and actually might still stand a chance at happiness.

He'd known he wasn't the only reason she'd come back. She needed to make amends to the people she'd wronged. He understood her need to do that. He had some of his own to take care of as well.

And while Lottie was always on his mind, this morning his thoughts were on his own grown children and mending fences. He reminded himself that he hadn't talked to his oldest son, Treyton, for months. Their last conversation hadn't gone well. Treyton had called him an old man who knew nothing about running a ranch. The words still stung, even though he knew that his son had been trying to hurt him. His eldest thought he could run the McKenna Ranch better than his father could. That was debatable.

He feared that Treyton was a lot like Lottie's oldest son, CJ. Both wanted power and money. He didn't think either really wanted the daily responsibility of actually running a ranch.

It wasn't just Treyton who had him thinking of all he'd done wrong raising his offspring. He picked up the book lying on his desk. It had come by special

messenger this morning. On the back cover, it said
This tell-all rivals even Peyton Place *for the sex
and secrets that go on in the Powder River basin
of Montana.*

Holden cringed as he turned the book over. Under the title *Dirty Business* was the author's name,
Bailey McKenna, his daughter. Bailey had sent him
a copy with a note inserted in the pages of the book.
It read *You don't have to read it. But I thought you'd
like a copy before it comes out so you can prepare
yourself. All the names have been changed, but
you'll know who you are.*

He'd never read anything more frightening except for the ransom note when his now-adopted
daughter Holly Jo had been taken. Prepare himself?
He looked up to find his housekeeper, close friend
and confidante standing in his office doorway. "I
thought you were going for a horseback ride?"
Elaine asked.

"I am. Did you get one of these?" he asked.

"Mine came yesterday. I read the whole thing
last night. Couldn't stop myself. Your daughter is
one hell of a writer."

"Really?" He couldn't help the doubtful face he
made. Bailey had always been his black sheep. For
years he had no idea who she was. He now understood part of the reason why she'd avoided him. Yet
he still didn't fully understand her.

"You should read it," Elaine said. "She did change
all the names, but you'll recognize everyone."

"That's what I'm afraid of." He looked at the

book in his hand. "Sounds like there will be a lot of lawsuits."

Elaine shook her head. "People would have to admit that they are Amy X or Jud Z." She laughed. "It's a fun read. I heard she was working on another book."

"I hate to think about what."

"A novel about the daughter of a pig-headed rancher."

"Very funny." He hesitated. "Tell me you're kidding."

She laughed. "Read the book, Holden. Your daughter wrote it. It's already a bestseller. You should be proud of her."

"I am," he said.

"Make sure you mention that to her," Elaine advised. "*After* you read the book."

His cell phone rang, and he saw it was Charlotte. His heart did that little whoop-de-do it always did. "I have to take this," he said to Elaine, who nodded and left. He picked up. "I'm so glad you called."

"Tilly's having her baby. I'm here at the hospital. I didn't think you'd want to miss the birth of your first grandchild. We've let Cooper know, but I thought—"

"I'll be right there." He disconnected. "Elaine!" he called as he rose from his desk and picked up his Stetson.

She came racing into the room, looking worried.

"It's Tilly. She's at the hospital having the baby. You want a ride?"

"I'll take my own car."

"All right," Holden said. "I'm going, then. Lottie's there."

Elaine nodded, smiling. "I'm so glad she made it. I'm sure Tilly is too."

"Yes, I forget how close the two of you are," Holden said. "Also, how good you are at keeping her secrets." He'd only found out recently that Elaine and Lottie had been friends for years. All that time, Elaine had been trying to get Lottie to forgive him and urging him to do what he could to get them back together—all in secret.

Elaine pretended to hold a key and lock her lips, making him laugh. His first grandchild was being born and he was going to see Lottie. He felt suddenly older than his almost sixty years, yet excited to be alive right now.

"Go," Elaine said. "I'll let everyone else know."

The drive into town was the longest of his life. By the time he reached the hospital, he had a granddaughter and Lottie was waiting for him on the bench outside the hospital. She smiled as he took a seat next to her.

"We're grandparents," she said and placed a hand on his knee and looked up at him. "Cooper's in there with her now. I thought I'd give them a few moments."

He met her gaze. "I'm so glad you're back."

She nodded. "Me too. Are you ready to see your granddaughter?"

"Yes, but not just yet. I've missed you. Now that

you're back, I don't want to waste a moment. Tell me that after all these years, we're going to be together."

Tears filled her eyes. "It's what I want more than anything."

He broke out in a huge grin. "Marry me, Lottie." A tear ran down her cheek. He caught it with his thumb pad before reaching into his pocket and pulling out the small velvet box he'd held on to for years.

Looking into her beautiful green eyes, he flipped it open and took out an emerald ring—the stone the same color as her eyes. "I've had this ring for years, Lottie. I never gave up hope." He slipped off the bench and got down on one knee, glad he could still do that and get back up. "Will you finally be my wife?"

It HAD BEEN so long coming that for a moment Charlotte only stared at the ring. She'd spent so much lost time being angry and hurt because Holden had married another woman when she knew he was in love with her and always had been.

She looked up, met his blue eyes and saw all the love still there. Smiling, she held out her left hand. She refused to think about what could have been, what should have been. She'd wasted far too much time when all she'd ever wanted was this man. It was never too late, she told herself. Not when you loved each other the way the two of them had for years.

"I would love to marry you, Holden McKenna," she said.

He slipped the ring on her finger. Of course it fit perfectly. She looked down at it, and then she cupped his wonderful face in her hands and kissed him. She didn't have to ask for forgiveness for making him wait all this time. She saw it in his eyes. She'd caused them both so much pain, but that was behind them as he took her into his arms and held her tight.

"I think we should keep this to ourselves for now and let this be Tilly and Cooper's day," she said.

He nodded. "But after today, I want to tell the children. I'm hoping they'll be happy for us. Happy or not, I'm happy."

"Me too," she said. "I suppose you're hoping for a long engagement?"

His eyes widened in alarm before he realized she was joking. "Not a chance. We've already lost too much time, don't you think?"

She did. "We could elope."

He shook his head. "You the deserve the wedding you should have had years ago."

"No looking back," she chided. "That's our new deal. Only looking to the future. You know I don't need a big wedding."

"But maybe the community does," he said, and she nodded. "They've put up with our rivalry for years. The least we can do is throw them a party."

Charlotte smiled, still bowled over by this. She and Holden were finally getting married. They'd spent years unable to keep their hands off each other—even when they should have. "Does this mean no more sneaking down to the creek to make love?"

"One of my favorite memories," he said. "Except for the times you chased me off with that bullwhip of yours."

"I've retired it."

"Good to hear."

"You heard that I got CJ out of jail and the charges have been dropped," she said. "I hope it wasn't a mistake, but I had to do what I thought was right. I changed. Maybe he can too."

Holden didn't look hopeful about that, but quickly said, "I've hoped the same thing with Treyton." He shook his head. "Our sons are a lot alike."

"Except Treyton hasn't been behind bars."

"Not yet," he said with a sigh. "But I fear he's headed in that direction. CJ was at least trying to get the Stafford Ranch. Treyton doesn't seem to have any interest at all in his family ranch."

"They aren't going to be happy about the wedding, you know," Charlotte said. "My fault for turning my son against your family."

Holden took her hand. "Lottie, this is a new beginning. Our sons will come around or they won't. A lot has changed. Cooper and Tilly are married and now have a daughter of their own. Oakley is married to Pickett. There aren't any hard boundaries between our families anymore and I'm glad of it. Of course there are going to be problems, but we'll deal with them."

He drew her to him again, and she pressed her

face against his strong shoulder before pulling back to admire her ring. "Holden, it's beautiful."

"Oh my God, you're . . . you're *engaged*?"

They pulled apart to see Oakley standing over them, her mouth open.

Charlotte looked up at her daughter. "Holden just asked, and I accepted. We're going to have a large wedding so we're going to need help planning it. I hope I can count on you."

"You're really doing this?"

"We are," Holden said. "I believe congratulations is in order, don't you, Lottie?"

"Or at least best wishes," she said.

Oakley was still staring at them. "I never thought I'd see the day." She seemed to shake herself before she broke out in a grin. "Congrats. Does Tilly know?"

"No one does but you," Charlotte said. "We'll put something in the local shopper, but I think word will get out on its own, don't you? But let's make this day Tilly and Cooper's."

Her daughter nodded, still looking dazed. "When is the wedding?"

"The sooner, the better," Holden said, taking her hand. "Your mother and I are in love."

"That isn't anything new," Oakley said. "Where do you plan to live?"

"We still need to iron out the details," Holden said. "But I hope she will live on the McKenna Ranch." He looked over at her. "If you want, I'll build us our very own house."

"We have time to talk about it," Charlotte said,

reflecting how different all of their lives would have been if she'd been his bride living in that house all those years ago. But then, they wouldn't have the children they did or have lived the lives they'd had.

She felt a surprised sense of accomplishment for having built her own ranch with little help. Same with raising her children, even if she did wish she could do that part all over again, knowing what she did now. Still, her life had made her a strong woman out of necessity, and she couldn't help being proud of that.

"Oh, wait until everyone hears," Oakley said. "Treyton is going to flip when he hears about this. Not to mention CJ."

"Let us worry about that," Charlotte and Holden said in unison as they rose to go see their first grandchild together.

BACK IN THE HOSPITAL, Charlotte was surprised to see her son Ryder had gotten here so fast. She was even more surprised to see that he wasn't alone. He had a pretty young woman with long curly coppery red hair, fair skin and jade-green eyes with him. She was stunning—much like her mother had been, Charlotte thought with a jolt as she recognized her.

As large as the state of Montana was, it never failed to astonish her how small it seemed when it came to running into people she knew or had a connection with.

"Mother," Ryder said, not appearing all that happy to see her. "I heard you were back."

She'd left the ranch for him and Brand to run without a word. She'd known he and his brother would do a great job. She would make sure that they knew that. She'd neglected both of them in the past. Ryder probably thought that nothing had changed.

"Ryder," she said, giving him an awkward hug. "It's good to see you." Before he could answer, her gaze went to Victoria. Wasn't that her name? The last time Charlotte had seen her, she was just a child.

"Victoria Forester," the young woman said before Ryder could introduce her.

Charlotte saw Victoria give her a questioning look. Maybe the girl hadn't been too young to remember after all. "I knew your father," Charlotte said so the woman didn't have to wonder.

Ryder put an arm around Victoria. "We just stopped by on our way to dinner. We're doing a night out on the town." He seemed almost protective of the young woman. Charlotte wondered how close they were. Closer maybe than even Ryder realized.

"Don't let me stop you," she said. "It was nice to see you again, Victoria." With that, Charlotte turned and went out in the hall where Holden was waiting for her.

But not before she heard Ryder ask, "What was that about?"

Whatever Victoria answered, Charlotte didn't hear. Where in the world had Ryder found this young woman? Was it serious? She couldn't help but wonder if Victoria had taken after her father.

"THAT BABY WAS so adorable," Victoria gushed as they drove to the café after they'd congratulated Tilly and Cooper and left. "They looked so happy."

Ryder hadn't said anything since leaving the hospital. She suspected he was still shaken after running into his mother—not to mention realizing that Charlotte knew Wendell Forester, had apparently been to his house and had recognized Victoria.

"Our parents met at our house years ago when I was just a girl," Victoria told him. "I probably only remember because my mother and I came home. She grabbed her favorite vase and threw it at your mother before demanding she leave and never come back."

Ryder groaned. "Do not tell me my mother and your father had an affair."

She shrugged. "My mother suspected as much, but if they did, it was short-lived. I never saw your mother again or heard her mentioned."

He shook his head. "Charlotte must have been between husbands."

"Small world, huh?" Victoria said with laugh. "It's not like we're related."

"No, but . . . it is still creepy." He shook his head as he parked again near the café. There were fewer vehicles than before. Climbing out of the pickup, he came around to open her door as if they were on a real date. Victoria was touched and saw people inside looking through the windows at them, definitely curious. If they only knew.

The moment Ryder opened the door to the café, she caught the aroma of roast beef and felt her stomach growl. He saw her rub her belly and chuckled as they found an empty table where he pulled out a chair for her. She felt the stares of everyone in the café, including the waitress.

"Thanks, Penny," Ryder said when the woman brought over two glasses of water and a menu, which she put in front of Victoria.

"Ryder, you already know the special tonight. What would you like to drink? Do I need to run across the street for something . . . stronger?"

"I'd love iced tea," Victoria said and looked at him. "And the special," she said, handing Penny the menu. She figured it was the roast beef since she'd already smelled it. But it didn't matter. If Ryder was having it, so was she.

He smiled. "I'll take the same, including the iced tea."

"She thought I was going to be difficult, didn't she?" Victoria whispered, leaning toward him. "Is it me, or are all your dates difficult?"

Ryder chuckled and seemed to relax. "I haven't had much time to date."

"What? One of the most eligible bachelors for miles around?"

"I'm serious. Brand and I have had a ranch to run all by ourselves."

"But now your mother's back."

"Right. I have no idea what she has in mind. I can't see her taking over again, but she might. With my mother, I never know."

"You sound so thrilled."

"Mother is . . . difficult. Now with CJ back too . . ." He shrugged. "I still can't believe he was at the ranch. I knew he wouldn't abide by any rules our mother set. He never has." He shook his head. "I'd hoped you wouldn't have to meet either of them. My mother can be worse than my sisters when it comes to butting into other people's lives."

"You are so lucky to have so many people who care about you."

Ryder didn't look like he felt lucky. Their specials arrived, roast beef, green beans and mashed potatoes with brown gravy, a roll and banana cream pie for dessert.

Victoria couldn't believe how hungry she was, even though she'd had that huge breakfast. Maybe it was the fresh air and exercise, or maybe it was being here with Ryder instead of her friends who were always watching their weight—and hers too.

She ate with abandon, looking up to find Ryder grinning at her. She recognized that look in his eyes and wasn't surprised when he said, "Want to go dancing after dinner? The Deacon Brown Blues Band should be startin' up over at the bar by the time we finish. It's a band out of Wyoming. I was thinking we could make a night of it."

Victoria broke into a huge smile. "Saturday night in Powder Crossing. I want to experience it all with you."

THAT WAS WHAT Ryder was afraid of. Experiencing it all, as he later pulled Victoria into his arms on the dance floor at the bar. He worried about how hard his heart beat with her in his arms. At the café, he'd looked over at her and realized that he never wanted this night to end.

But it would end. Tomorrow. He wasn't sure how she would get back to Billings. Maybe he'd take her. He could imagine what Brand would say if he took off with Victoria tomorrow. He tried not to think about it as they moved to the music. Just as he tried not to think too hard about how she felt in his arms.

Maybe what worried him the most was that this woman who'd sneaked into his life had practically met his entire family even though he'd hoped she wouldn't during her short stay. His family was going to make more of this than it was. She would be leaving tomorrow.

Maybe.

He assumed that her father would send someone for her.

The thought of her leaving filled him with a strange kind of dread. He'd been ready to send her packing the next morning. Hell, he'd thought she'd be on the phone calling her father to come get her. Now he realized he didn't want her to leave.

The thought rattled him. Right now, holding her this close, smelling that girly scent in her hair, swaying to a slow song, she felt too right in his arms. Her bare skin felt warm from the sun as their arms brushed. Her green eyes were as bright and inviting as a dip in a mountain lake. He kept thinking of how excited she'd been when she'd mastered driving the flatbed truck. She'd done better than he'd expected.

A thought hit him like a cold drink of water from the creek. Maybe like the horseback riding, she already knew how to drive a stick shift. How could he tell what was real and what was a con? After all, look who her father was.

He'd told himself to just enjoy the weekend. Like now. The problem was that he was enjoying it too much, enjoying her too much. He could already imagine the hole she would leave when she left.

And she would leave. This wasn't her life.

Her eyes sparkled like emeralds as she looked up at him and he felt a hard tug at his heart. Be careful, he warned himself. But even as he did, he knew that what Brand had said before he'd left was true.

"She's having fun on the ranch, but you know she's not staying, right? This isn't her life. It's a kick for a few days, but ultimately that old life is going to call her back. You don't want to fall for this girl."

"I know that," Ryder had said, irritated at his brother for thinking he needed to be reminded. "I'm counting on her leaving so I can get back to work."

"Me too," Brand half joked. "I could use the help. But seriously, I've seen the way you look at her. She's getting to you. I just don't want to see you get your heart broken."

"It wouldn't be the first time," he said glibly.

"Yes, it would," Brand said seriously. "None of

the girls you've dated ever had you looking at them like this."

"You're wrong. I know this is temporary. I'm just enjoying myself. I wouldn't be surprised if someone showed up tomorrow to take her home," Ryder had said, realizing how true that was. Like he'd told Victoria, he'd been waiting for a helicopter to land, and just like that she'd be gone.

All that had been easy to say to his brother, but now with her in his arms, Ryder didn't kid himself. He could fall so easily for this woman—at least the one he'd glimpsed today on the ranch. She'd been so different from the one he'd met at the airport, the one he'd seen on the social media posts. Except that party girl, big city Victoria was still her deep down. This weekend was just a blip, only a glimpse of her in his life. Like his brother said, she was enjoying herself because it was only for a couple of days.

Cursing silently as the song ended, he told himself to enjoy it while it lasted. He'd deal with whatever came tomorrow. But tonight, he just wanted this time with this beautiful, sexy woman. It had been too long. Just the scent of her and the way she smiled at him had his pulse pumping. He never wanted this night to end.

THE TWO OF them ended up closing down the bar, laughing on the way out with their arms around each other. In the pickup on the ride home, they'd joked about the day and night they'd had. Ryder found himself questioning if he'd ever felt so close to any woman before. He hadn't. He kept thinking about his brother's warning, wondering if it was already too late.

He'd barely known this woman twenty-four hours. Was it possible to fall for someone that fast? He knew what his sister Tilly would say and smiled to himself at the thought that Oakley would understand even if Tilly wouldn't.

As he drove up to the house, they both fell silent. Yes or no? The answer hung between them. Ryder had never fallen into bed with a woman on the first date. Often not even the third date. He wasn't playing hard to get. He just didn't get intimate unless he felt something deeper. Often, he didn't. He thought about Brand, with all his good advice. Hadn't he slept with Birdie not long after she'd climbed in his bedroom window?

He parked in front of the house and turned off the engine, the battle going on inside him. One voice was saying *Go for it. You only live once.* The other was saying *You'll regret it because you'll only get more involved and it will hurt more when she leaves.* And she would leave.

Ryder opened his door and hurried around to open Victoria's. On the doorstep before they headed inside to go to their separate parts of the huge house, he stopped her, turning her to him. She'd said at the airport that she'd never kissed a cowboy. He didn't want her only cowboy kiss to be the one from earlier, as electrifying as it had been.

The moon bathed the night in a silver glow. He could hear the breeze in the cottonwoods along the river, feel the humidity rising from the water and smell the fertile earth as he pulled her to him. An owl hooted at them from a nearby tree. Farther away he could hear a horse whinny from the barn.

His gaze locked with hers in the shine of the moon. What he saw sent his heart pounding and his body responding. There wasn't a chance in hell that he wasn't going to kiss her. He slowly lowered his mouth to hers, felt her arms encircle his neck as she moved closer, pressing her body to his, making him catch his breath. The kiss was all heat and passion and unresolved desire.

When the outside light flashed on, Ryder jerked back, then swore under his breath.

"Your brother?" she whispered, turning away from the bright light.

"Yep." The light had the same effect as a bucket of ice water thrown on him. It was just the reminder he'd needed—but sure as the devil hadn't wanted. "I need to go check one of our mares that is about to foal," he said, stepping away from her. "I had a great time tonight."

"Me too," she whispered, looking as disappointed as he felt. Maybe a little relieved too. Saying goodbye would be much harder if they were lovers. In fact, it could be near impossible.

"Good night." He turned and walked away, mentally kicking himself as he thought about literally stomping his brother's ass.

CHAPTER TEN

VICTORIA FELT THE same disappointment she'd seen on Ryder's face when the light had come on. Neither of them had wanted to stop what they were doing. But at the same time, the kiss had been so dreamy and wonderful, she felt as if she was floating as she climbed the stairs to Tilly's room. The whole day had been like out of a dream, and tonight . . .

As she lay down on top of the covers and stared up at the ceiling, she thought about the horseback ride, learning to drive the truck, dancing almost every dance, all of the slow ones in Ryder's arms. She hugged herself at the memory, then forced herself to rise and get ready for bed. It was late, and life on a ranch started with the sun, and she only had one more day here, she told herself as she climbed between the sheets.

She didn't think she would be able to sleep, her mind too busy as if trying to avoid thinking the one scary thought. She was falling for the cowboy. She thought of this latest kiss. It put the first one to shame, she thought with a chuckle, yet that first one had set a fire in her. This one tonight . . . If that light hadn't come on when it did, she'd be curled up next to Ryder in his bed down in the wing where he and his brother lived.

Rolling over, she thought about her friends back home. They'd understand the attraction—who wouldn't if they met Ryder Stafford?—but other than a roll or two in the hay . . .

She moved to lie on her back, telling herself that her friends would be right. This was fun, but it wasn't her life. She was no ranchwoman. She closed her eyes, reminding herself that she was going home tomorrow. But all she could see was Ryder as they waded together in the middle of the Powder River side by side, the sun warming them along with their closeness. Had she ever felt that comfortable with a man she was attracted to? Other men paled next to Ryder. She could almost imagine herself living here with him.

Her eyes flew open. She could imagine herself having his children, raising them here on this ranch, teaching them to ride and drive trucks and feed cattle. She'd never imagined herself married living in one city or another. Was that because it had never been her dream?

The long day finally caught up with her. Her eyes closed and she fell asleep, dropping into the waiting darkness.

It seemed like only moments had gone by when Victoria was startled awake by a clap of thunder. She looked to the window. A flash of lightning blinded her for a moment as the glass seemed to rattle. Rain began to pour from Montana's big sky,

pelting the glass as the wind picked up. A tree limb
groaned as it scraped against the house. At least that
was what she thought it was.

She hated thunderstorms. They terrified her. This
one was louder than any she'd ever heard. It felt
as if the house was going to come apart. She was
reminded that she was the only one sleeping in this
section of the house. The brothers had their own
wing on the other side of the kitchen. The house had
begun to make all kinds of noises she hadn't heard
before. Suddenly, she couldn't stand to be alone in
this part of the big house for another second.

Throwing herself from the bed, she raced for
the door. Not even bothering to grab something
to cover her shortie pj's, she tore down the stairs.
Flashes of light and huge booms of thunder followed her down to the first floor as if the storm
had settled right over the house. As rain beat at
the windows harder, she ran down the hall past the
kitchen.

Ryder had pointed out the other wing where he
and Brand stayed. She threw open the door and saw
a covered area that connected the separate part of
the house. It should have been dry beneath the roof,
but the wind blew the rain sideways, drenching her
to her skin before she reached Ryder's room.

She trembled hard from fear and cold as she
pounded on his door, hoping it was the right one.
When he opened the door a few moments later, she
was so relieved she threw herself into his arms.

"Vicky, what in the—"

"I hate thunderstorms," she cried against his shoulder. "I got so scared."

"It's all right." He closed the door. "You're soaking wet. Come on, let's get you into some dry clothes." He led her deeper into what was more like an apartment than a bedroom. "Take those off and I'll get—"

But before he could walk away, she drew him back and kissed him.

"Vicky?" he whispered as he pulled back to look at her questioningly. Lightning lit the sky outside the window. She could see the desire in his eyes. He wanted this as much as she did.

She pulled her wet pajama top up over her head and dropped it on the floor. His eyes widened as he took in her naked breasts in the next flash of lightning. Then his gaze met hers as she dropped the bottoms to her feet.

WARNING BELLS CLANGED in his head, but Ryder ignored them as he lifted her into his arms and carried her over to the bed. He quickly stripped off the boxers he'd been sleeping in and crawled up on the bed to join her.

He held her chilled body until it grew warm, until they both became aware of their bodies' attraction to the other. *You still have time to back out.* Ignoring that annoying voice, he bent to kiss her dark nipples, cupping her full breasts. She cradled his head as she opened her body to him, and he no longer heard warnings or paid any attention to his doubts as he trailed his tongue down over her flat stomach to her center.

Her body responded to his touch like an expensive car. She arched against his mouth, as she buried her hands in his hair. He felt her shudder against his mouth and lifted his head. Her hands drew him to her, pressing the flats of her palms to his chest, kissing his already taut nipples.

They explored each other's bodies until they were breathing hard and grasping for each other with a need that he, for one, had never felt before. Vicky drew him down on her. Her eyes widened, and he slowly entered her. Her body was beautiful, ripe and throbbing. She moved with him to the pounding beat of the rain as they rode out the storm until she shuddered under him, and he let himself climax in a final burst of lightning.

Thunder rumbled in the distance as they collapsed on the bed. He spooned her against him, holding her, never wanting to let her go.

"You rescued me," she whispered once they'd both caught their breath.

"You didn't need rescuing. Not to mention that my motives were suspect at best," he said with a chuckle. "I couldn't stand Claude, and I was angry at your father."

"I was going to say I was sorry that I involved you in my mess with my father, but I'm not. It's the most impulsive thing I've ever done, but I'm so glad."

"You were desperate. Once I met your father and Claude, I understood."

"It would have been an unbearable weekend, so thank you. I owe you."

"That's just it, Vicky . . . You don't owe me anything."

She turned in his arms to smile at him. "As I recall, I promised you a night you'd never forget. I never break a promise." Her gaze locked with his as she reached for him again.

"Vicky—" The rest of his words died on his lips as she kissed him.

CHAPTER ELEVEN

SOMEONE WAS POUNDING on the door. For a startled second, Victoria forgot where she was. She felt Ryder go rigid next to her for a moment before he leaned over and kissed her, then leaped up calling, "Just a minute." She watched him in the semidarkness of the room as he pulled on briefs and a T-shirt before he went to the door.

He cracked it open only a few inches. She heard Brand's voice, then Ryder saying, "I'll tell Vicky," before he closed the door and turned to her. "It's time."

Still half-asleep, she glanced at the clock by the bed. Four-thirty in the morning? Surely not breakfast.

"It's Sunny. She's about to foal," he said as he pulled on jeans and a shirt. "You don't want to miss this," he said, sounding excited, even though he must have seen dozens of horses born on this ranch. "Hurry and get dressed and come out to the barn." He stepped to the bed, kissed her again, his gaze as much as the kiss telling her how much he'd enjoyed last night. Then he left, closing the bedroom door behind him.

She lay there for a moment, not wanting to leave

the warm bed. She remembered last night, their lovemaking, and hugged herself. She hadn't meant for that to happen but didn't regret it. Couldn't. It had felt so . . . right.

It would have been easy to just close her eyes and go back to sleep in the warm hollow Ryder's body had left in the bed. Why was she so tired? Brand said it was the higher altitude air that had worn her out, or it might have been the long horseback ride or driving that big truck or dancing until the bar closed. Not to mention making love not once but twice.

Brand couldn't know she was in his brother's bed, could he? She felt as if he was challenging her to show his brother how wrong she was for him. She wouldn't put it past him. She could tell that Brand thought she was too soft, too fragile, too spoiled, too much of a city girl.

Right now she figured that, but determined she threw her legs over the side of the bed and hurriedly dressed in one of Ryder's shirts. It had quit raining as she crossed over to the house and ran upstairs to get dressed. She'd show them both what she was made of, she thought as she left the house in the cold darkness and made her way to the barn.

As she walked in, her nostrils filled with the once-strange smells that now seemed familiar. She heard Ryder and Brand encouraging the mare. Drawing closer, she saw the horse moving around the stall nervously. She could see what appeared to be one small leg protruding from the back of the horse.

"Foals come out front hooves and face first," Ryder said when he saw her and motioned her closer. He was talking to the mare, brushing his hand over her, speaking in a soothing tone.

"We're about to pull him out," Brand said. "Want to help?"

Heart pounding, she stepped into the large stall as another leg protruded. She stepped in and watched nervously as the mare circled nervously once more before lying down. Both brothers got behind the mare and began to pull on the colt's legs. Victoria hugged herself, hoping both horses were all right as the men worked.

It seemed to take forever and yet it was only a few minutes before the foul came sliding out and Victoria saw its tiny body and face inside a thin sack. She began to cry tears of joy. The brothers pulled off the bag so the colt could breathe. It lay there, so tiny, as the mare began to lick him.

"She's encouraging him to stand up," Ryder said. "He needs to get on his feet to make it."

Heart in her throat, all she could do was stand still, silently pleading with the colt to get up. It was such a beautiful scene, but she feared the colt wouldn't rise, and her heart broke at the thought. She could see the mare encouraging her baby to stand. Her heart pounded as she willed the little animal to stand.

And as suddenly as he came into the world, he was on his feet, wobbling, butt up. Victoria began to cry, covering her mouth, relief making her weak.

"He's going to be a strong little fellow," Brand was saying.

Ryder stepped over to put his arm around her, looking as awed by the birth as she'd been. To her amazement, once on the colt was on his feet, he began to try out those legs, and within minutes, he began to nurse as the mare too was back on her feet.

"It's such a miracle," she said, her voice breaking.

As the brothers finished taking care of the mare and her foal, Victoria sat on a stack of hay bales, content to watch baby and mother and the cowboys looking after them both. At some point she must have leaned over and fallen asleep because the next thing she remembered was sunlight streaming in through the barn door.

She could feel it on her face but kept her eyes closed, wrapped up in the warm memory of last night.

CLAUDE COULDN'T BE more anxious to finally get to Powder Crossing. He'd left the motel and driven to Miles City early this morning. Now he was cutting east toward Broadus. Who in their right mind would live out here, he thought as he crossed a mountain and dropped down into what he hoped was the Powder River basin.

He thought he would never get to Powder Crossing when all of a sudden it appeared on the horizon. But when he drove down the main drag of the town, he saw to his dismay that there wasn't much there. Fortunately, there was an old hotel, a bar and a café. And at least there was a place to get gas at the fuel station/convenience store for when he finally got to leave.

Not having any idea where to find the Stafford Ranch, he parked in front of the Cattleman Café and went inside. It was after the morning rush so there were only a couple of older men at one of the tables. Both looked at him, frowned and went back to their breakfasts. Wen had advised him to try to blend in. Not to wear a suit. Try to look local.

As he noted the two locals frowning at him, one in worn blue overalls and the other in just as worn canvas pants, he couldn't imagine why he would want to look like them. But he had stopped at an outdoor store in Miles City, bought himself some canvas pants, a flannel shirt and a pair of Western boots. He hated the feel of all of it and felt ridiculous. At the first wide spot in the road, he'd changed into a pair of designer jeans he'd brought along with a hoodie and his running shoes.

Now he took a seat in the café, trying to ignore the two men who would occasionally turn in his direction with questioning looks. The place smelled of bacon and biscuits. When an older woman, her hair a cap of tight gray curls, came out of the back, she grabbed a menu, a glass of ice water, a cup and a pot of coffee before she approached him.

"Coffee?" she asked as she set down the cup and started to fill it. "Cream and sugar?" He just had time to nod before she reached into her pocket and produced several small containers of cream and some sugar packets. She handed him the menu. "Special is bacon, two eggs, biscuits and gravy."

He thought of his boss and smiled. "I'll take it." Before she could ask how he liked his eggs, he told her, "Over easy."

She gave him an abrupt nod and took off with the coffeepot to go refill the ranchers' cups.

The breakfast was delicious. He ate every bite and enjoyed it so much that he'd wished he had taken a photo of it first to send to Wen. Too late now, he thought.

When the woman came back to clear the table, he asked, "Can you tell me how to get out to the Stafford Ranch?"

She eyed him suspiciously. "You have business out there?"

"I'm a friend of Ryder's," he lied. "He said if I was ever in the area . . ."

She still looked skeptical but said, "I'll make you a map. You might want to call first, though. This time of year, they aren't around the house much, though I think they've already moved their cattle."

"The life of a rancher," Claude said, wondering what ranchers did other than move cows around.

The next time she came by, she brought a map she'd drawn on a napkin. She gave him a cup of coffee in a to-go container for the road, he paid his bill and, feeling good and confident this wasn't a wild-goose chase, left.

Once in the SUV again, though, he had to go over his game plan in his mind. It was risky, but at this point, he felt he had nothing to lose. And it wasn't as risky or as dangerous as plan B, let alone C.

He couldn't help but think about what he'd already been through as he drove out the county road toward the Stafford Ranch. He'd flown up here with Wen thinking he was almost family. He'd foolishly thought that even if he and Victoria didn't hit it off this time, Wen would have been able to bring his daughter to heel.

Instead, she'd pulled a fast one that neither of them had seen coming.

Claude had never had any trouble getting women. It still irked him that this spoiled brat had his future in her hands. Worse maybe, he had come to hate his job, especially the way Wen treated him. He had to do something to fix that or he was going to quit. Wen would destroy him if he quit, but he couldn't be expected to take this much abuse.

As he drove, he thought about how to get back into his boss's good graces. Wen wanted the Stafford Ranch; he'd made that much clear. There was only one way Claude could see him getting it—short of figuring out how to buy a place that wasn't for sale. Victoria would have to marry Ryder. Apparently, his boss thought that Claude showing up at the ranch would force her into the rancher's arms—if not his bed.

Claude felt he had two options. Push Victoria into a marriage with the cowboy to make his boss happy. He really couldn't see that happening, knowing Victoria. She was an obstinate, incorrigible woman. The second option was to make sure the cowboy and the princess never got together.

He loved that idea because it was the perfect way to get back at his boss for making him come out here, expecting him to grovel for his daughter. Tough decision, he thought, smiling. This trip to Montana had opened his eyes. He didn't care about his job anymore. His self-respect was on the line. He wanted more than anything to get out of his contract, even though he knew he didn't stand a chance in hell—and Wen knew it. Which meant the man wasn't going to fire him, no matter what he did. Payback felt good.

As he saw the sign to the ranch ahead, he slowed, knowing there was only one answer. Plan A. The risky one, but still less dangerous than the other two. With this one at least, he wouldn't go to jail.

VICTORIA HEARD THE sound of a vehicle engine and opened her eyes. She'd fallen asleep on the bales in the barn? The realization made her chuckle. Back in the city, she'd always needed pills to sleep. She certainly hadn't the last two nights here on the ranch. She sat up and stretched.

"Have you been here all night?" she asked Ryder when he came out of the new mama's stall. She caught a glimpse of the foal and couldn't believe how well he was getting around already.

"There wasn't much night left after the birth,"

Ryder said as he moved to the open barn door at the sound of a car door slamming. "Looks like we have company," he said. He didn't sound surprised, but she saw his disappointment and quickly stood.

"Who?" She began to brush herself off, afraid it was Ryder's mother. She didn't want anyone seeing her with hay in her hair and looking a mess, but especially his mother. Why she wanted the woman to like her she couldn't have said yesterday. Today she felt more invested in this ranch, in this life, in Ryder.

When she reached the open barn door, though, she saw their visitor was the last person she wanted to see under any circumstances. "You have to be kidding. What is *he* doing here?"

"I would imagine your father sent him to get you," Ryder said.

"My father didn't mention it when you texted him where I was going, did he?"

"He didn't answer my text at all."

"Enjoying yourself?" Claude asked her as he walked over to them, ignoring everyone but her. She felt him take her in, not missing a thing. In the wee hours, she'd thrown clothing on half-asleep and was still wearing Ryder's shirt that was far too large for her. Claude had also caught her after having just woken up on a hay bale. She hated to think what she looked like—or what Claude thought had been going on. She didn't want to hurt the man or antagonize him. She just wanted him to leave.

Claude cocked a brow and said, "I see ranch life agrees with you."

Then again, she realized she didn't give a damn what he thought. "What are you doing here?" she and Ryder asked in unison.

"Seeing if you're all right," Claude said, still only talking to her and pointedly not looking at Ryder. "Your father was worried."

"I doubt that," she said. "So what are you really doing here?"

"Well, it sure as hell isn't to win you back," Claude snapped. "It's pretty clear what you've been doing."

"That's enough. You're not welcome here," Ryder said, as if tired of being ignored by the man. "Get off my property, or I'll have you arrested for trespassing."

Claude finally acknowledged him with a frown. "Seriously? Do you really not have a clue what's going on here, cowboy?" he said and shook his head. "You actually think Victoria just happened to ask for your help to save her from me? Ryder, it was a setup from the get-go. Wen wants your ranch, and he will literally do anything to get it—including enlisting his daughter to go after you." He glanced from Ryder to Victoria and back. "Apparently, it's working."

CHAPTER TWELVE

RYDER BALLED HIS hands into fists. He heard his brother deeper in the barn say behind him, "Easy, bro." He knew the kind of man Claude Duvall was, and so did his brother. If Ryder did what he'd wanted to do since the moment he'd met Claude, he would have already hit him and be facing assault charges and attorney fees.

Still, he ached to punch this jackass, even though he knew his brother was right. Claude was the kind of man who would call the sheriff, press charges and then hit him with a hefty lawsuit.

Knowing that made him want more than anything to punch this SOB's lights out. "If you drove all the way here to the ranch to warn me about Wendell and his daughter, you wasted your time. You should have just called."

Claude chuckled. "You don't believe me. Okay, so she hasn't been asking lots of questions about your ranch, showing an interest, reeling you in with those eyes and that body of hers? She hasn't told you how much she's enjoyed being here, loves it all, right?" He lifted a brow again as he smirked at Ryder. "She hasn't crawled into your bed on some excuse?"

He must have seen that the last hit its mark because Claude's sneer turned into a full-on smile.

"Cowboy, you've been had by the best. Wen and Victoria are an unbeatable team. You think this is the first time he's used her to get what he wants? Think again. He used her to reel me in. Why not you?"

Ryder looked down at his boots for a moment before glancing over at Victoria. He almost flinched when he saw the truth in her expression even as she quickly tried to deny it.

"Don't listen to anything he says," she said, but it wasn't her usual fiery defense. He knew at least some of it was true. Wendell Forester had used her to get what he wanted in the past. Probably had made a game out of it. Victoria was up for a good romp pretty much anytime, he figured.

"You have to believe me, that isn't what is happening here," she said. "None of this was planned. You know it started as a prank when I saw you in the airport. But then one thing led to another and . . ." She sounded close to tears. "Claude's lying."

Ryder thought about all of it from the moment he'd laid eyes on her at the airport to how she'd lured him in. If Forester had had a hand in it, then he'd played him perfectly. Maybe even that scene in the bar in Billings had been part of it, forcing Ryder to play the protector, get her away from her father and Claude and take her to his ranch.

If so, Ryder had played right into the gambit. He'd swallowed it all, hook, line and sinker. He'd taken the bait.

Yet even as he thought it, he didn't want to believe she'd been playing him. Not on their horseback ride. Not when he'd taught her to drive the truck. Or when he'd held her in his arms when they were dancing. But especially last night when she'd showed up at his bedroom door soaking wet and shivering.

If it had all been a ruse, then he'd been taken for a ride like a hick fool. He'd made love to her, gotten swept up in the emotion and done the one thing he swore he wasn't going to do. Had she known that once they made love, she would have had him right where she wanted him?

Ryder realized that he wouldn't put anything past Wendell Forester and maybe his daughter too. "He's lying," Victoria said again, but it lacked conviction. He could feel her gaze on him, his hands balled in fists at his side as he looked at Claude. "Does your boss know you're here?"

"Wendell *sent* me here to act as a catalyst—his word—to push her into your arms as I attempted to grovel and try to win her black heart," Claude said. "You think I don't know what she's like?" He chuckled again. "I've been where you are, so to speak. Wen used her to reel me into the worst contract of my life."

"Claude, don't—"

"What?" he said, turning to her. "Didn't you get around to telling the cowboy about you and me, Victoria?"

Ryder didn't dare look at her. He could feel the way her heart dropped, because his own had done the same thing. She and Claude had a past. No wonder the man had thought he had a chance with her.

"It isn't what you think," she said. "He's making more of it than it was."

"Claude, if you've come to take Wendell's daughter back to him, be my guest," Ryder said, his voice sounding stronger than he felt. "Victoria only came here for the weekend. As far as I'm concerned, the weekend is over."

With that, he turned on his bootheel and headed back into the barn.

VICTORIA WATCHED HIM GO, wanting to run after him. But some of what Claude had said was true, and Ryder knew it. She'd known that her father wanted Claude to go to work for him. It wasn't like they'd discussed it. She'd just known to be on her best behavior that night at dinner. But she'd known she was luring Claude in, and she'd felt guilty for doing it, given the way it had turned out for the man.

But she hadn't led him on the way he'd insinuated, and she'd certainly never encouraged him when it came to marriage. That had never been on the table.

But with Ryder, it had started as a fluke. She'd suspected her father was to up something when he'd told her she needed to meet him in Billings at the airport. She'd complied, hoping it had nothing to do with getting her married off. But she'd feared that was exactly what her father had in mind.

So when she'd seen Ryder standing there in his

Stetson, she'd done what came naturally: trying to
beat her father at his own game and using the handsome cowboy to help her.

She'd just never thought it would turn out like
this or that she would feel like this when it came
time to leave. This was all her fault. How could
she have thought that she could have a fling with a
man like Ryder? Other men might have been happy
for only that, but not this cowboy. She'd seen how
deeply he felt about life, his ranch. Shouldn't she
have known that he didn't take intimacy lightly?

Victoria had thought she could protect her heart
even as he'd taken her in his arms. She'd been such
a fool. She'd gone too far. She'd fallen in love with
the rancher. Last night she'd given away a part of
herself, a part she'd never shared before. Last night
making love with Ryder had left her shaken by its
impact. Her feelings for him ran so much deeper
than sex. Then waking up in his bed and racing out
to see the birth of the foal. She felt invested in not
just Ryder, but the ranch and this life. It was as if in
such a short time she'd become part of it.

But he was right, she thought, her heart breaking as she watched Ryder walk away. Their deal
was just through the weekend. She had known this
would end, but she hadn't wanted it to end like
this. Tears burned her eyes. She'd come to know
this cowboy. Last night had meant something to
him too. She'd looked into his eyes, and she'd felt
their connection, something as strong as his love
for the ranch and her love for him.

She loved him. She'd expected that admission to come as a shock, but it didn't. She thought of the way he'd touched her life. Neither of them had been expecting this. But that didn't make it any less true.

With a silent curse, Victoria turned around to face Claude and snapped, "Wait for me in the car." Then she headed for the house to get her things. All she had were the clothes she'd been wearing when she'd left Billings with Ryder. She thought about that night, the beginning of what she'd hoped would be an adventure she could tell her friends about. But it had turned into so much more.

What she hadn't expected was that she would feel the way she did right now. She didn't want to leave. She knew that was ridiculous. This wasn't her life. It had always been just a weekend adventure with a recall date stamped on it. So why did it hurt so bad to see Ryder's disappointment and feel her own so painfully it made her want to double over? Worse, she knew she'd never see him or this place again once she left. Even if her father got what he wanted, she would never come back to Stafford Ranch because Ryder and his family here would be destroyed. Wendell would destroy it out of greed, and Ryder would always believe that she'd helped him do it.

In Tilly's room, she took a moment to catch her breath before she stripped down, took a quick shower and, finding the clothes she'd worn here, changed back into the woman who'd hitched a ride with a cowboy. When she was finished, she stood in front of the mirror. She didn't look any different, but she certainly felt as if she wasn't the Victoria Forester she'd been before and never would be again.

At the sound of a car honk, she gritted her teeth. Was she really going to get into that vehicle with Claude after what he'd done to her?

What choice did she have? She still didn't have her purse, so no money or credit cards or phone. She could call her father on the landline downstairs, but her pride wouldn't let her. Also, she had a feeling he would just tell her to catch a ride with Claude or walk. She'd run out of options.

As she went downstairs, she hoped she wouldn't have to face Ryder or Brand or anyone else in the family before she left. Fortunately, she was spared. There was no one around as she stepped outside.

Claude was waiting impatiently behind the wheel as she climbed into the passenger side of the SUV and slammed the door. "About time."

"Aren't you afraid that I might kill you?" Victoria asked as she put on her seat belt. "You should fear for your life."

"Take it up with your father," he said as he started the engine. "I'm just doing my job."

"What are you talking about?" she demanded. "He told you to come here and humiliate me?"

"No. He suggested I try to win you over. He even promised that if I did, he would let me out of my contract with him. But screw that. I never wanted you, spoiled princess. I despise you. I only wanted the money. So ruining your chances with Ryder Stafford was just the fun part for me because what your father really wanted was the Stafford Ranch. Now there is no way in hell he'll get it. As for you . . ." he raked a disgusted look over her ". . . you get your comeuppance from a cowboy." He laughed. "Ironic, isn't it?"

"When I tell my father what you did—"

"Honey, I have nothing to lose. Your old man has taken my dignity and my honor and my self-respect. Now he'll take my money and ruin my life. I'd like to kill him, but disgracing his daughter will have to do. At least for now."

"You are such a bastard," she said as he drove away from the Stafford house and down the lane to the country road. As they passed through the stand of cottonwoods, she tried to see the Powder River. She caught glimpses of it in the rays of sunshine cutting through the trees. Her heart ached because the river seemed to symbolize Ryder in her mind. She would always remember the feel of the sun as she and Ryder sat on the rock in the middle of the river, the sparkling water all around them on the perfect summer day.

She closed her eyes, hating the tears that welled behind her lids. This shouldn't hurt as much as it did.

"YOU'RE JUST GOING to let her go?" Brand asked as Ryder came deeper into the barn. He could see where his brother had been shoveling out one of the stalls. Grabbing a shovel, he swore under his breath and stepped into the next stall. Of course Brand had heard every word that had been spoken.

"Don't want to talk about it."

"She really got to you, didn't she?"

He kept shoveling, hearing his brother stop to lean on his shovel.

"I was skeptical at first," Brand continued. "But even if it was planned, you got to her too."

Ryder stopped shoveling for a moment. "It was never going anywhere. We come from two very different worlds. Not to mention if we got together, her father would have what he wanted from the beginning—the Stafford Ranch."

"That's the part that doesn't make any sense," Brand said. "If Forester sent his flunky here acting as a catalyst like he said, then it didn't work. He drove the two of you further apart, not closer."

Ryder shook his head. "All I know is that I don't trust the man, and she's a lot like him."

"What worries me is that as badly as he wanted the ranch, I can't see him giving up so easily," his brother said. "What if he's found another way?"

"I can't imagine what that would be." He shook his head. "I hope I never hear the man's name again," he said pointedly and started shoveling again. As he did, he tried not think about Vicky, but images of her kept coming back fast and painful. Her on the horse, her in the creek, her driving the flatbed, her smiling up at him on the dance floor, her in his bed making love.

She'd left her mark on not just him but the ranch.

He feared he wouldn't be able to banish her memory every time he climbed behind the wheel of the truck or rode up into the mountains to that spot she had loved so much. He didn't want to believe it had all been a lie, a plot, a ruse—to what? Trick him into marrying her so her daddy could get his hands on the ranch some way.

That was the worst part. He'd begun to see her here on the ranch as his wife. He hadn't realized how much that image had seemed so real; he'd almost believed it. He'd thought about their children and the life they would have had. Even then though a part of his brain knew it was only a dream. But a dream so real he thought he could reach out and touch it. He'd never felt like that ever before.

The women he'd dated were from the area and knew this life. With Vicky he'd seen the ranch through her eyes in a whole new way as if there was something magical about his life.

Well, that magic was now gone, he told himself as he continued to work. He could hear his brother in the next stall doing the same. For a moment, it felt as if it had all been a dream and none of it had happened.

"I suppose we won't be naming the new colt after her, then," Brand said, making him swear.

WENDELL TAPPED ON CJ Stafford's apartment door, hoping the older Stafford brother was ready to back up his claims. He couldn't see how CJ thought he was going to get possession of the ranch. The man was living in an apartment in Miles City, and he'd just barely escaped going to prison. No wonder he was skeptical about the cocky former rancher.

All he could think was that CJ better be telling the truth. The man didn't know who he was dealing with otherwise. Wendell felt grumpy after spending the night in a motel. He'd gotten up this morning ready to do business or head home. CJ had insisted he come by the apartment. Wendell suspected the man didn't want him going by the Stafford Ranch. While CJ had promised to make it worth his time, he was definitely having his doubts.

"You and I really need to talk," CJ had said on the phone. "I can get you what you want. Stafford Ranch. Lock, stock and barrel."

"And what do you get out of it?" Wen had asked.

CJ had chuckled. "Money. That doesn't bother you, does it?"

"Not in the least."

He knocked again, growing impatient that he'd had to wait even a few seconds before the door opened. He took in the cocky man standing in the doorway. He saw at once CJ's resemblance to his brother Ryder. Both had the thick head of blond hair, those deep green eyes and similar handsome looks.

The difference was also just as apparent. There was a callousness in this man that verged on cruelty. Wendell could see it in the set of his jaw, in the cold depth of the green eyes, in every cell of his body. CJ had a chip on his shoulder and an ax to grind.

He was a loose cannon, since this was personal for him. He wasn't just after the money. He was after vengeance.

That alone should have warned Wendell that this was a mistake.

"Come on in, and let's talk business," CJ said, stepping back to allow him to enter.

He hesitated, good sense trying to win out over greed. He wanted that ranch for what lay beneath it. Methane gas and lots of it. He would make a fortune because he didn't give a damn that the wells might ruin the water supply or at some point be abandoned and poison the soil and even the groundwater.

Against his better judgment, he stepped in. The apartment looked unlived in—almost more like a staged scene than a real residence.

"Can I get you something to drink?"

Wendell declined, surprised that there were glasses and dishes in the cabinets of the small kitchen as he took a seat on what appeared to be a brand-new couch. He knew instinctively that CJ hadn't put any of this here. Furnishing this apartment was the last thing the man would have done. Wendell had heard that his mother had pulled some strings to get him out. Knowing Charlotte Stafford, Wendell just bet she had.

He watched him pour himself a Bloody Mary. "How long have you been out?"

CJ chuckled. "Did a little background check on me, did you? I would expect nothing less. That concern you?"

"Only if you're planning to do something that will get you sent back in the can before I get the ranch."

"A man after my own heart," he said. "You want the ranch. I can get it for you. The question is how much are you willing to pay me for it? A Bloody Mary all right with you?"

Wendell nodded. "But first, I'd like to know how you think you can get the ranch free and clear? Your mother, I believe, is still the owner, and you're one of five possible heirs."

"That's true, but I'm my mother's favorite."

"Still?" He glanced around the apartment. "Then, why are you living here and not on the ranch?"

CJ smiled. "This is only temporary. My mother's idea for the moment. She got all the charges against me dropped. She's waiting for me to prove how much I've changed." He chuckled as he carried over the two drinks, one of them overflowing. What looked like blood splattered on the new rug in front of the couch.

"You're on probation," Wendell said, worried this man wouldn't be able to hold it together long enough to get the ranch. "As I understand it, one little misstep and you're back behind bars."

"You let me worry about that," the eldest Stafford said as he handed him his drink and took a seat at the other end of the couch. The one thing CJ Stafford wasn't short of was arrogance, Wendell thought. Not that it was a bad thing, he told himself.

CJ took a sip of his drink, then looked down the length of the couch at him with those ice-cold green eyes. "How badly do you want the Stafford Ranch?"

CHAPTER THIRTEEN

CLAUDE TURNED UP the radio, wanting to drown out the dire thoughts circulating in his head. He knew that he'd crossed a line. He told himself he didn't care. All he could think about was getting off the Stafford Ranch, getting out of Montana and especially handing over Wen's daughter and telling them both what he thought of them.

Victoria would tell her father what he'd done, making it look as if she'd been in on it and ruining her chances with Ryder. But Claude was tired of playing games with these two. He was going to walk away from the job. Wen wouldn't sue him—unless he wanted some of the crooked things the man had done to come out.

Who was he kidding? Wen was vindictive enough that he'd sue no matter what. All Claude could do was wash his hands of this entire mess—once Wen flew him back to Dallas in the private jet. It would probably be the last private plane he'd ever get to fly in. No one would hire him after this.

He shoved that thought away. A man could take only so much, he told himself. All he wanted to do was to drop the princess off at the hotel and head for the airport. After she talked to her father, he figured Wen would be happy to fly him back to Dallas to be rid of him.

Victoria reached over and snapped off the radio. "You realize that he's going to make your life miserable, don't you?"

He snapped the radio back on and turned the volume up even louder.

She turned it off again, keeping her hand on the knob, daring him to touch it. To touch her.

"I know enough about you and your father to make both of your lives miserable, princess."

She laughed. "Try that on my father and he'll bury you."

"I don't think so. He might not care about things coming out on him, but you . . . He won't want the mud to get splashed on his precious daughter."

Victoria looked around as if searching for something to hit him with. Like father like daughter, he thought. He couldn't get this over with soon enough.

As THEY NEARED the town of Powder Crossing, Victoria was heartsick. For a while, she'd felt like one of the Stafford family. She'd liked that feeling, getting to see Tilly's baby, meeting the rest of his family, even Ryder's mother. It even helped to realize Charlotte Stafford was a lot like her father, as ridiculous as that sounded. What she hated most was that now they would all believe that she'd come here at her father's bequest in an attempt to steal their ranch.

How could she leave with them believing that? She couldn't, she thought as she reached in the back for the wrap she'd tossed back there when she'd gotten in the vehicle. It was the same one she'd worn over her dress the night she and Ryder had left the hotel for the ranch. She'd been so angry with Claude that she'd wanted to strangle him with it and had been afraid she would unless it was out of her reach.

But as she picked it up now, she spotted her purse on the back seat. Unsnapping her seat belt, she got on her hands and knees and reached in the back to snatch it up too.

"Why didn't you tell me you had my bag?" she demanded as she turned back around and refastened her seat belt. Opening her purse, she checked to make sure her phone was inside, along with her money and credit cards, and looked up to see that they were driving through Powder Crossing, and would be out of town soon.

"Let me out!" she demanded, startling Claude. He kept driving. *"Let me out now!"* He gave her a smirk.

Pulling out her phone, she called her father. "Maybe you'd like your boss to tell you to stop this damned car."

"Hang up," Claude bellowed. "Hang up!"

"Daddy? It's Victoria."

Claude made a swipe at the phone as if to knock it out of her hand, but she ducked away, avoiding his hand.

Turning away from him, she cried, "Claude has kidnapped me! He's going to kill me. Help! No, stop!"

Claude threw on the brakes. She would have gone through the windshield if she hadn't buckled her seat belt again. "Get out!" His voice sounded raw with emotion. She had the feeling that he was getting close to the end of his rope with her and her father. Who could blame him?

She grabbed her door handle and practically threw herself out.

"Victoria!" She could hear her father still on the phone as Claude peeled out, burning rubber as he sped away.

"You shouldn't have sent Claude after me," she said into the phone. "Now I'm going to see that you never get the Stafford Ranch." She disconnected and dropped her phone back in her handbag.

As she looked around town, her anger slowly evaporated. Now what? she thought. Seeing the Open sign at the café in the distance, she began to walk. With each step, she promised herself she would do exactly what she'd told her father she would on the phone. She knew he had a plan to get the ranch—other than her marrying into the Stafford family—and that was what worried her. Her secret weapon was that she knew how her father operated, so maybe that would help.

Also, she thought that maybe Wendell Forester loved his daughter enough not to break her heart.

On that thought, she had her doubts, but she could hope, couldn't she?

The hard part would be convincing Ryder to trust her ever again.

CLAUDE WASN'T SURPRISED when he'd barely gotten rid of Victoria before his phone began to ring. He let it go to voice mail. But it immediately rang again. Grabbing it, he planned to turn it off, but realized he needed to end this. Why not now?

"What?" he snapped into the phone as he drove. He'd never been so happy as to see Powder Crossing in his rearview mirror—and Victoria Forester with it.

"Did you hurt my daughter?" Wen said, his voice low and deadly.

"The drama queen? I wish. I just dropped her off on the main drag of Powder Crossing like she'd demanded. I never touched her. She's your problem now because I quit."

"Claude," he said reasonably, "you know you can't do that."

"So sue me."

"Oh, I will. I'll drag your name through the dirt and leave you penniless."

Claude began to laugh. "She's just like you, a coldhearted bitch. I've had more than enough of both of you."

He could hear Wen breathing hard, trying to control his temper. "I'm sensing that you're angry."

"You think?"

"What do you really want?"

"Not your daughter, I can tell you that much. You couldn't pay me enough money to marry her."

"Since that isn't on the table, what is it you want?"

"You have nothing I want." Except a ride back to Dallas in the company jet. He knew he should get off the phone. Wendell Forester was the devil, and he was after Claude's soul. Right now, Wen was just fooling with him, trying to establish his price.

"Claude, I can make all your dreams come true. Isn't that why you came to work for me in the beginning? I don't want to lose you as my associate."

Associate? What a laugh, he thought. "You despise me as much I despise you. I'm tired of being your flunky, Forester."

"We can work with this," Wen said reasonably. "I'm going to get the Stafford Ranch no matter what Ryder Stafford says. That should make you happy."

Claude shook his head and pulled over to the side of the road. His hands were shaking, his heart thundering in his ears. He would like nothing better than for that cowboy to lose everything. But it wasn't enough. What was his price? "I want Victoria to pay too," he said. "Cut off her money."

The connection went so quiet he thought his former boss had hung up. Everyone knew how Wen felt about his daughter. Claude feared that he'd asked too much.

Then he heard a sigh. "I'll do it if you promise not to quit, because I need you. I have a job for you that I think you'll enjoy. You'll be working with CJ Stafford. He's going to help me take the Stafford Ranch. I want you to do whatever he needs to make that happen."

"And as soon as I'm done with this last job, I want you to fly me back to Dallas in the jet."

"All right."

"And Victoria?" he asked, not willing to give an inch.

"Just as you want. She's now on her own."

ONCE IN THE CAFÉ, Victoria ordered pancakes and bacon. She couldn't believe how hungry she was. In one day's time, she'd gotten used to the ranch meals. She couldn't bear the thought that for a moment she'd almost been one of the family and her father and Claude had snatched it away without a thought to what she might want.

She could feel the locals in the café watching her, wondering about her. She wondered about herself as well. Ryder thought she was like her father. She was . . . to some extent. But not in the way Ryder thought.

The rancher and this life had gotten under her skin. That was the only way she could explain it. She couldn't leave. Not yet anyway. She couldn't let her father take Ryder's ranch. She'd seen how much he and Brand loved the place. Her father could never understand that kind of love. He had always been about the money. Only lately, he'd gotten so much worse.

The problem was stopping him. He'd never listened to her—not when she'd told him she wasn't marrying one of his yes-men or when she'd tried to explain why she worked at a nonprofit. What made her think she could make him see reason now?

Earlier when she'd made Claude let her out on the street, she'd been so sure of what she had to do. Right now, though, she was beginning to realize that she had no plan and no power. Her father was determined that he knew what was best for her.

Which meant that even if he knew how she felt about Ryder, he would still take the ranch. Because she knew her father and how he operated, which was why he would be hard to stop if he thought he'd found another way to get what he wanted. Her hope was that if she could convince him otherwise, he might back off just this one time.

But first, she had to convince Ryder that she'd never been part of a scheme to steal his ranch and that he needed to be concerned about what her father was now up to. She feared it was dangerous.

Her breakfast came. After her worry about what her father was up to, she'd lost her appetite, but she made herself eat some of it. The breakfast was nothing like the one she'd had at the ranch. She thought of Ryder and Brand sitting around the table giving each other a hard time. She'd always wished for a sibling, never getting to experience what Ryder had in spades. Did he know how lucky he was? She thought he just might.

By now, the brothers would have eaten and were probably out doing chores. She hoped the foal was doing well. She wondered what he would be like when he was grown. Brand had joked about naming the colt after her. The thought made her heart lift like a balloon. But the thought of never seeing him grow up pricked that bubble of joy, letting all the air out.

She pushed her plate away, only half-eaten. When the woman Ryder had called Penny came over, she gave her a credit card to pay for her bill.

"I'm sorry," Penny said, returning quickly. "I ran it twice." She shook her head and looked embarrassed.

"Just a moment," Victoria said and checked her phone. Just as she suspected, there was a message from her father that read When you mess with the bull, you're going to get the horns.

Putting her phone away, she checked to see how much cash she had and quickly paid her bill. On her way out of the café, she stopped at a bulletin board covered with posts offering babysitting, cleaning services, car repair and finally vehicles for sale.

She pulled off a number and made the call. Fortunately, the vehicle was still for sale and only a block away. The Montana summer day was so beautiful she enjoyed the walk. She'd never get over how blue the sky was out here. She thought of the night sky she'd stood under after she and Ryder had returned from the bar last night. She'd never seen so many stars. She felt sad to think that she might not see another sky like that.

The faded red pickup sat out front of a small shop that was being run from the man's garage.

"Hello?" she called as she approached.

A gray-haired man came out of the garage, shading his eyes. "You the lady who called about the pickup?" he asked as he stepped from the darkness of the garage, wiping his greasy hands on a rag. Somewhere in his late sixties, she saw he had the hood up on an older-model car he'd been working on.

"I am. Is this it?" she asked, stepping over to the red pickup.

"That's her, but I don't think she's for you," he said, taking in her dress and high heels before shaking his head.

She smiled. Did he think she was too proud to drive an old pickup? "Why?"

"It's a stick shift."

Victoria chuckled. "Not a problem. I can drive it. Mind if I start her up?"

"Help yourself. She runs like a top. Worked on her myself."

The engine started at once and purred. "Sounds good," she said. "I'm a little short of cash, though. What's the best you could do on her?"

The man studied the ground and chewed at his cheek for a few moments before he shook his head. "She's worth every dime I'm asking."

Victoria looked around the clean cab. "She was yours?"

"Yep."

"You took good care of her. She have a name?" she asked, knowing the pickup would.

"Mabel," he said, ducking his head as if embarrassed.

"Mabel," she repeated, liking the sound of it. Not only had she learned to drive, she now had her first automobile—if she could afford it.

"Named after my wife. She's now deceased."

"I'm so sorry." She gripped the wheel, sensing that Mabel would have liked her having the old pickup. "I'd like to buy Mabel. I promise to take good care of her. Is there any chance you could throw in a tank of gas?"

CJ KNEW HE was going to have to lean on some of his former friends in order to pull off his plan. Forester had said he would provide help, but CJ preferred to work with men he knew and could trust over the tycoon's right-hand man, Claude Duvall. But Duvall might make the perfect fall guy if things went south.

"I thought I told you to never call me again," Treyton McKenna snapped in answer to the call.

CJ laughed, unconcerned. If Treyton really hadn't wanted to talk to him, his old rival wouldn't have picked up. "You're going to want to be in on this."

Treyton swore. "I don't even want to know."

"Yes, you do. I'm almost to your place now. See you soon."

"Seriously, CJ, I don't—"

He hung up before the man could argue further.

It was no surprise to find Treyton standing outside the shack he lived in, holding an automatic rifle. CJ pulled up, smiling at how he and a McKenna had been in business together not all that long ago. He'd made Treyton a lot of money and provided him with a whole new profitable enterprise while he'd been behind bars. The man owed him.

CJ climbed out and walked toward him, knowing Treyton wouldn't use the weapon. He was bluffing. He'd always been a jerk. The McKenna family had pretty much disowned Treyton except for his father. Holden didn't have the sense to realize that his son had no redeeming qualities and let him go.

"I don't want to hear it."

CJ shrugged. "Then, I won't be able to change your mind."

"Heard you're living in an apartment in Miles City." Treyton had perfected the mocking tone he used with most people. It was no wonder he lived out here in the badlands alone instead of on the McKenna Ranch. But it did make it easier for CJ to con him into doing most anything he wanted.

"The apartment is perfect," he said lying through his teeth about that. He hated it, found it humiliating. He should be out at the ranch in his wing of the house. He should be running the ranch, but that, he realized, was an old dream that he had to let go. He had a new plan thanks to his mother.

"The apartment is perfect?" Treyton mocked.

CJ grinned. "How else could I have met with Wendell Forester there this morning without anyone being the wiser?"

Treyton let out a grunt. "Right, Wendell Forester, the billionaire developer. Did this new you serve him a cup of tea?"

"No, a Bloody Mary, if you must know. His daughter's been staying out at the ranch after hooking up with Ryder. Maybe you heard."

His eyes widened a little, even though he denied any interest. Clearly, Treyton hadn't heard.

"I've promised Wendell the Stafford Ranch for a very large sum of money. Maybe you would be interested in some of it."

Treyton frowned. "You running a con on Wendell Forester? Oh, you really are playing in the big leagues now." He laughed. "You swindle him, and that man will have you killed and buried out here in the badlands."

"It's not a swindle. It's a straight-up business deal," CJ said.

"Just one problem, as I see it. You don't have the ranch. In fact, you can't even stay there. Come on, CJ, quit wasting my time."

"Right, you're *so* busy." CJ looked away, grinding his teeth and trying for patience. "Do you really think I don't have a plan? I'm going to get control of the ranch. I'm going to sell it, and I'm leaving the country. You can stay here and live like this, or you can help me and spend the rest of your life on a beach far away from here. You want in on this or not?"

"I never liked beaches. The sand. It gets between my toes, you know?" But he lowered the rifle. "What's my cut?"

"Five percent."

"Ten percent," Treyton said, thinking he was in a bargaining position.

"Fine," CJ said. "Ten percent of over ten million dollars. Let's see how much that would be," he said, pretending to run the numbers in his head.

Treyton's eyes had gone as big as silver dollars since the man was capable of counting. "Who do I have to kill?"

CHAPTER FOURTEEN

CLAUDE WASN'T LOOKING forward to meeting another cowboy, especially from the same family as Ryder. He'd had his fill of Montana and couldn't wait to leave. But Wen had offered him a deal. His last job for the man. Both Victoria and the cowboy would suffer. Then he'd be on the jet, sipping Wen's expensive booze and winging his way back to Dallas a free man.

He was delighted that Wen was going after the cowboy's ranch with both barrels firing. He'd seen what his boss could do when he set his mind to something he wanted. Claude couldn't wait to see what Ryder thought of Forester when he came at him in his take-no-prisoners mode. Wen would get the Stafford Ranch, whatever it took. Ryder didn't stand a chance.

As for Victoria, he smiled to himself as he neared Miles City. If Wen had done what he'd promised and cut her off, her life as she'd known it was over. Little Rich Girl was now poorer than Claude. She'd always depended on her father, working that rinky-dink job that paid squat and living like a queen, thanks to Daddy.

He wondered what she would do. He realized that she might even come crawling to him for help in the future. That thought certainly ticked up his mood as he parked in front of the apartment number Wen had given him.

The man who answered the door was enough like Ryder to be his evil twin. The resemblance was striking, but where Ryder might be a nice guy, CJ Stafford didn't even pretend to be.

"You know how to shoot a gun?" CJ barked, but didn't even wait for an answer as he shoved a weapon into his hands. "I didn't think so. But where you're going, you can learn." He handed him a couple boxes of ammunition. "Practice with some tin cans out behind the place where you'll be staying." He must have seen Claude's dislike for guns. "What exactly is it you do for Forester?"

"Whatever he asks."

CJ raised a brow. "He tell you to do whatever *I* ask?"

Claude hated to admit that he had. "What do you need me to do?"

The evil twin laughed. "I'll let you know. For starters, I need you to go back out by the Stafford Ranch." Claude started to object, but he waved it off. "I suspect you aren't any more welcome there than I am. I need to know who comes and goes from the ranch." He handed him a map. "There's an old place on the other side of the river. You can hide out there. It's pretty primitive, so buy yourself some good binoculars and what you'd need if you were camping out for a couple of weeks. Once you get there, call me. Stay there and report to me. Got it? My number's on the map."

Pretend he was camping out? He'd never camped out in his life. This sounded like the last thing he wanted to do, but it was his last job for Wen, he reminded himself. He said, "Sure. Why not?"

"Good thinking. That's it. Get movin', and if you're smart you'll learn to shoot the gun."

Claude wasn't CJ Stafford. He really doubted he'd ever have a use for a gun. But he didn't argue. Instead, he went back out the door he'd come in, map in one hand, gun in the other, ammunition weighing down his jacket pocket. What the hell had Wen gotten him involved in? Maybe more important, what was his boss doing working with CJ Stafford?

In the SUV again, he stopped at a grocery store, stocked up what he might need for a couple of weeks and considered the map. He had no idea what to expect of this old place he would apparently be hiding out in and spying on the Stafford Ranch. At least that part sounded all right.

He bought plenty of snack food and drinks. At the last minute, he stopped at a sporting goods store and picked up a camping stove, a pan, utensils, a bedroll, a cot and lantern and anything else to make this assignment not be pure hell. He charged it all to Wen on the company credit card.

The drive was just as boring as the other time he'd made the trip out to the Stafford Ranch. He kept thinking of Victoria spending the night in the barn, hay in her hair, looking like something the cat had dragged in, as his mother used to say. Maybe she was cut out for ranch work. More than likely she was doing the rancher—and apparently anywhere he wanted.

He found the turnoff to the old place just past the Stafford Ranch and drove up the hill to where he found an abandoned house. It looked rough, but it wasn't leaning too badly, and it had a roof. He hated to think what it would be like inside, though. He parked the SUV behind it and got out to inspect the dilapidated structure, wondering what he would do if it was as bad inside as he anticipated.

When he pushed open the back door, he was glad to see that someone had been here and cleaned it out. It smelled musty, but he didn't see any rodents around, so he made the call to CJ, letting him know he'd made it.

Then he set about turning the place into his makeshift temporary home. He hoped he wouldn't really be here for weeks. The things he did for Wen, he thought with a curse. If that wasn't bad enough, now he was working for CJ Stafford, who he thought just might be even more dangerous than his egomaniacal boss.

RYDER HAD BEEN in the barn with his brother when he heard a vehicle coming up the road toward them. Brand had been busy saddling up to ride out after a neighbor had called to inform them that they had some fence down in a far pasture. "Go on and check the fence. I can let the mare and colt out into the pasture," he told his brother.

Brand, who'd always been the more curious sibling, walked his horse over to the open doorway and stepped out to see who it was.

Ryder heard him say, "Well, I'll be. I didn't expect that."

Unable not to, Ryder walked out to join his brother who elbowed him and pointed at what had just driven up in the yard. "Didn't expect it, but I guess we should have," Brand said with a chuckle.

From where they were standing, Ryder saw the older-model faded red pickup that had pulled in and recognized it—just as he did the woman who had climbed out.

The moment he saw the high heels and then those long bare legs exiting the truck, he swore. "What the hell is she doing in that pickup, let alone back here?"

"Beats me," Brand said, chuckling.

Ryder stalked toward Vicky, wondering what she thought she was doing showing up here again. His mind fought with his heart. No matter what she and her father were up to, he wasn't interested. His heart, however, couldn't help beating faster at the sight of her. Damn, he thought. That woman had done a number on him.

She held up a hand as he approached. "Hear me out. Please."

He'd been trying his best to forget Victoria Forester

ever existed. He'd told himself all morning that at least he would never have to lay eyes on her again. She'd get in that private jet and wing her way back to her famous life. Shoot, by tonight, he'd told himself, she would be partying with her friends. He hated to think what she'd be telling her friends about the cowboy she hadn't only kissed.

After she'd left earlier, he'd been working to put the whole thing behind him. Unfortunately, he kept having flashbacks of the two of them in his big bed, both of them naked as a jaybird. He'd told himself he would forget what she looked like. He wouldn't remember those flecks of gold in her green eyes any more than he would remember the feel of her lips on his. The sweet sound of her breath escaping as he touched her.

Seeing her again brought it all back in Technicolor. *What was she doing here?* A half-dozen questions leaped into his head. What had she done with Claude? Why was she driving Hank Armstrong's old truck? What part of *Get lost* had she not understood? He'd thought he'd made himself clear that she wasn't welcome here ever again—as much as it had pained him to do so.

He opened his mouth, not sure which question to ask first. What came out was "What did you do with Claude?"

"I didn't kill him, if that's what you're worried about. I wanted to, but I didn't."

Ryder shook his head. "Where—"

"Hank Armstrong in town sold me Mabel. He was worried I couldn't drive it because—"

"It's a stick shift," he said for her. "What are you doing here?"

"I came back to try to help you keep your ranch."

He lifted a brow. "I beg your pardon?"

"I know my father. He isn't giving up. If anything, he'll do whatever he has to do now to get what he wants. He's up to something. I don't know what, but I'm afraid he's found another way to get the ranch."

Ryder shook his head. "Why would I—"

"Trust me?" Now she interrupted him. "Because no matter what Claude said, I wasn't running a con on you. I don't expect you to believe me right now, but . . ." She looked around the ranch for a moment. "Being here with you, I was more myself than I've ever been. I couldn't leave like that."

He was swamped with such a rush of emotions he felt off balance. He wanted to believe her, but so much was at stake. How could he trust this woman? How could he not if she was telling the truth?

His heart thumped hard in his chest as if begging him not only to believe her but also to not let her go. Ryder told himself he couldn't trust his heart any more than he could trust this woman.

Unfortunately, even though he had the heart of a fool in love, he wanted to trust it.

VICTORIA FEARED HE didn't believe her and that he'd never trust her again. Maybe she'd been too impulsive, forcing Claude to let her out on the edge of

Powder Crossing, then buying a pickup and coming back here. But she'd had to. Just as she had to make him understand. "Ryder—"

"You want to see Vic?" Brand called from the barn doorway, clearly ignoring the angry look his brother shot him.

"Vic?" she asked and heard Ryder groan as she passed him on the way to the barn. Once inside the cool darkness, she breathed in the familiar scent and went to the stall where the mare and foal were.

"I thought you were going to check that fence," Ryder said pointedly to his brother.

Neither Vicky nor Brand paid him any attention.

"Oh, he's so beautiful," she said of the new colt. "I swear he's gotten bigger since I saw him earlier."

Brand chuckled at that. "We were about to let them out into the pasture," he said. "Glad you didn't miss it." Then he grinned and shook his head. "You really did come back."

She met his gaze. "I had to."

Brand nodded. "Try not to break his heart."

For a moment, she thought he was talking about the new colt. Then Ryder walked past her and opened the back of the stall to let the mare and her foal out into the pasture. The foal took off at a run after his mother. Victoria felt her throat close, and her chest hurt. She couldn't help getting choked up as she watched the colt chasing after the mare. Her gaze went to Ryder leaning against the fence watching mother and son.

Her heart ached at just the sight of him. She

wanted to reach out, press her palm against his back, feel his strength through the sun-warmed fabric of his shirt. She wanted to touch him so badly that it made her ache inside. She felt her eyes fill with tears at the thought that he would turn her away again.

"I would imagine you two have something to talk about and I have some fence to check," Brand said loud enough for his brother to hear. He tipped his hat at her and whispered "Good luck" as he picked up his horse's reins from where he'd ground-tied them earlier and swung up into the saddle.

Victoria joined Ryder at the fence to watch the horses. Beyond them, she could see Brand riding off through the summer grass. They both seemed to watch him go, neither acknowledging the other.

She found herself holding her breath, half afraid of what Ryder would say, let alone what he'd do now that his brother was gone.

Securing the gate on the pasture, he turned to her. "Let's go up to the house to talk."

IN FRONT OF a window that he cleaned the dust from, Claude had set up a viewing station, realizing that CJ had been right. He was high enough on the hill that he could see who came and went from the Stafford Ranch. He'd found an old wooden box, and taking his binoculars over to the window along with it, he surveyed the property. He was glad that he'd spent a whole lot of Wen's money to get the really good binoculars. He could see everything and zoom in on faces and license plates.

As he watched, he saw a dull red pickup turn into the ranch. He'd followed it in until it disappeared behind the trees and reappeared down by the barn. With a shock, he'd seen the woman who'd climbed out.

Victoria? He should have known she'd head back out there. But what was she doing in that old truck? More important, how was Ryder going to react? The cowboy would have to be a fool not to run her off again. But Claude would bet that the woman had made a fool of her share of men, and Ryder wasn't the exception.

Claude had watched her disappear into the barn with both cowboys. Minutes ticked by. A cowboy came riding out on a horse headed north across the endless prairie. Where was Victoria?

His cell phone rang. CJ Stafford. He picked up. "Yeah?"

"Are you watching the ranch? Anything happening?"

Claude thought about mentioning Victoria and wasn't sure why he didn't. "A cowboy just rode off. I think it was—" He'd been about to say Ryder when he saw him come out of the barn with Victoria. "It wasn't Ryder. Another brother?"

"Brand. Where was he headed?"

"He just rode north out across the pasture."

"Good," CJ said. "You're doing great. Let me know when he comes back." He disconnected, apparently only interested in Ryder's brother.

Claude, though, was more interested in Victoria as he zoomed in on her as the cowboy led her toward the house.

RYDER STEPPED INTO the living room, then turned to face her. Clearly, he didn't think this would take long so he didn't bother to offer her a seat. "What are you doing back here?" he asked again, as if still having trouble believing that she'd had the gall to return after the damning things Claude had told him—and she hadn't denied them.

Now that she was here, she had no idea how to reach Ryder. She could tell by the set of his shoulders and the rigid way he stood that he was angry and hurt and didn't trust her. But if he would give her even half a chance and a little time, she would prove herself to him.

The problem was, she didn't know how much time they had. How much time she had before he threw her off the ranch. Or worse, her father got hold of the ranch.

"It's not over," she said quickly, realizing that she could be talking about her feelings for him. "I'm not sure why Claude said the things he did to you, but he is still working for my father. Which means they have a new plan of attack, and I think your brother CJ might be involved."

She could see that even the mention of CJ and her father in business together upset him.

"Your father is not getting the ranch no matter who he is teamed up with," Ryder said.

"You don't want to underestimate him," Victoria said. "I think it will come down to how desperate your brother might be to gain control of the ranch and whether or not his real interest is the ranch—or what it's worth in cash." She saw that she'd struck a nerve. "You said he wasn't supposed to come out to the ranch and yet I met him upstairs. Clearly, he doesn't play by the rules—and neither does my father."

"Sneaking onto the ranch is one thing. Getting control of it?" Ryder shook his head, but she could tell he was worried. He knew his brother better than she did, but she suspected if he was anything like her father, this ranch would soon be up for grabs and her father would be waiting with the cash.

"You said CJ is your mother's favorite. Also let's not forget that our parents know each other."

"My mother would never make a deal to sell the ranch," he said emphatically, but she got the feeling he was trying to convince himself more than her. Hadn't he said that Charlotte had left for months and had only recently returned? Maybe her interest in the ranch had waned.

"It might depend on what kind of leverage my father has," she said.

Ryder stared at her in horror. "Are you saying he might have something on my mother that he could blackmail her into selling him the ranch?"

She could only shrug. "All I know is that he has found a way to get the ranch that doesn't involve me or you." Victoria saw his expression and felt her heart break. "I'm so sorry. If I hadn't approached you at the airport—"

"Propositioned me, you mean?" he said, but there wasn't a lot of bite to his words.

"That too," she agreed. "My father already wanted your ranch, but once I got involved, I might have made it worse. That's why I came back here today. I couldn't just leave. I know my father. He's angry at me right now, but I might be able to reason with him and get him to back off."

"By agreeing to marry Claude or some other fool he picks for you?" Ryder was already shaking his head. "No way. This is my battle. I'm not going to let you sacrifice yourself for—"

The front door flew open, and Brand stumbled in, his hand over the left side of his chest, blood oozing between his fingers. "I rode out to check that fence we heard was down. Someone took a potshot at me."

AT THE HOSPITAL, Ryder paced the floor of the waiting room, anxious to hear about Brand's condition. He'd been agitated before Brand had stumbled in bleeding and telling them he'd been shot.

Now Ryder was incensed. He'd called the sheriff, who was on his way. Sheriff Stuart Layton had been at a wreck over by Broadus.

"Who would do this?" Ryder demanded as he paced, not that he expected Vicky to have the answers. But it was damned suspicious since she was the one who'd warned him her father wasn't going to stop—no matter what he had to do.

"My father wouldn't shoot anyone," she told him as if she knew what he was thinking.

"What about Claude?"

"I doubt he's ever fired a gun in his life," she said. Their gazes met, both thinking the same thing. "Your brother?"

He swore and pulled out his phone. CJ's phone went straight to voice mail. He called his mother. "Where is CJ?"

"I beg your pardon? Hello to you too, Ryder."

"I don't have time for niceties, Mother. Brand's been shot."

She let out a cry. "Is he—"

"He's in surgery here at the Powder Crossing Hospital. Where is CJ?" He heard a chair scrape and his mother moving through what sounded like a restaurant, then silence again for moment. "Your brother didn't shoot Brand. He was just sitting across from me having brunch."

"What a coincidence that he just happens to have you for an alibi," Ryder snapped.

"Brand's in surgery?" she asked, ignoring his implication. "Did the doctor say how serious it is?"

"No. We don't know anything yet. I just know CJ hasn't been out twenty-four hours and Brand gets shot."

"I'll call Holden and let him know. We'll come down to the hospital," his mother said, reminding him that Brand was his half brother. And the result of one of his mother's and Holden's little get-togethers out at the creek, a secret that had only recently been exposed. Not even Brand had known. Holden hadn't known until recently either. "Have you called the sheriff?"

"Stuart just walked in. I need to go." He pocketed his phone and hurried over to the sheriff. "Someone took a potshot at my brother. Sound familiar?"

The same thing had happened to Oakley not all that long ago. When caught, CJ swore it had been an accident. He'd almost killed her.

"Where is your brother?" the sheriff asked.

Ryder wasn't surprised that was Stuart's first question. "Having brunch with my mother. Convenient, huh?"

The sheriff nodded, as if not surprised that CJ would have an airtight alibi.

As the doctor came out, he and the sheriff turned. Victoria was on her feet. "How is he?" she asked.

"Luckily, the bullet didn't hit anything vital," the doctor said. "He'll be laid up for a while, but he'll survive." Even though the hospital was small, the doctor had taken care of his share of gunshot wounds.

"I'll need that bullet if you have it," the sheriff said. "Also, I need to speak with Brand."

"It's a .22 slug. I'll see that you get it, but you can't talk to Brand yet. He's still in recovery. It will be a couple of hours at least before he's awake enough to make sense. I'd suggest you come back later."

"Thanks, Doc," Ryder said and turned to the sheriff as the doctor walked away. "This has CJ written all over it."

Stuart didn't argue the point but asked, "Why would he want to shoot Brand? It would appear that whoever shot your brother wasn't trying to kill him shooting him with a .22."

"Or was a piss-poor shot," Ryder said. "If it was me, I'd see if Treyton McKenna has a .22 rifle lying around."

The sheriff groaned. "Everyone in this county has at least one .22 rifle lying around, but I'll drive out and talk to him and pickup up whatever .22 he has. Again, why would CJ or Treyton want to shoot your brother?"

"Does CJ really need a reason other than he hates our family?" Ryder snapped. "Same goes for Treyton."

Stuart shook his head. "He just got out of jail. If he breaks his probation, he's going back behind bars. Worse, he could be looking at prison. Why would he risk it?"

Ryder looked at Victoria for a moment before shaking his head. "I don't know." The sheriff had a point. If CJ was after the ranch, why take such a foolish chance? And what was shooting Brand going to get him?

"Maybe it was an accident," the sheriff said. "Some kid with a .22 rifle not realizing how far a bullet can travel." Stuart saw his expression and quickly raised his hands. "Don't worry. I'm taking the slug as evidence, and after I talk to Brand, I'll go check out the spot where he was shot and take a drive out to Treyton's place. In the meantime—"

"Don't even say it. You don't want me getting into it with CJ," Ryder said.

"I think that's good advice on any given day," the sheriff said. "You both might want to leave since I'd like to speak to Brand when he's ready. I could have someone call you when your brother can have visitors."

Ryder rubbed a hand over his face and realized that he hadn't introduced Victoria to the sheriff, who was now studying her openly. "This is Victoria Forester, my . . . houseguest."

Stuart raised a brow. "Forester?" Ryder had called him numerous times to have Forester's men thrown off the ranch.

"Don't ask," Ryder said.

The sheriff smiled and nodded. "Nice to meet you, Ms. Forester."

"Vicky," she said. "Nice to meet you, Sheriff. I just wish it wasn't under these circumstances."

He nodded. "Might want to stay close around the ranch until we find out what's going on," Stuart said, then tipped his Stetson and headed off down the hall in the direction the doctor had gone.

CHAPTER FIFTEEN

OAKLEY, TRUE TO her promise, had kept quiet about the engagement. Charlotte and Holden had both wanted Cooper and Tilly to enjoy some time with their new baby without anyone stealing the limelight.

They'd known that the moment the news hit the county, it would spread through the Powder River basin like wildfire. Word got out when Holden called the church to make arrangements for the upcoming wedding, and tongues began to wag. Rumors circulated just as quickly. Bets were being taken that it would never happen. Bets were also being taken on who would show up from the family.

But it was doubtful that anyone in the county aware of the feud between the two families wouldn't show up. Everyone would expect fireworks—and not the kind that you had to light. Anything could happen at this wedding when you threw the McKennas together with the Staffords—especially with CJ Stafford out of jail. Which was exactly why Holden planned to hire security.

"The church isn't going to be large enough," he'd told Lottie after they'd taken a seat at the café.

Earlier they'd stopped by the hospital to find Brand in stable condition and recovering from the surgery, which had gone well. Neither of them mentioned who they thought might have shot Brand, preferring to agree with the sheriff that it had been an accident.

"Maybe we should get married at the fair-grounds," he joked in a back booth where they were having coffee and pie. They'd gone to Billings to get the marriage license and do some wedding shopping and only just returned.

"Or elope," she suggested again, taking a bite of the lemon meringue that she so loved.

He shook his head. "No one would ever believe we actually did it if we don't have a big wedding right here in Powder Crossing. No, we have to make this an event, a sign that all the animosity between us and our families is over."

They ate for a moment in silence. "Have you told Treyton yet?" she finally asked.

"I'm sure he's heard. What about CJ?"

She seemed to hesitate. "I was going to tell him at brunch yesterday, but I chickened out. I didn't want to spoil a nice meal with him. I've had so few. He already knew about the engagement and made a point of not mentioning it. Maybe he thinks that if he ignores it . . ."

Holden was quiet for a moment. "We knew that this wasn't going to be easy."

"Their loss if they don't come around," she said. "I'm not worried about it." But he could tell she was worried because he was too. He wished he wasn't.

Both CJ and Treyton could be unpredictable when things didn't go their way. He didn't want trouble at the wedding and made a mental note to check on that security he'd called for.

It wasn't until Charlotte went back to her room at the hotel and he drove to the ranch that he decided to bite the bullet and make the calls to his children about not just the engagement, but the wedding. Treyton didn't pick up. No surprise, so he had to leave both announcements in a voice mail.

His cell phone rang. He saw it was Lottie and picked up. "Anything new on Brand's condition?" he asked, recalling how upset he'd been when he'd found out that the young man was his son—and Charlotte had kept it from him. He pushed the memory away. No looking back at the past, she'd said. It was good advice. Too much water had already flowed under that bridge. He focused on the future.

"I spoke to the doctor when I went over to see him again. Just a few more days in the hospital, and he should be released," she said.

"I talked to the sheriff," Holden said. "The bullet was a .22 like when Oakley was shot. But it doesn't match CJ's rifle, which is still in evidence."

"I really don't believe CJ had anything to do with it. I'm not sticking my head in the sand, believe me. He at least didn't fire the shot," Lottie said. "He was with me having brunch, but everyone suspects he's behind it. Holden, I'm scared. What does the sheriff think?"

"Stuart still thinks it could have been an accident, some kid with a rifle," Holden said.

"But what if CJ or Treyton heard about the engagement and upcoming wedding and wanted to hurt us?"

"By shooting our son? That makes no sense. Lottie, I'm sorry, I'm getting another call. I need to take it," he said as he saw it was Pickett calling. "I'll call you back."

"Pickett?" he said into the phone, hating that he'd had a bad feeling when he'd seen who was calling. He knew that Pickett and Oakley desperately wanted children. They'd recently gone through a miscarriage.

"I thought you should know," Pickett said. "Someone set a fire out by our new house. We got it out in time, but there is no doubt that it was arson. I think it might be about Oakley since she was the only one home at the time."

Holden swore under his breath. He knew exactly what Pickett was trying to tell him. First Brand and now Oakley? The common denominator was CJ Stafford. "Is everyone all right? Oakley?"

"No one got hurt. Oakley had the fire almost out by the time we got there, but I think someone needs to pay CJ a visit," Pickett said.

Holden wished he wasn't thinking the same thing. "Let's let the sheriff handle this, please. I'll call him right now. Stay at the house. I'm sure he'll have questions."

He disconnected and called Lottie. He quickly told her what had happened.

"I know it sounds like CJ, but I can't believe he'd

do this and so quickly after being released. Let me talk to him," she said. "Please, I'll handle it. If he's behind either of these incidents, I'll know. I'll have his probation revoked and he'll be behind bars by tonight."

"Just be careful," Holden warned. "If he is behind this, I can't see him admitting it, let alone going back to jail without a fight."

"I'll be fine. I'll call you."

With that, she disconnected, leaving him with a bad feeling she was underestimating the danger she might be putting herself in. He called her right back to insist he go with her, but only got her voice mail. "I'm going with you to meet him. Don't go alone. Call me!"

IT WAS STRANGE. Oakley had been thinking about her brother when she saw the flames. At first, she'd thought they were a mirage as they rushed toward the house through the tall dry weeds left from the construction site around the house. Pickett had ordered the sod for the yard, but with the house just now finished, he hadn't had time to do anything more. He still had a ranch to work.

Born and raised on a ranch, she knew the dangers of a wildfire. She called Pickett at once since she knew he was working close by today, then she ran out the back door and grabbed the garden hose attached to that side of the house.

She was busy fighting the fire when Pickett rode up with a couple of ranch hands. The fire had spread, but she'd managed to keep it away from the house. Between all of them, they were able to put out the blaze before it could spread.

Hot, sweaty and smoky, they stood looking at the charred land. She glanced at her husband and saw his jaw muscle working as he took in how close the fire had gotten to the house. A moment later, he walked out to the edge where the fire had started, the men going with him.

She knew by his body language that he'd discovered the same thing she had. Someone had purposely started the fire. She placed a hand over her stomach, thinking of the secret she was keeping from everyone, especially her husband. They'd both gotten too excited the other times she'd been pregnant only to have it end suddenly, leaving them desolate and feeling broken. They both wanted children so badly. It had seemed so unfair.

That was why she couldn't share the news. Not yet. Not until she was far enough along that there was a better chance it would last this time. She hadn't even taken a pregnancy test yet. Her body felt different, and she was determined that this time she was pregnant and it would last. If it didn't, Pickett would never have to know. She would suffer the loss alone and spare him.

"Are you all right?" he asked as he walked back to where she was standing.

She nodded and removed her hand from her belly. "Someone started it, didn't they?"

"Yep." His gaze said he knew who it was. CJ.

Her brother had tried to kill her twice. Why not a third time?

"We don't know it was him," she said, though neither one of them believed that. "Let the sheriff handle it. Please, Pickett. Promise me."

He studied her for a few moments, then gave in and nodded. "I'll call Stuart." He stepped away to make the call, but still she worried. She couldn't lose her husband, and she couldn't trust her brother. CJ didn't want her to be happy. He wanted everyone to be as miserable as he was.

For a moment she was tempted to tell Pickett about the baby she was carrying so he knew what was at stake here and why he had to be careful and not confront CJ. There was too much bad blood between the McKennas and the Staffords still. This child would need a father.

But she realized, knowing her husband, if he knew she was pregnant it would only make him more protective of her and the baby growing inside her. So she kept quiet. Soon she would tell him, she told herself. Soon she would feel safe enough to tell him.

CJ HAD BEEN waiting for a report from Claude updating him on what was going on at the Stafford Ranch. Last report Victoria and Ryder had left, but had returned to the ranch together. They'd hurried into the house, and Claude reported that he hadn't seen them since. No sign of Ryder's brother.

"Keep up the good work," CJ had told him and

smiled to himself as he'd hung up. No sign of Brand because he was in the hospital.

He quickly put in a call to Treyton. "Brand's in the hospital recovering. Haven't heard anything about a fire out at my sister's new house yet, though."

"A little impatient, are you? You'll be hearing about it. I just got a report from an associate of mine. Apparently, it was put out before it reached the house, but I'd say you made your point—whatever that point is. Does this have something to do with the news about your father and my mother?"

"What news?" he asked, telling himself it was probably the same old thing. If they weren't arguing about water rights, it was land. Even though Charlotte had supposedly forgiven Holden, CJ knew it wouldn't last. She could pretend that she had changed, but he and his mother were too much alike. The two of them never forgot any slight or injustice toward them. Where did she think her eldest son had gotten it from if not from her?

"Our parents are getting married," Treyton said, dropping it like a bomb.

"What?" CJ felt his whole body go numb. "No. Like hell they are."

"It's true. They're engaged and already planning the wedding. I thought you would have at least heard about the engagement. They're planning a huge wedding in just over a week. Apparently, everyone is invited. Cooper made a point of calling me to warn me not to cause any problems. Like I need my little brother telling me what to do. Can you believe that crap?"

CJ couldn't believe any of it. "They can't get married," he said more to himself than to Treyton. "That would ruin my whole plan."

"They've set the date. I heard it's coming out in the shopper this week. They aren't wasting any time. If you're thinking of riding into the church to stop it, I'd think again. Heard my father hired a bunch of security guards. Knowing him, he probably told them to shoot on sight if I turned up. Like you could get me to that wedding. But sounds like it's happening no matter what we think about it."

CJ swore. "It's not going to happen. You hear me? We aren't going to let it happen."

"How are *we* going to stop it?" Treyton asked sarcastically. "It's one thing to terrorize your family. Wait, you aren't planning to kill one of them, are you?"

"Not unless I have to," he said as he realized he'd just have to step up the timeline on his plan. "I'll call you if I need you."

"I'm not going to prison because of you, Stafford. Don't forget. You owe me money already. You'd better get your hands on that ranch."

CJ hung up, cursing under his breath. He couldn't believe his mother was going to marry McKenna. All that talk of forgiveness. That was what this had been leading up to, hadn't it? He should have known.

His cell phone rang. His mother. Perfect timing.

AFTER PICKETT'S CALL, Holden was even more worried about Lottie. He tried to reach her several more times with the same results. Voice mail. "Don't meet CJ alone. Call me. There's been a fire outside Oakley's new house. Someone intentionally set it. Lottie, for the love of God, be careful." He put down his phone, hoping he wasn't too late. *Call, Lottie. Call. Don't go alone.*

After all this time, he couldn't lose her. Nor could he rein her in, he reminded himself. Charlotte had always been her own woman. Like him, she'd made mistakes, and many of them they'd made together. He wished she'd talked to him about getting CJ out. But she would have known that he would have advised her against it. Not that she would have listened if she had bothered to ask him. He suspected she hadn't told him because she feared he might try to stop her. He suspected she was trying to make up for the past and was smart enough not to try to stop her.

When it came to their individual families, they would have to be careful. Some boundaries needed to be upheld, especially when it came to their offspring. Just this morning he'd seen an ad on television about his daughter Bailey's book being released nationwide—right before his and Lottie's wedding. When it rained, it poured, he thought about his family. He was worried enough about what Treyton would do on the wedding day.

But with CJ out of jail, Holden worried that his and Lottie's oldest sons might team up again. He knew Treyton had been involved in that meth lab at the old ranch on their property. But his son had apparently destroyed any evidence before the sheriff could get there. Holden suspected Treyton and CJ had been in business together—and feared they might be again. They were both cut from the same cloth, both the result of growing up caught in the worst of the bitter rivalry between the two families.

Too nervous to think about all the mistakes he'd made as a father and to worry about Lottie at the same time, he picked up the early copy of his daughter's book that she'd sent him. Apparently, Bailey had been working on this book for years as she searched for the man who had attacked her. He read the dedication.

This book is dedicated to the man who saved me, the love of my life, the man I'm going to marry, Stuart Layton.

They had married, eloping without telling anyone. Holden wished now that he and Lottie had done that. They could be on their honeymoon right now instead of her going to meet with CJ.

He studied the book in his hand, afraid to read it. A tell-all about the people of this area of Montana? He couldn't imagine anything good coming out of it, even with the names changed. He wasn't sure he wanted to read about people he knew even if it was about how their secrets had affected their lives in this unique place where he'd grown up. He turned to the first chapter, thinking it would help get his mind off Lottie. To his surprise his daughter's writing grabbed his attention. He read the whole chapter, then picked up his phone and called his daughter. Voice mail. Did anyone actually answer phone calls anymore?

Holden sent a text.

I just started reading your book. Bailey, you're an amazing storyteller and a beautiful writer. Congratulations on your first book!

Then he turned to the next chapter and began reading again, impressed how she had captured the area and its people in a light that made them seem as unique as the Powder River basin itself.

CLAUDE WONDERED HOW long he was going to be forced to stay in this old house on the side of the hill, watching the Stafford Ranch. He hadn't seen Victoria and Ryder for a long time. He could well imagine what they were doing in the house. He cursed in disgust. He hoped CJ was telling him the truth about taking down these people.

Unfortunately, Wendell Forester was the one who would gain everything he wanted, and CJ too if whatever they were up to worked.

Seeing movement down at the ranch, he picked up the binoculars and focused on Victoria as she came out the front door, followed by her cowboy lover. She and Ryder appeared to be going back into town. He wondered if a person could die of boredom as he lost interest and began to look around the ranch.

The place was huge with few roads, so it was no wonder that he'd spotted the dust being kicked up first. An SUV crossed, headed toward the foothills between the two ranches. He followed it with the binoculars, zooming in to see a Stafford Ranch pickup parked in the trees, and recognized CJ leaning against it as if waiting.

Claude quickly found the SUV again as it turned and headed for the spot where CJ Stafford was waiting. A secret meeting? He couldn't help being curious about who was driving the SUV.

He didn't have to wait long. The driver continued up the road to come to stop a few yards from the pickup. CJ hadn't moved. He lounged against the side of the truck, waiting for whoever it was who'd come to meet him. Claude groused at the sight of the arrogant bastard. Whatever he was up to, he thought he had the upper hand.

The door of the SUV finally opened, and a statuesque older blonde woman stepped out. CJ's mother? He watched her close her door, but she didn't move toward CJ. Instead, like him, she seemed to be waiting for him to make the first move.

CJ finally pushed himself off the side of the truck, seemingly irritated as he closed the distance between them.

What was this about? Claude wondered. But even more interesting, had CJ forgotten that he was up here watching everything that happened near the Stafford Ranch through his powerful binoculars?

CHAPTER SIXTEEN

ON THE WAY into town, Victoria could tell Ryder was still worried. Brand had come out of surgery fine. The doctor said he should have a full recovery. It was the phone call from Brand's room from Sheriff Stuart Layton that had Ryder concerned. "What did the sheriff say?"

"Just that he would meet us at the hospital. That's all I know."

If Ryder was worried, there was probably a good reason. "I've been trying to call my father."

He looked over at her before turning back to his driving. "Let me guess. He isn't taking your calls."

"He must realize that I'm going to tell him to stop." She saw not just skepticism, but incredulity on Ryder's face. "I know it's a long shot, but there is no one else who can reason with him. He loves me. At least, I think he does."

Ryder shook his head. "He's trying to get you to do what he wants. The only way he's going to back off is if you do." He shot her another glance. "Don't do it. Not for me. I'd never forgive myself for putting you in this position."

"Don't worry, I'm not going to agree to anything." But even as she said it, she was aware that her father had never gone this far before. He'd threatened to cut her off financially in the past, but hadn't. She'd actually never thought he would. He knew she made little at the nonprofit center. But did he also know that she loved teaching there? She doubted it. He'd always encouraged her to quit the job, saying that he made plenty of money for her future.

Victoria now realized how dangerous that was, depending on him. No wonder he thought he could tell her what to do. Still, she didn't understand why he had cut her off now. That was what scared her. It was as if he'd had enough of her not doing what he wanted. He wasn't fooling around anymore.

Is that what this was about? Or was it guilt? He was making a move on the Stafford Ranch, and maybe it had nothing to do with her. Maybe he'd given up on trying to force her to do anything. He was just taking the ranch because he wanted it and hadn't given any thought to her.

She hated to think what he might do to get what he wanted. Worse, maybe there was no way to stop him. Maybe it was too late.

Ahead, the town of Powder Crossing appeared on the horizon. She turned her worry to what the sheriff had to tell them. Her father couldn't have had anything to do with Brand being shot or the fire out by Oakley's new house. She knew how cutthroat Wendell Forester could be, but he wouldn't stoop to violence, would he?

Inside the small hospital, they found the sheriff waiting for them in Brand's room. Ryder went straight to his brother's bed. Victoria was happy to see that Brand was sitting up. Even his color looked good, although she could tell he was still in some pain.

"I don't want this to turn into another McKenna versus Stafford war," Stuart said. "Brand agrees. The shooter wasn't trying to kill him."

"Just as the fire out at Oakley's wasn't meant to burn down the house?" Ryder snapped.

"That's what I'm saying," the sheriff said. "Someone is using scare tactics."

"My brother could have been killed," Ryder said angrily. "Scare tactics, my ass. We all know CJ's behind it."

"CJ didn't fire the shot. Nor did he start the fire," Stuart said. "He has an alibi for both."

"Then, it's one of his buddies," Ryder said. "You know he's behind this."

"Let's say you're right," Stuart said. "What's his goal? I really doubt it is just to torment the family, given how much he has to lose."

"My father is trying to buy the Stafford Ranch," Victoria said. "CJ has been in contact with him."

"How would these incidents get him the ranch?" the sheriff asked.

"I don't know," she admitted. "But I suspect they're tied to each other."

Ryder swore. "Wendell Forester is also trying to force Victoria into marriage with a man named Claude Duvall. I hate to think this is his latest tactic."

She shook her head. "His form of intimidation is legal, threatening lawsuits, dragging people into court for years. This isn't him."

"I think she's right," Brand said. "This is CJ. So what are you going to do about it, Sheriff?"

Stuart sighed. "I'm going to talk to him. I've been trying to find him. He's been a little hard to pin down."

"Talking to him won't help," Ryder said.

"You're probably right. That's why I called you here today," the sheriff continued. "You need to be on the lookout for more trouble, and don't—whatever you do—confront CJ. If he's behind this, we all know that threatening him will only make him worse. I don't know what your mother was thinking getting him out of jail and seeing that the charges against him were dropped."

"You aren't the only one," Ryder said. "But even from jail or prison, my brother is dangerous. Maybe that's what he's trying to tell us. We all know what he wants. The ranch and us gone."

"Kind of like the same thing Wendell Forester wants," Brand said and looked over at Vicky. "You think the two of them might be working together?"

She swallowed the lump in her throat. "Is there any way CJ can get his hands on the ranch?"

IT WAS JUST like his mother to make him come to her, CJ thought. He glared at her, thinking how sorry she was going to be, before finally walking over to where she stood. She thought she was still in charge. She'd soon find out how mistaken she was.

"Why did you get me out here, CJ?" she asked.

"I wanted to talk to you about something, and I didn't want to be interrupted." He could tell that she was annoyed, but she was also nervous. She didn't like meeting out here, just the two of them. She was afraid of him.

Good, he thought as he hid his smile. She should be afraid.

Not that he wasn't a little nervous too. He told himself this was going to go just the way he'd planned it. She'd forced him to do this, forced him to move up his timeline, but the plan he'd come up with had always ended this way. He wasn't backing down. She had pushed him into a corner, and the only way he could survive was to push back.

"If this is about my engagement to Holden," she began but stopped as if she must have seen his expression. "I was hoping you wouldn't try to fight me on this, CJ. You know I've always loved him."

He lifted a brow. "Maybe not always, but then again, as they say, hate and love are kindred spirits."

"I don't believe that's what they say, but you're right. I did tell myself that I hated him. He'd hurt me, and you, of all people, know that it is easier to hurt people back than to forgive."

He ignored that. She wanted to believe that they were the same. Maybe they were, except she wanted to change. He didn't. Which meant she had no idea what he was truly capable of. But she would soon enough. "He'll hurt you again, but I really didn't get you out here to talk about Holden McKenna."

He moved a few feet from her, impatient to get this settled, but hating that he'd had to move up his plan because of her. Hearing about Wendell Forester trying to buy the ranch had set the fuse. The engagement and upcoming wedding had lit the flame. There was no stopping it now. He had to move quickly, something he hadn't wanted to do. He'd hoped to lull his mother into thinking he really had changed.

Instead, she'd forced this. She had only herself to blame. Now she was about to see her son for what he truly was, what he'd always been. She'd spent years believing she'd made him this way. Maybe. But he could have been born like this. They would never know.

He met her gaze. "We have a problem."

Her eyes narrowed. "Please don't try to stop me from marrying Holden."

As if he really cared. He just couldn't allow her to marry anyone until he got what he wanted. "It's your funeral. No, that's only one of the problems, Mother."

She instantly looked wary. "CJ, we had a deal."

"Yeah, about that. I'm changing the terms, and you're not going to like them. You're going to sign the Stafford Ranch over to me, lock, stock and barrel."

"*What?* That's ridiculous. I'm not going to do that." She started to turn back to her vehicle as if to leave. He knew how stubborn she could be. He was a lot like her. "If you don't, I'm going to have to kill them all."

She froze. He could see her gathering her strength and fighting to control her temper. That was something else they had in common. She was just better at controlling her fury and channeling it.

After a moment, she turned to face him. All the color had drained from her face, and yet she stood tall, determination and an even stronger emotion burning in her gaze. "What are you talking about?"

"I've never made it a secret that I wanted the ranch to myself."

"No, you never have. You don't care at all about your brothers and sisters, especially Ryder and Brand who have been working the ranch by themselves with you and me gone. You would just take it from them?"

He said nothing, and she stared at him as if finally seeing him. From the disgusted look on her face, she didn't like what she saw as she made up her mind. Would he actually do it? Or was he just bluffing?

Come on, Mother, which is it?

When she spoke, her voice was tight with pain. "You would kill them."

CJ nodded and smiled. "Only if you forced me to."

She breathed, her nostrils flaring. "Aren't you afraid I'll have you sent back to prison?"

"I wasn't planning to kill them myself. I can do it just as easily from behind bars."

She seemed to stagger under the weight of his words. "I didn't make you like this."

"Keep telling yourself that," he said with a chuckle. "It doesn't matter. All that does matter is that you realize I'm dead serious. Brand's recent so-called accident?" He smiled and saw her cringe. "Oh, I bet you haven't even heard about the fire out at Oakley's new house. Don't worry. She's okay, and so is the house. Those were just warnings about how easily it could happen. Don't make me do it, Mother. I think you now know I won't hesitate to destroy them all to get what I want."

"I won't sign the ranch over to you," she said emphatically.

He laughed. "Oh, I think you will. I didn't want to do this, but you've left me no choice. If you don't sign the papers I've brought, I'm going to kill Holden first."

"CJ! No!" Her cry died on her lips as she stared at him. But the look on her face told him everything he needed to know. She hadn't taken him seriously until this moment. She hadn't really understood how much he hated Holden. Now she knew. He wouldn't hesitate to have him killed. In fact, he planned to kill him before he left the country with all the money from selling the ranch, once it was his. But he wasn't about to tell her that. She wanted to believe he loved the ranch the way she did. She thought he was just greedy and selfish. Surely she didn't still believe that somewhere inside him there was good?

"As a matter of fact," he said, glancing at his watch, "if I don't make a call within the next seven minutes, Holden will be dead." He looked up at her. "Your choice, Mother. But understand . . . he'll only be the first if you don't sign these papers."

CHAPTER SEVENTEEN

CHARLOTTE STARED AT her son. If it had been anyone but CJ, she would have called his bluff, but her son wasn't bluffing. She'd finally realized what he was capable of when he'd shot his sister and then later hired two men to kill Oakley if she got in his way. His sister had been trying to keep him from drilling on the ranch. Like now, he'd wanted the money it would bring. He hadn't given a thought to what it might do to the ranch the rest of the family loved.

That shocked her the most. She'd actually thought CJ wanted the ranch because it meant something to him. But now she had no doubt that he was going to force her to turn it over to him so he could sell it. Had she really believed he could change? Or had she thought she could control him?

She was wrong on both counts, she realized, blood hammering in her temples. She could feel the minutes ticking away while she stood, saying to herself *This is your son*, as if she didn't believe she could have given birth to this monster. Or was he right and she had made CJ like this?

"Mother?" he said, glancing pointedly at his watch.

One look into the icy-cold depth of eyes so like her own and she had to stifle a shudder. "Let me see the papers."

He turned to walk back to his pickup, opened the door and pulled out an envelope. Of course he had them all ready for her to sign. He'd planned this and probably had from the moment she'd said she would get him out of jail, out of the charges against him, if he could change. How he must have laughed at her foolishness, she thought as he turned back to her.

She wished she'd brought her gun or the bull-whip she always carried on her horse. But she knew her son. Even faced with a loaded gun and the promise of death, he wouldn't have made the call to save Holden.

Her body trembled with fury and fear. She tried to still her hands from shaking as she took the papers and the pen he handed her and moved over to the hood of the SUV. Even if she hadn't gotten him out of jail, he still would have done this, she realized. He couldn't let her marry Holden because then he would have had no way of getting the ranch and the money.

Her eyes blurred for a moment. She blinked and swallowed the lump lodged in her throat. The document had been drawn up by an attorney. It all looked legal and binding. CJ was no fool. He knew what he wanted, and he'd gone after it his whole life, knocking down anyone who got in his way.

He'd fooled her for so long, playing on her love

for him. He'd never gotten along with his siblings. She'd seen his cruel side and tried to love him more than the others believing he needed it more. Now she could admit that she'd pampered and protected him because she'd seen something in that little boy that broke her heart even as it scared her.

Neither of them were pretending now, she thought. He was no longer trying to con her to get what he wanted. The mask was off. He was everything that she'd feared, and she would have to live with whatever she did right now.

"Ticktock," he said behind her.

She turned to the last page, knowing she was signing away the ranch she'd worked for her whole life. She'd thought her children and grandchildren would keep the ranch going long after she was gone. Once she signed these papers, the Stafford Ranch would be history. CJ would sell it. He'd probably already made a deal with Wendell Forester, she realized.

Closing her eyes for a moment because of the pain and the anger in her, she opened them and hurriedly signed the papers. "Make the call."

He snatched up the papers, and suddenly she was terrified that he'd go back on his word. But surely he knew what she would do if he did. The document would have to be notarized and still she would have a three-day waiting period to change her mind. Their gazes locked for just an instant before he pulled out his phone and placed the call.

She noted how he didn't have to tap in the

number. He already had it ready because he knew she would sign. "Abort," he said into the phone. "Got that? Good." But he also must have known what she would do if he killed Holden.

He disconnected and folded the papers. "I'm sorry it had to be like this. We can finalize this in town."

Charlotte couldn't speak, her throat so tight she could barely breathe. "Why?"

He frowned, looking confused. "You've always known that I wanted the ranch for myself."

"But you don't really want the ranch. You just want the money."

CJ seemed to consider that, then laughed. "Why pretend? You're right. I want what's mine, and then I'm out of here. You won't ever have to see me again."

She stared at him, wishing so much that things were different. That he was different. "You didn't even try to change, did you?"

"Maybe if you had picked me up when I got out of jail, let me come home to the ranch . . . What am I saying? It probably wouldn't have made a difference. But maybe I would have tried at least for a little while. Then you had to go and get engaged. You're really throwing a big wedding? Don't worry about sending me an invitation. I won't be in town." CJ folded the papers and smiled as he pocketed them.

She said nothing, feeling numb after her earlier fury and fear. She watched him pull out his phone and send a text.

"I should get going," he said, looking almost un-comfortable. Maybe he still was capable of feeling shame, she thought. "Have to plan the rest of my life."

Her heart lodged in her throat at the fear of who he'd just texted and why. Her family was still in danger. Holden was still in danger. "This isn't just about the money or destroying the ranch, is it?" she said, fighting to breathe. Her chest felt on fire, her heart nothing but charred embers. "You can't stand to see me with Holden or your sisters happy with men from the McKenna Ranch."

CJ's gaze snapped to hers, and she saw the an-swer she'd already known. He no longer tried to hide the truth, yet he still lied as if it came naturally. "Why would I care about the McKennas?" he spat out. "I'm leaving here, and I'm never looking back. Unless, of course, you do something ill-advised like try to have me arrested, then who knows what kind of damage I can do from behind bars? Otherwise, I'm leaving the country. You'll never see me again."

She didn't believe him. She didn't even think he believed it. He thought the money from the ranch would fill that hole where his soul should have been. She knew different. He couldn't stand the thought that life would go on without him once he was gone and everyone would be happy and forget about him. He would destroy not just their livelihood but their lives before he was finished unless she stopped him.

When the money wasn't enough, he would want to inflict pain, just as he was doing now. That was why he wasn't going to kill her, even though he knew there was a chance she could have him locked up behind bars.

He'd taken the ranch, but she couldn't let him take anything else from this family. He always said the two of them were alike. He had no idea.

"You realize I was forced to sign those papers under duress, therefore they aren't legal," she said, knowing he expected her to put up more of a fight.

"But you won't go back on it," he said smugly. "Because you know me. I'd take out my disappointment on everyone you love—especially if I was behind bars. This way, you're rid of me. Isn't that really what you want, Mother?"

There he was, that insecure little boy she'd doted on, yet he'd never felt loved enough. Because he knew he didn't deserve it?

"What I want is for you never to hurt anyone else," she said as her heart broke at the thought of what she was about to do. For a moment, she wasn't sure she could inject the poison that was about to come out of her mouth even as she knew she had to. "Do your . . . friends know you're coming into all this money?"

"What are you getting at?" he demanded as he glanced around as if he thought someone was already watching him.

"Just that you've used them to do your dirty work. When they find out what you're getting for it compared to what you offered them, I'm just afraid they might turn on you."

"You don't know what you're talking about. They're too smart for that."

She shrugged. "Like you said, you're leaving the country. It's not like they could stop you if they resented you. I just worry about the people you hang out with. Treyton, for one." She told herself that she would go to hell for this. The thought almost made her laugh. She'd done much worse things in her life. Treyton had shot her son and tried to burn down her daughter's house for money because CJ had told him to do it.

"What about Treyton?"

"I would think he'd be the last person you could trust, given the way you feel about the McKennas. Yet Treyton was the one you got to shoot Brand and start the fire at Oakley's house, wasn't he?" she said, seeing the truth and hurriedly dripping more poison into his ear. She knew her son's insecurities and now heartlessly played on them. "Even if you could trust him, Treyton will always have that to hold over your head in case one day he needs a get-out-of-jail-free card."

CJ shook his head as if trying to shake off his own his own fears and self-doubts at her words. "You don't know what you're talking about. You'd like to see my friends turn on me, wouldn't you, Mother."

She knew he didn't have any real friends, and that made her even sadder. Tears filled her eyes. "I'm just really sad for you."

He laughed. "What is this? Reverse psychology?

You think I'll feel bad and give you back your ranch? Think again. I'm fine. I'm better than fine. I finally have everything I want. Don't you think I see what you're doing? You're just trying to stir up trouble," he said, glancing over his shoulder again. "You're hoping my friends betray me."

"I'm sorry, but my own son turned on me, so I know it can happen. I didn't mean to upset you."

"Sure, you did," he said, trying to laugh it off. "But you're wrong. I don't have to listen to any more of this." But he didn't move. He kept standing there as if waiting for her to say something to reassure him because she would see that her words had done their job. Her heart broke at what she'd done. "You're just messing with my head. We're done, Mother."

Yes, they were. She felt a horrible sense of loss, but she reminded herself that she'd lost her son a long time ago. Now she was trying to save the rest of her family. "Goodbye, CJ." She turned and walked back to her vehicle, forcing herself not to look as broken as she felt. She had wanted to believe he could change. She was the fool, and it had nearly cost her family their lives.

She didn't know how long CJ stood watching her go like the angry boy he'd been, but by the time she slid behind the wheel, he was roaring off down the road as if being chased.

VICTORIA LEFT RYDER and his brother alone and went outside the hospital to make the call. She hadn't spoken to her father since her call to force Claude to let her out of the car in Powder Crossing. While she'd left messages, he hadn't gotten back to her. She knew he was avoiding her. A part of him still wanted her to believe he wasn't as bad as she thought.

Which meant he was up to no good and she had a pretty good idea of what it was. He was going to get Stafford Ranch no matter what he had to do. But if there was any chance that she could stop him, she had to take it.

The phone began to ring, and she braced herself. She wasn't looking forward to this, knowing how badly it could go. Her father had a bad habit of not listening and only hearing what he wanted to.

She felt that Brand might be right. Did her father want the Stafford Ranch badly enough that he would work with a known criminal? Unfortunately, she feared he would. Having already suspected what CJ Stafford would do to get what he wanted, she thought Wendell Forester might have found the perfect partner.

"Victoria?" her father said, startling her out of her thoughts as he answered the call.

She tried to read meaning into the way he'd said her name. He was angry at her, that much she knew. But there was also hope in his voice. She hated to think what he was hoping for. Where there might have been something between her and Ryder, there wasn't anymore. He didn't trust her, and she couldn't blame him. After all, she was her father's daughter, right?

Now she was ready to do whatever was required to keep her father from getting Stafford Ranch. She felt she owed Ryder that. But she also knew that her father seldom lost. Money and power often won out, she knew so well.

"I'm calling to ask a favor," she said, getting right to it.

"Really?" He sounded amused, probably because he knew she had nothing to really bargain with. But she was still his daughter, and she wanted to believe he did care about her.

"I want you to leave Ryder's family alone. You don't need this ranch. I'm asking you to let it go."

Silence, then he cleared his voice and asked, "Don't tell me you're falling for the cowboy?"

The question surprised her because it hadn't been about the fake engagement. "What if I am?" she demanded defiantly, angrier at herself than her father. What if she was?

"Oh, Victoria," he said, sounding sad.

She waited for him to say more. When he didn't, she felt a lump rise in her throat. "What's going on, Dad?" She hadn't called him *Dad* in years.

"I'm sorry, sweetheart, but it's too late. I've already purchased the Stafford Ranch."

CHARLOTTE SAT BEHIND the wheel, shaking so hard that she was afraid she wouldn't be able to drive.

Fear that CJ had lied, and that Holden was still in danger, finally made her pull herself together. She called, fearing she was too late.

Holden answered on the first ring. "Lottie, are you all right?"

Her heart lifted as tears burned her eyes. "Where are you? I need to see you."

"I'm at the ranch."

"Stay there. Don't even go outside. I'll be there in a few minutes."

"Lottie, you're scaring me."

She disconnected. Her hands trembled as she started the engine. She gripped the wheel, her knuckles white with rage and pain and fear, but mostly heartbreak. Her son was gone. So was the ranch. She had to accept that. Now what she had to do was keep her family and the people she loved safe. She knew they would all want her to have CJ thrown back in jail and void the papers she'd signed.

None of them had seen the look in CJ's eyes. But she had. There was no doubt he would do what he said. He had his so-called friends like him who thumbed their noses at the law and thought vengeance was an honorable pursuit. CJ would get his revenge against the family he had always believed was against him because that was who he was.

Charlotte couldn't wait another moment. She had to see Holden. She needed his help. Putting the SUV into gear, she drove off from the hillside and down to the road that turned into the McKenna Ranch. She told herself that CJ was smart enough to know that if he hurt Holden before the ink dried on those papers, she would come after him and it wouldn't be to have him put in jail.

Like he said, he could kill from there. He wanted the money from the sale of the ranch. Until he realized he wanted more, everyone should be safe—as long as she could convince everyone not to do anything that would make CJ change his mind.

She made one call on the way into town. "I thought you'd like to know that Treyton McKenna shot Brand," she told the sheriff when he answered. "CJ was behind it, but I need you to do me a favor. I don't want either of them taken in for questioning yet. But if you just wanted to pay Treyton a visit, that would be good."

"What are you up to, Charlotte?" Stuart asked suspiciously.

"My son CJ just stole my ranch and sold it to Wendell Forester, but I need him free just a little longer. I'm trying to keep my family safe. I need you to trust me. It will all make sense soon, I hope."

"Charlotte, I hope you know what you're doing," the sheriff said.

"Me too, Stuart. Just be careful. CJ is more dangerous than he's ever been."

Ahead, she saw the turnoff to the ranch and slowed, her heart in her throat. As she pulled up in front of the McKenna Ranch house, Holden came rushing out. He had her vehicle door open and was taking her in his arms almost before she could turn off the engine.

"We need to get inside," she said as she reached up to touch his cheek. He must have seen the fear in her gaze and felt it in her trembling body because he quickly ushered them into the house and called Elaine to get them all something to drink.

Once in his office, Charlotte downed her shot of bourbon and told them what had happened. Just as she'd expected, Holden was furious and wanted to call the sheriff to pick up CJ and put him back behind bars.

"I already spoke with the sheriff," Charlotte told him. "He knows that Treyton is the one who shot Brand and had someone start the fire out at Oakley's house. I'm sorry, Holden."

He shook his head and shot to his feet. "I want to take care of both of them before they do any more damage."

"Holden, you heard what she just told you," Elaine said, trying to help calm him down. Charlotte was so thankful that the two of them had been secret friends all these years. Elaine was the voice of reason to Charlotte's destructive temper.

"What would you have me do?" he demanded. "CJ can't be trusted not to go back on his word. Lottie, CJ stole your ranch, and my son helped him."

"We have to keep everyone from going after CJ or Treyton. He's already made a deal with Wendell Forester to buy the ranch. Once he gets the money, maybe he really will leave the country as he said."

Holden scoffed. "You don't believe that any more than I do."

"No," she said. "But he has to believe that I do. The money won't be enough for him. Would you come with me to tell Ryder? Brand will have to be told too. He's still in the hospital. Then you'll need to tell Cooper and Tilly and Oakley and Pickett. They have to trust that I know what I'm doing. You have to trust me too."

She could see that even Holden was skeptical. If he ever knew what she'd done . . . She pushed the thought away. Her whole life she'd done what had to be done no matter how objectionable. She'd hoped that she'd put that behind her. Holden would figure it out. She just hoped he would forgive her.

"You have a plan to get your ranch back?" Elaine asked.

Charlotte shook her head. "It's gone. Wendell will drill methane wells, take whatever treasures there are from the land, and then he'll sell it."

"And I'll buy it back for you," Holden said.

She smiled at him, thankful for him. "We'll see. What matters to me is our families and the people we care about. We have to keep them safe from CJ."

"There's only one way they'll be safe from CJ," Holden said angrily.

Charlotte knew he wasn't talking about having her son thrown back in jail, but Elaine didn't.

"He can get to everyone from jail or prison," Elaine said. "Brand got shot and Oakley's new house could have burned down. CJ had an alibi for both. He's not doing his own dirty work. He has people to do that, so he can hurt people even if behind bars. He told Charlotte as much, and I believe him."

He cursed under his breath. "Lottie, I've known you my whole life. This isn't like you to just accept this situation without a fight. I don't understand how he could get you to sign those papers."

"I already knew that he was behind the so-called accidents with Brand and Oakley," she said and raised her gaze to lock with his. "CJ told me that he had someone ready to kill you if he didn't call them within a few minutes."

"You thought it was Treyton," Holden said with a curse.

"I don't know if it was him, but he's involved," she said. "I hate to be the one to tell you that."

"Oh, Lottie," he said and reached for her hand and squeezed it. "I have known for a long time now that Treyton is involved in illegal activities. I've suspected he and your son have been working together. They need to be stopped."

She could see how badly he wanted to take care of Treyton and CJ himself. "Right now, it's just the loss of the ranch. I can live with that. The other . . . I can't. I don't think you can either."

He nodded and rose. "Then, we better start telling the family before they hear about it from someone else. I always worried that our rivalry might end in a war that could get our kids killed."

"That's why we have to keep that from happening. That means not telling them the truth. They have to believe that I sold the ranch."

Holden shook his head. "Your sons may never forgive you."

"That's a chance I'll have to take. If they knew that CJ blackmailed me . . ." She didn't have to finish. Both Elaine and Holden knew what would happen.

CHAPTER EIGHTEEN

"WHAT'S WRONG?" RYDER said as he joined Vicky outside the hospital. She looked pale and shaken, her eyes full of tears. "Vicky?"

She looked up at him and shook her head before wiping at her tears. "I just talked to my father. He said he's already purchased your ranch."

"*What?* That's not possible. Why would he say that?"

"He told me he was sorry," she said, her voice full of emotion. "I believe him, that he's sorry and that it's true. He now owns Stafford Ranch."

Ryder was shaking his head as he stepped back, knowing there was only one way it could be true. He pulled out his phone and called his mother's number. She answered on the second ring. At just the sound of her voice, the truth came crashing down on him. His legs went weak as his heart threatened to pound from his chest.

"You didn't," he said into the phone. "You wouldn't. How could you?"

"Ryder, you have to understand—"

He disconnected, feeling as if a mountain had been dropped on him. For a moment, he didn't know what to do. "She sold it. No," he said, realizing what had happened. "She gave it to CJ, and he sold it to your father."

She nodded. "I wish there was something I could do."

Shaking his head, he couldn't look at her as he said, "I'm sorry, but I have to ask. Tell me you had nothing to do with this."

"You know I didn't," she said, her voice breaking. "I only came back to the ranch because I thought I could stop it. I thought my father wouldn't do it if he knew that I'd fallen for you. But he . . ." She swallowed and couldn't seem to go on.

Ryder raised his gaze, took in the devastated look on her face and knew she was telling the truth. He had wanted to believe what Claude had said about her because he was getting too involved with her. He had kept telling himself that it could only end in heartbreak. He'd been scared, wanting to push her away—just as he did now.

He reached for her, dragging her to him to hold her tightly. She wasn't her father. She knew what the ranch meant to him. Her heart was breaking for him. He could see all of that as she hugged him back.

"This is my fault," she said against his chest. "If I hadn't involved you at the airport—"

"This isn't your fault," he said as he released her. "Your father was already after the ranch. That's why I was at the airport. I thought if I told him to back off, he would. You and I just got caught up in family politics. This is my mother's doing. She's the only one who could sell the ranch. She did it for CJ. It's the only thing that makes sense."

Vicky drew back. "But I thought you said she loved the ranch?"

"She loves Holden McKenna more, and now she's marrying him. Yet I still can't believe she would do this to Brand and me, let alone my sisters."

"She's protecting Brand and the rest of you," Vicky said. "We all think CJ put him in the hospital and almost burned down your sister's house. Your mother must believe the same thing. Maybe she loves all of you more than the ranch."

He knew she could be right. *Of course* CJ was behind the shooting and the fire. Their mother would know that. It was CJ's plan, probably had been the reason he'd tricked her into letting him out of prison. She had wanted to believe that he could change because she had.

"Charlotte Stafford, at least the one I grew up with, would never have let CJ get away with this. Never. It's just not like her to cave like this. CJ conned her or blackmailed her or threatened the family. It's the only thing that makes sense. If I could get my hands on my brother, I would—" His cell phone rang. Sure enough, it was his mother. "I need to take this."

Ryder stepped away a few feet as he tried to rein in his temper. He wanted to yell at her, to blame her for CJ, to let out his grief at what she'd done in a burst of angry words. "Mother," he said as he answered the phone.

"I'm sorry. I did what I had to do," she said, sounding like the woman he knew.

"He blackmailed you. You need to go to the law, and he needs to go prison."

"That won't help anything," she said quickly. "I need you to keep the rest of the family from going after him. You all need to let me handle this. He has an alibi for the shooting as well as the fire. He can get to us from prison and will."

Ryder didn't know what to say. "He's that dangerous? And yet you want to leave him out on the street to do even more damage? If this is your way of handling things . . . Mother, you can't believe that he won't—"

"I know. It isn't what I wanted, but in this case I had no choice. I made a mistake when it comes to CJ. I owe you all an apology for that. But right now, he is more dangerous than he's ever been. I need you all to stay clear of him."

"You know he sold it to Forester?"

"I assumed that was his plan. That means he has the money. I'm hoping he leaves the area, the state, the country like he said he would."

Ryder began to laugh. "You believed him?"

"No. But please, let me handle it. I'm depending on you to keep everyone calm until this is over."

"It's already over, as far as the ranch goes."

"Don't worry about the animals," she said as if she hadn't heard him. "Holden will see that they all get moved over to his ranch. As for CJ, we both know it won't be over until he's gone—and not just out of the country."

He disconnected and turned to look at Vicky. "I don't know what is going to happen now, but it probably isn't going to be good. This isn't your fight. There is no reason for you stay."

"There's one reason," she said as she took a step toward him. She stopped a few inches from him. He could see the question burning in her gaze. "Are you sure you want me to leave?"

He wanted to say the words that would let her go. He couldn't understand why she wouldn't want to leave. The one constant he'd had in his life was the ranch, and now it was gone. The only thing he knew was ranching. His mother had put aside money for each of them since they were born from the ranch proceeds, so he had money. But not enough to buy his own ranch. How could he ask her to stay when he didn't even know what he was going to do or where he was going to live?

She touched his cheek, her gaze holding his. "The only way I'm leaving is if you tell me you don't want me here."

He swallowed around the lump in his throat. "That's not going to happen," he said as he reached over to cup her shoulders and pull her to him. "I just don't understand why you'd want to stay."

Vicky looked up at him. "Don't you?" She leaned in to kiss him.

Dragging her closer, he deepened the kiss, wanting

to do more than that. As he drew back, he realized where they were: in downtown Powder Crossing. Not that there was much traffic this time of day or most times of the day, but his family was already the talk of the town. He didn't need to add to it.

"How much time do we have to get off the ranch?" he asked, thinking about the animals more than their personal belongings.

VICTORIA PULLED OUT her phone and called her father.

"Victoria." He sounded surprised that she'd called him back.

"How long do we have before you take possession of the ranch?" she asked.

"*We?* Surely you aren't going to stay around Powder Crossing. I would think you've had enough of Montana and cowboys. You can fly back with Claude. He'll be returning to Dallas probably tomorrow. Once you're on the plane, I'll reinstate your allowance and reactivate your credit cards."

"How long before you take possession of the ranch?"

Silence, then, "I planned to take immediate possession, but I could give you twenty-four hours to say goodbye. But then I want you on that plane."

She disconnected and turned to Ryder. "We have twenty-four hours. Maybe we should make the most of them."

FROM THE ABANDONED house on the hillside, Claude saw Ryder and Victoria through his binoculars returning to the ranch. They seemed thick as thieves, all wrapped up in each other, as they'd gone inside the house. He doubted this was the kind of information CJ wanted him to call about. But he was bored out of his mind, so he made the call.

"Nothing much is happening at the ranch. Just saw Ryder—"

"It's over."

For a moment he wasn't sure what was over.

"You're done. You can go back to wherever you came from," CJ said.

"I haven't gotten paid," Claude said, hating the way this small-time crook talked to him. It was one thing to let Wen berate him, but not this cowboy criminal.

"Talk to your boss," CJ said and hung up.

He had a bad feeling that CJ was right. Whatever the two of them had been up to, it was over. Which meant that his boss had gotten what he wanted—the Stafford Ranch. How had he done it so quickly? Not that it mattered. What did this mean for the cowboy Victoria only moments ago had been snuggling with? Maybe the two of them didn't know that her daddy had bought the ranch.

Didn't that mean Wen would be kicking them out? Maybe they had come back to pack. But if Wen had kept his word, he would have already cut Victoria off. So where would she go now? Poor princess, he thought, smiling.

She was broke, and now her boyfriend was losing his ranch. Maybe the cowboy didn't deserve it, but once Wen set his mind to something, there was no stopping him. Claude knew that for a fact. If he'd ever questioned just how coldhearted Wendell Forester could be, he didn't now.

Wen didn't answer the phone when he called. Claude left a message, then disconnected and looked around the old house he'd been hiding out in. Wen was avoiding him. Just as he would forget the promise he'd made him to pay him and put him on the jet home.

Claude realized that he was no better off than Victoria or her cowboy. He was just waiting to find out what other dirty job his boss was going to give him, because Wen would never let him go. How did he find himself in this position time and time again? What was wrong with him?

"Thanks for the expensive binoculars," he said as he began to pack up, unsure where to go now, but he really didn't want to do this anymore. Last time he'd tried to quit, Wen had talked him out of it. Because he needed him.

Not this time, Claude promised himself. He'd go back to Billings. The least Wen could do was let him take the plane home early. He wouldn't tell his boss his plans until he was back in Dallas.

He picked up the gun CJ has given him. Maybe he'd hang on to it. Maybe he'd even try a little target practice behind this place before he left here.

RYDER TOOK VICKY'S hand and led her down the hall-way to his wing of the house. It seemed a lifetime ago that she'd appeared looking like a drowned rat at his bedroom door. He opened the door, his arm around her, and the two of them stumbled in to fall on his bed.

If this was now Wendell Forster's ranch, then they planned to enjoy it until he took possession. Tomorrow, Ryder would worry about what to do with the animals. Vicky said they had twenty-four hours. He figured Wen had only given them that because of her.

Right now, all he cared about was the woman in his arms as he freed her of her clothing and buried his face between her breasts. She giggled as she worked the snaps open on his shirt and placed her warm palms against his flesh. Desire like he'd never experienced before raced through his veins like hot lava. He lifted his head to look into her eyes.

"You do know what's happening here, right?" he asked.

"I sure hope so," she answered, smiling.

"I love you, Vicky, and that scares the hell out of me since I've never felt like this before."

"Scares *you*, cowboy? How do you think I feel? I really thought this would be one weekend, something to tell my friends back home about. But once I got to know you and your family . . ." She shook her head. "I can't imagine going back to that life. I can't imagine leaving you."

He drew her close and kissed her, pulling her over on top of him. "I don't know what the future holds. Doesn't that scare you?"

"It probably should, but it doesn't because I feel like you, and I could do whatever we wanted as long as we're together."

He nodded. "I'm not broke. But I don't have enough to buy a decent-sized ranch, nothing like this one that my mother spent her life building."

"I do have some money of my own that was left to me by my grandmother in a trust fund that I've never touched. I think we'll be just fine."

Ryder smiled, shaking his head. "So you did have access to money without your purse and your phone. You could have used the landline to hire a helicopter to pick you up at any time without your father's help."

She nodded. "I could have. If I had wanted to."

"Instead, you bought an old pickup with what cash you had and came back."

Vicky grinned. "I did because I couldn't stay away from you. Also, I had to warn you about my father."

"I already knew the lengths he'd go to. I just wasn't sure about his daughter."

Vicky kissed him, then pulled back. "Are you sure now?"

"Oh, I'm sure," he said, rolling her over so he was on top. "I'm sure I want you in my life no matter what."

CJ HAD NEVER seen so much money. Forester had advised him to get it into a foreign bank account as quickly as possible. But he had other plans. It had taken time, but he'd had the money transferred to his bank account. Then he'd driven to Miles City, walked into the bank and demanded all of it in cash.

"We don't keep that kind of money here," the bank manager had told him.

"What's the most I can get today?"

"Under the Bank Secrecy Act, you are limited to $10,000 of cash per day."

CJ told the manager what he thought of that, but took out the ten thousand. "I'll be back tomorrow."

He'd moved out of the apartment, not sure what to expect. He didn't think his mother would do something foolish like set the law on him, but he wasn't sure. Also, he had a feeling that his brother Ryder might not take the news about the ranch well and would come looking for him.

So he'd made himself scarce before going back to the bank and picking up his cash. Now back at his hotel room, he poured the bills all out on the king-size bed. The money floated like dried leaves around the bed. Not nearly enough, but he'd add it to each day until he could cover himself with the cash.

CJ told himself that only then could he die a happy man. He took a couple of selfies with his money. He wanted to gloat, but there was no one he could really gloat to. Nor could he put the photo up on social media. He wasn't that reckless.

When Treyton called wanting to be paid, he hated that he was going to have to give away any of these beautiful bills. He took a handful hundreds, then called Treyton back and set up a meeting place. Then he checked to make sure that his gun was loaded—just in case Treyton got greedy. They might have been partners in crime, but Treyton was still a McKenna, and after this their business dealings would be over.

CLAUDE CALLED HIS boss again. "I need to get paid," he said on the message this time. "Otherwise, I'm going to start talking to the press, the cops, anyone who'll listen."

Five minutes later, Wen called back. "Talking, huh? You sure you have anything interesting to say?"

"Try me." He touched the cool metal of the gun in his jacket pocket. "Where would you like to meet?"

"You're right, we should get this over with so we can move on," his boss said. "I'm on my way to talk to a geologist about doing some methane drilling at my new ranch property. I just passed the fairgrounds. There's no one around. Why don't you come out here, since it sounds like we have some things we need to settle." He told him how to get there.

"See you soon," Claude said, wondering why Wen would want to meet in some place so private or if it was just handy for the tycoon. Either way, he was fine with private, he thought and patted the gun. He'd found he was a pretty good shot knocking old tin cans off the fence behind the abandoned house. Not that he would be shooting anything that small—or that far away, he told himself.

He would never have thought he was capable of murder. But working for Wendell Forester had changed that. The man had humiliated him for the last time. Wen would pay him, or he would be sorry or worse.

CJ had given him the gun, he realized. Hopefully it was registered to him. Claude couldn't help but grin. If push came to shove and he did what he really wanted to do—put a bullet in Wen's black heart—then he would wipe his prints from the gun and leave it at the scene. He especially liked the idea of CJ going down for the murder. Wouldn't that tie things up neatly?

Ahead, he saw the outline of bleachers and several large buildings. A large SUV was parked next to one of the buildings. He hoped Wen had been waiting for a while, knowing how much he enjoyed it.

Don't get too cocky, he warned himself. Shooting tin cans was one thing. Actually killing Wendell Forester was another—as much as the thought made him feel better than he had in a long time.

Claude parked and climbed out. He didn't see Wen until he approached the vehicle that his boss must have rented back in Billings. The man was standing on the far side in the shade.

"Took you long enough," his boss snapped, then reached into his pocket and pulled out a wad of bills and thrust them at him.

"What is that?" he asked, looking at the wrinkled bills but not touching them.

"Money. That is what you want, isn't it?"

Claude laughed. "It's going to take a hell of a lot more than that."

Wen narrowed his eyes. "I'm not going to let you shake me down, Claude. I'll give you your paycheck when we get back to Dallas. In the meantime, this is the best I can do. Take it or leave it."

He put his hand on the gun resting in his pocket. He realized that if he pulled it out, he would be forced to use it. He snatched the money out of the man's hand. "I want you to call your pilot and tell him to fly me back to Dallas today just as you promised."

"I'm going back in a few days. You'll have to wait until then. Victoria is coming with us." Wen started to turn back as if to get in the SUV and leave.

"Are you sure about that?" Claude asked, making him turn back to look at him. "I just saw her with the cowboy, and she didn't look like she was going anywhere but to his bedroom."

"You leave Victoria to me. I know my daughter. She might think she's fallen for Ryder Stafford, but without his ranch . . ." Wen shook his head. "She'll be coming back to Dallas. She's had her fun, and now she's going to do what is best for her." Wen began to walk away again.

Claude laughed. "She might surprise you." He had his hand on the gun again. "Where are your bodyguards?"

His boss stopped midstep and turned to look back at him yet again. "I fired them."

"Aren't you afraid someone might try to kill you?"

Wen seemed to freeze. "Do you know something I don't?"

He smiled at that. "The next time I call you, pick up or you'll wish you had." With that, he walked toward his rental. If he had pulled the gun, his boss would have laughed in his face. No, he had a much better way of dealing with Wendell Forester. Plan B.

As he climbed behind the wheel, he saw that Wen hadn't gotten into his rig. Instead, he stood next to it, frowning as if he might be worried about what Claude would do next.

He should be worried. He had only himself to blame.

CJ NEEDED TO wrap things up before he made his plans to leave the country. As much as he had hated putting the money back into the suitcase, he knew he had to get it into an offshore account or two. He couldn't cart that much money around and even leaving it for a little while had him worried someone might take it.

But first he had to settle up with Treyton McKenna. The drive out to Treyton's place in the badlands made him glad he was leaving. He no longer needed to be in business with Treyton or anyone else. His mother was right. He couldn't trust anyone.

He tried to assure himself that he was home free, but he was worried about his money back at the hotel. He needed to get it stowed away somewhere safe, then get out of Montana. He wasn't sure where he could go—someplace that he couldn't be brought back because of the ridiculous probation. Let them try to bring him back, he thought as he came over the last rise in the road and saw Sheriff Layton's patrol vehicle.

Acid rushed to his stomach even as he told himself that Treyton was too smart to turn on him. Yet there he was, standing in the yard with the sheriff as if they were both waiting on him. Earlier, he'd texted Treyton he was coming out to finish their business. "What the hell?" he said under his breath.

His first instinct was to turn around and make a run for it. But there wasn't a place to turn around and they'd already seen him. Running would make him look guilty, and unlike Treyton, he had nothing to be guilty about.

As he continued up the road, he furtively stuffed the stack of hundreds he'd had lying on the seat next to him into his jacket pocket. If this was a setup, Treyton was a dead man. Trying to stay calm, he parked and got out. No reason to worry, he told himself. Just as there was no reason to act surprised to see the two of them together.

"CJ?" the sheriff said. "I had a feeling we'd be seeing you. Treyton kept trying to get me to leave. Glad I didn't miss you. I had this ridiculous idea that the two of you were in league."

CJ shot a look at Treyton, but couldn't read his expression. "We grew up on ranches adjacent to each other. I wouldn't say we're in cahoots."

"Wouldn't you?" Stuart said. "I thought the two of you hated each other's guts."

"There something you want, sheriff?" CJ asked. He didn't have time for this. He needed to get back to the hotel. He was worried someone would steal his money. He just wanted to finish his business and leave. "I didn't mean to interrupt your visit with my former neighbor. I can always visit some other time." He started to turn back to his rig.

"Actually, I'm glad you're here, CJ." The sheriff smiled. "I was here confiscating Treyton's .22 rifle. You might have heard that Brand Stafford was shot."

CJ shook his head. "Maybe you heard I'm living in Miles City. I haven't heard anything."

"Well, what I heard is that your mother turned her ranch over to you," the sheriff said, no longer smiling. "Want to explain to me exactly how that happened?"

"Not really. It's between me and my mother, but I think everyone knows that I was always her favorite."

The sheriff nodded. "I'd ask what you planned to do with the ranch, but I also heard you've already sold it to Wendell Forester."

"All perfectly legal, Sheriff."

"Unless I can prove that you coerced your mother into giving you the ranch," Stuart said.

"That what my mother told you?"

The sheriff laughed. "If she had, you'd be in handcuffs by now. But it's only a matter of time before you go to prison. I really doubt she'll get you out again, don't you? Sorry, I can see that I'm boring you. I'll leave and let you visit with your former neighbor and, as I recall, former nemesis."

CJ watched Stuart walk to his SUV and drive away before he turned to Treyton. "Tell me you didn't shoot someone with your own .22 rifle."

"I don't know what you're talking about."

He considered Treyton for a long moment before he pulled the stack of hundreds from his jacket pocket, thumbed through them and put them back in his pocket. "Guess we're done here, then." He started to walk back to his ride, thinking about what his mother had said. He couldn't trust anyone, especially Treyton.

"Where do you think you're going?" Treyton demanded behind him. "You owe me a lot of money."

CJ turned quickly, closing the space between them. Treyton didn't have time to react. CJ plowed into him, driving him to the ground and ripping open his shirt. The fall knocked the air out of Treyton's lungs. He lay on the ground, gasping for air.

"Are you wearing a wire, you bastard?"

"No!" He was sucking in air and trying to fight him off as CJ tore open his jeans, dragging them down to Treyton's ankles.

He blinked in confusion, his pulse thundering in his ears. The sheriff hadn't been out here hooking Treyton up to a wire to frame him? Treyton hadn't been setting him up? It was just his mother putting that crap into his head. Getting to his feet, he stumbled back.

"What in the hell is wrong with you?" Treyton

demanded, pulling his pants up. "You think I turned on you?"

It was exactly what he'd been thinking. It was too much of a coincidence that the sheriff had been here. He glanced toward Treyton's house, little more than a lean-to, yet there were curtains—and they were closed. "Who's inside that shack of yours?"

"No one. Seriously, are you losing it?" Treyton said as he inspected the damage to his shirt. "You owe me for this shirt. Just pay me, and we're through."

"Pay you for what?"

His old adversary gave him an impatient look. "Getting a little paranoid, are you, CJ? Might be your guilt over what you did to your mother. You didn't fool anyone. Everyone knows what you're like."

"You've always been jealous of me." CJ found himself watching the house. Someone was in there. The sheriff hadn't come out here alone. Stuart would have known that CJ would suspect that Treyton was wearing a wire and check. Treyton resented him, always had. Of course, he would want him gone since he'd taken over the business CJ had started after he'd gone to jail. He realized he'd been a fool to ever trust him.

"I'm not going to stand out here and argue with you," said Treyton. "Pay me what you owe me, and we're done. After that, don't call me ever again to do your dirty work. You got what you wanted. Now pay me. I know you made a bundle when you sold the ranch to Wendell Forester. If you try to cheat me—"

CJ expected the cops would come busting out of the house any moment after Treyton had laid it all out for them. He hadn't admitted everything, but there was no doubt Treyton was going to sing.

The curtain moved inside the house. At least he thought it had. "You made a deal with the cops," he yelled as he pulled his weapon and opened fire.

Treyton had already gone for his own gun as if he'd been ready for this.

CJ got off a shot, but his former business partner got off two, both dead center. He felt them burn through him as he fired again and again, even as Treyton took the bullets, dropping to his knees, his weapon falling from his hand.

He emptied the clip. As everything suddenly went silent, CJ looked toward the house again and saw a cat sitting in the window, batting at the curtain. No one had come out to arrest him because the cops hadn't been in there.

He frowned as his legs gave out, and he fell over on the ground. Only yards from him, Treyton lay motionless, the ground next to him dark with his blood. He hadn't betrayed him after all, yet CJ knew he would have eventually. He knew he couldn't trust anyone. His mother had been right about that.

CHAPTER NINETEEN

CLAUDE CURSED HIMSELF all the way back to Powder Crossing. *You lie with dogs and you're going to get fleas.* His mother's old expression echoed in his head. There was no doubt now about his future. Wendell Forester was going to use him, then throw him away or just get right to it and ruin him.

He couldn't believe how excited he'd been when his boss had invited him to come to Montana for the weekend. He'd flown in the private jet, believing he was going to marry Victoria. True, the first time they'd met, things hadn't gone well, but Claude had thought given a little time, he could win her over— and if not, Wen would make her marry him.

He'd seen himself as Wen's son-in-law with his own private jet, his own tailored suits, his own corner office with floor-to-ceiling windows. Even though he'd known that Victoria would make his home life miserable, he'd been ready to make a deal with the devil to get the life he'd only dreamed of.

Now, after every humiliating thing he'd done for Wen, the man wouldn't even let him fly home in the company plane. Instead, he was just supposed to wait around until Wen and Victoria were ready?

Well, he would see about that, he thought as he drove through Powder Crossing and headed for the Stafford Ranch. He knew where he could find Victoria. She'd been his ticket all along, just not quite in the way he'd hoped.

Wen would do anything for his precious princess, wouldn't he?

Claude was about to find out as he drove up into the ranch yard. He didn't even hesitate as he got out. This was going down. He wasn't changing his mind or second-guessing himself. He knew what he had to do.

He started toward the house, but then heard voices down by the barn. Turning, he headed in that direction, knowing that Brand was still in the hospital. From what he'd heard, there wasn't much staff other than a cook who only worked two meals a day and lived in town. He'd gotten the impression that Brand and Ryder had downsized the staff, running the house by themselves until their mother returned. No wonder Wen thought he could get the ranch. Clearly, it was vulnerable as its future was up in the air with Charlotte Stafford holding the purse strings and being out of the picture.

The voices grew louder. Ryder and Victoria sounded quite intimate as they laughed and talked about some horse called Vic. Had the rancher named a horse after her?

That just made Claude more determined to do this. Maybe he'd hoped that his usual good sense would have talked him out of this plan by now. No such luck, he thought.

At the open barn door, he stopped to peer inside and let his eyes adjust to the dimness, then he slipped in. The two were so engrossed in each other that they didn't see him as he picked up a shovel leaning against one of the stalls.

It only took a few steps to come up behind Ryder. The cowboy hadn't heard him: he was too enamored with Victoria. Claude swung the shovel, catching him in the side of the head before either of them knew he was there. Claude thought he'd have to hit him again. Or maybe he just wanted to. But the cowboy went down like a bag of rocks and didn't move.

By then Victoria was screaming, racing forward to fall to her knees beside the rancher. Claude grabbed her arm and jerked her to her feet. "Come on, princess. You and I have a flight to catch."

She kept screaming and trying to claw and kick him. He only tightened his hold on her, half dragging her. He was bigger and stronger, and he wasn't going to take any shit from her. As they reached his rental, he'd finally had enough of her trying to scratch out his eyes, and he backhanded her. Her head bounced off the side of the SUV, and she slumped as if he'd cut the strings on a marionette.

Scooping her up, he put her into the passenger seat and pulled out the zip ties he'd bought before he'd left Billings. Hadn't he known it would come to this?

He glanced toward the barn, but there was no sign of Ryder. He hadn't wanted to kill him, but at this point did it really matter? He was kidnapping the only daughter of one of the wealthiest men in America, a man he already knew was a coldhearted bastard who would probably have him killed.

But damned if he wasn't getting back on that private jet to Dallas today, and he was taking Victoria with him.

BAILEY MCKENNA STARED at the box of books the delivery driver was holding before she finally reached for it. When she'd gotten the advance copies to share, it still hadn't felt real. But this made it all too real.

"Thank you," she said and turned to take them inside to the kitchen. Setting the box down, she stared at it, almost afraid to open it to see stacks of books marking years of her work now in print.

"You should be proud of what you wrote," her editor had assured her. "The way you wrote it, the book is fun to read. You have a tongue-in-cheek way of writing about people on the edge. It's comedic, yet fascinating. That it's all true makes it even more salacious."

Bailey had insisted the names stay changed before it went to print. When she'd originally written about the people of the Powder River basin, she'd been angry and hurt and scared. That had all changed when the man after her had been caught and killed. But that was only partially why she no longer felt a need to get back at anyone.

Since writing the book, she'd fallen only more deeply in love with the man she'd eloped with last weekend. That love had left no room for anger, hurt or fear. For the first time in her life, she believed that love was the most powerful of all emotions, able to conquer all.

With that thought, she grabbed a knife and opened the box. She felt a surge of excitement as she pulled back the cardboard flaps and saw the stacks of her first book. She caught her breath. The cover was more beautiful than the cover art that had been proposed. It was of the Powder River in all its glory and the people who meted out an existence along its shores. It, like the people, were the basis of her stories. People who often fought every day to survive there.

With awe, she picked up one of the books and ran her thumb across the raised gold letters of her name. Her dream had been to write a novel one day. She hadn't planned this book. It had practically written itself as she investigated the families, looking for the man who'd almost killed her when she was seventeen. She hadn't seen his face, but she'd known he still lived in the basin. She wrote down the stories she uncovered, and now here they were.

At the sound of a vehicle driving up outside, she looked to the window and saw her husband get out of his patrol SUV. She held the book to her chest, knowing it was going to cause him some pain because of the chapter on his mother. She had tried to get the chapter out of the book, but her editor had convinced her that what had made her book so powerful was that it was honest.

Stuart knew she'd written about him and his parents but not what he'd found out about his mother. He'd assured her not to worry about it, that he doubted he would read it. They both knew he would end up reading it because he'd been haunted by his memories of her for years and needed to know if they were true or not.

Bailey had known that there would be an uproar over the book once it hit the market. She'd already been threatened by one family who got wind of its publication. But now it was on sale.

She took a deep breath and let it out as the sheriff came through the door. He headed straight for her, drawing her close to kiss her.

"Bailey," his whispered against her lips, sending shivers across her skin. As he drew back he saw the box, his eyes lighting up. "Your books?"

She could only nod, both excited and a little scared, much like when Stuart had asked her to marry him. Now his wife, she didn't want anything to spoil their happiness.

He reached for the book she was holding and studied the cover. Like her, he ran a thumb over the raised gold letting, then looked up at her and smiled. "Congratulations, author. What would you like to do to celebrate?"

"Stay home and curl up with you."

Stuart shook his head even as he reached for her, drawing her into his arms again. "Anything you want." She snuggled against him, never having felt such love.

"How was your day?" she asked.

"I saw CJ Stafford and Treyton McKenna together today."

"The black sheep of the two families are friends?"

"Friends?" He shrugged. "Business associates. I'd bet money on it. I've suspected they were involved in that meth lab they burned before I could raid it. Treyton now has his own place out in the badlands." He pulled back, immediately changing topics. "I'm buying you dinner in Miles City. Then maybe a show? I want to celebrate this with you. What do you say? We can curl up when we get home."

She studied him for a moment, seeing how much he probably needed this more than she did. She smiled and nodded.

"Good," he said as he put down the book without opening it. "Let me change." Later he'd pick it up again, she knew. She'd dedicated it to him, the man who'd saved her from her very own monster. The man who loved her. The man she'd married.

Bailey hugged herself. She'd never dreamed she could be this happy. She couldn't help but worry about her brother Treyton. Their father was finally happy. He and Charlotte Stafford were engaged and would soon be married. She didn't want anything to spoil that.

VICTORIA SURFACED WITH a start to find herself bound and her mouth covered with duct tape in the passenger seat of a vehicle racing down a highway. Her gaze flew to the driver. Claude, she thought with a groan as everything came back. Ryder! She thought her heart would burst at the thought that Claude had killed him.

"Are you demented?" she tried to yell, but it came out a muffled groan behind the duct tape covering her mouth. "My father will have you thrown in prison." Again her words were more like muffled groans.

Claude let out a curse, reached over and ripped the tape from her mouth. She let out a cry of pain and saw him grin. She hadn't been afraid until that moment when he'd struck Ryder and taken her captive and she'd awakened bound and gagged. She'd always thought Claude was harmless. Now she saw that he wanted her to suffer. She felt a moment of regret for the way she'd treated him and said as much.

He laughed. "Easy for you to say now."

"Was Ryder all right when we left the ranch?" she asked, terrified of what he might say since he could have gone back and finished the job before they left.

Claude shrugged. "I didn't check."

She rode for a few moments in silence as she tried to assure herself that Ryder was strong. He would be all right. He had to be. Her heart lunged in her chest at the thought that he might die. She'd never felt about anyone the way she did Ryder. It had happened so quickly, yet she knew this was the first time she'd been in love, and the last. She'd always laughed about her friends wanting to find their so-called soul mates.

Whatever, she used to think. But in her heart, she knew that was exactly what Ryder was. He was her soul mate, and she his. It was funny how Montana had played a part in it, she thought. This place she thought she wouldn't like had seduced her. Ryder's love for this land and ranching had in turn drawn her even closer to him as if her fate was always going to lead her here.

Ryder had to be all right. Claude couldn't have killed him. If her hands had been free, she would have attacked him. "Where are you taking me?" she asked.

"To the airport. We're flying back to Dallas."

She studied him for a moment. "Did my father tell you to do this?"

"Your father doesn't tell me what to do anymore."

Still trying to assess what was going on here, she asked, "Did he fire you?"

Claude let out a bark of a laugh. "He just isn't calling the shots anymore. I am."

Victoria really doubted that, unless her father was dead. "Where is Wen?"

"Last I saw him he was going to get a geologist to inspect his new property . . ." He glanced over at her. "Stafford Ranch. Before he begins drilling."

That sounded like her father. "Does he know that we're flying back to Dallas?"

He nodded. "I called him as I drove out of Powder Crossing. Sent him a photo of you all tied up and unconscious. Told him I'd meet him at the airport because he's coming with us."

She stared at him. Earlier she'd been afraid because Claude had seemed so different. Clearly, he'd reached the end of his patience with her—and her father. But if he thought this was going to work, he'd completely gone off the rails. "My father won't just show up at the airport, and he certainly isn't going to fly to Dallas with us unless he's ready to do so," Victoria said as he drove. "He'll tell his pilot not to fly us at all. You're going to get to the airport and only be disappointed."

"I've been disappointed from the moment I met you and signed that contract to work for your father. He dangled you in front of me like a prize if I went to work for him. What a fool I was." He shook his head angrily. "I will fly home in the company jet because you're going with me no matter what."

Victoria sighed, shaking her head. "Do you really not know how far my father will go? He won't do what you want. But he will make you pay."

"He will when he realizes that I not only have you and that, unless he comes to the airport and agrees to leave with us, I will kill you."

She couldn't help being skeptical. "I don't think you're a killer, Claude."

He shot her a look, then he pulled the gun from his pocket. "I wouldn't bet on that, princess."

"You overestimate his love for me. He loves

money and power a hundred times over what he feels for me. He was trying to marry me off to you. Think about it. Does that sound like a man who loves his daughter?"

"Insult me again and I'll put the duct tape back on your mouth," Claude said through gritted teeth as he pocketed the gun. "I know what I'm doing. He'll show up. Your blood on his hands would be bad for business."

They were almost to Billings when he pulled off in a wide spot. She watched him get out and make three calls. She couldn't imagine who he was calling. She hoped her father didn't take the bait. He knew Claude. She also knew her father. He'd call Claude's bluff, and this time, he might be making a mistake that could get them all killed.

But as she watched Claude finish the last call, she saw that he was smiling as he headed back toward the SUV. What scared her was that he seemed . . . desperate, and way too sure of himself. She feared that she and her father had pushed the man too far.

"Any luck?" she asked as he slid behind the wheel and started the engine to pull back on the road.

He smiled over at her, and for a minute she didn't think he would answer. His smile was almost more frightening than his snarl. "You, your father and I are flying to Dallas this evening. The pilot is making the arrangements as we speak."

Claude was too happy. She had a bad thought. "My father's pilot?"

"He won't be flying with us. Maybe you hadn't heard, but your father fired his bodyguards. I assume you knew that they were both former pilots Wen hired as backups should his pilot be indisposed in some way. JJ Gibson is flying us. Your father used to make me call them with their orders for the week, so I had their phone numbers. JJ was still in Billings and happy to have a ride home."

She shook her head. "Claude, this can't end well. You have to know that my father will—"

"Bury me. I know, he's told me that numerous times. It's up to him what he decides to do, but he'd be smart to put a million dollars in my offshore account before we land in Dallas. Otherwise . . ." His gaze held hers for a few seconds, long enough that she could see how much he hated her. She couldn't even blame him. "Otherwise, he'll never see his princess again." He reached over and turned up the music, giving her a headache.

There was no way her father would give Claude a million dollars. As she watched him attempting to sing along with the rock music, she had a bad feeling that this wasn't even about the money. This was about vengeance. It was why her father was rich and not behind bars. He'd never let emotion cost him any money.

SHERIFF STUART LAYTON had just walked into his office when he got the call.

"I think something has happened to CJ," Charlotte Stafford told him. "I'm worried about my son."

"The son you didn't want me to arrest for stealing your ranch," Stuart said.

"That is hearsay," she said indignantly.

"I saw him yesterday out at Treyton McKenna's place," the sheriff said. "I did as you asked, not taking either him or Treyton in for questioning. I only confiscated Treyton's .22 rifle to check against the slug taken out of your son Brand's shoulder. The ballistics didn't match."

"I doubted he would use his own rifle," she said. "I have a bad feeling that CJ is still out there."

That catch in her throat caught his attention, as well as her words. "A bad feeling." He swore. He'd known when she'd contacted him that she was up to something. "I have no idea what's going on, but I don't like it, Mrs. Stafford."

"Don't *Mrs. Stafford* me, Stuart. I've known you since you were knee-high to a badger. I'm worried. Will you drive out and check or not?"

He sighed, worried about what he was going to find. "I'll head out there now and call you if I find him."

"Thank you, Stuart." Her voice broke again before she could hang up.

Swearing, he headed for the door. Stuart drove toward Treyton's place in the badlands outside of Powder Crossing, admitting he had a chip on his shoulder when it came to CJ Stafford and Treyton McKenna. While Stuart had been raised by his father, the local sheriff, lived in a small house in town and had a mother who'd run away, CJ and Treyton were spoiled-rotten ranch kids.

Both had never wanted for anything as the eldest in their ranch families. CJ even more than Treyton had no respect for the law. Worse, they'd never had any respect for him. After he'd taken over his father's job as sheriff, he'd had to deal with both of them. Arresting CJ and putting him behind bars had been a highlight.

Unfortunately, and without surprise, his mother had gotten him out, and trouble had soon followed— just as he'd known it would.

As he turned down the dirt road leading back into Treyton's property, he found himself slowing to pull out his shotgun. He had no idea what he was walking into, but his instincts told him it was going to be bad. As far as he knew the two hadn't started up their meth lab and human-trafficking business again, but one never knew with these two, he thought as he topped the hill. The first thing he saw was CJ's SUV parked where it had been before. The sound of his patrol vehicle's engine approaching sent a flock of carrion birds scattering across the barren yard like a scene from a scary movie.

That was when he saw what was on the ground.

CHAPTER TWENTY

HOLDEN HAD BEEN sitting in his home office thinking about his upcoming wedding when he got the
sheriff's call.

"Maybe you should sit down," Stuart had suggested.

His heart had almost stopped since his first
thought was Lottie. *Don't let it be Lottie.* He'd
waited almost his whole life for this woman. He
couldn't bear it if anything happened to her.

"It's Treyton," the sheriff said. "He's been killed."

The words had refused to register for a moment.
"Killed?" His first thought was a car accident.
His second was suicide. Which showed how little
he knew about his son. He hadn't seen Treyton in
months. Their last conversation had been his son
telling him that he was too old to run the ranch and
how disappointed he was in him. Like CJ, Treyton
had just assumed as the eldest son that he would
take over the ranch one day—even though he'd
hated ranching, seldom worked it and resented his
brother Cooper for doing so.

Holden could just imagine how Treyton had
taken the news that his father had a love child with

Charlotte Stafford. He'd been half afraid that Treyton might try to harm Brand when he heard.

He realized that the sheriff was still talking. "I had just seen the two of them together out there. It was obvious that they had some kind of business going on. CJ was acting . . . paranoid. It appears they had a shootout. They were both killed. I'm so sorry, Holden."

At some point he must have stood up behind his desk because now he sat down heavily as if his legs had been knocked out from under him. Treyton and CJ, both dead. "Have you told Charlotte yet?"

"No, I wanted to call you first," the sheriff said.

"Thank you, Stuart," he said, feeling as if he was in a bad dream. He disconnected as Elaine came into the room.

"What's happened?" she demanded at seeing his distress.

"Treyton is dead. He and CJ, both dead. Apparently they killed each other." Shoving himself to his feet, he said, "Stuart is going to tell Lottie. She's going to need me."

"What about you? Are you going to be all right?" Elaine sounded upset and worried.

He gave her a weak smile. "We knew this is how it would end with both of them, didn't we?"

"That doesn't make it any easier."

"No, but it's hard to be shocked. I'm just . . . sad." He shook his head. "They both had everything going for them as our oldest sons, but it was never enough."

Elaine nodded and wiped her eyes. "It's not your fault."

He smiled at that. "Of course it is. That's why I have to see Lottie. We both blame ourselves for the way CJ and Treyton turned out. The sheriff said he thought the two of them had some business together. That they took each other's lives . . ." He shook his head again. "I have to go. Are you all right?"

She nodded and wiped her eyes again. "It doesn't help that we've been expecting this, does it?"

"No," he said as he picked up his Stetson and headed for the door.

WHEN RYDER CAME to, his head aching, he immediately called the sheriff, but had to leave a message. "Claude Duvall just kidnapped Victoria Forester. I think he's taking her to Billings to the airport. They'll probably take her father's private jet." The dispatcher said she would give him the message.

Ryder was already disconnecting. He felt a little woozy, but not bad enough that it was going to stop him. He had felt worse after being bucked off a wild bronco at the rodeo. Grabbing his gun, he headed for his pickup. He had no idea how long he'd been out. Not that long, he didn't think. Maybe he could catch them.

Even as he thought it, he feared what he would do to Claude if he caught up with him before he reached Billings. His bigger worry was what the man might do to Vicky, he thought as he slid behind the wheel of his pickup, started the engine and hit the gas.

His phone rang and he quickly picked up, hoping it would be Victoria.

"This is Wendell Forester." The voice on the other end of the line sounded distraught. Claude must have already called him. "Tell me my daughter is with you."

"Claude knocked me out and took her," he said, roaring down the road, planning to take the shortcut. "He's on his way to the Billings airport. I've already alerted the authorities. I think he's planning to take your jet. I'm going after him. Give me her cell phone number. I think she has her phone with her."

Wen rattled off the number, but then added, "You're wasting your time. I called. It went to voice mail."

"The difference is she'll want to talk to me."

Wendell swore. "I'm already headed for the airport. I can handle Claude."

"Doesn't seem so," Ryder said as he drove. "Unless you put him up to this."

"You have such a low opinion of me."

Ryder swore. "Do you blame me?"

"It was just business."

"Really? Destroying people's lives is just business for you? When we get to the airport, Claude's mine. Don't get in my way or you're going down with him." He disconnected and called Vicky. The phone was answered on the second ring—but not by her.

"Ryder? I thought you were dead," Claude said into the phone. "You must have a very hard head."

In the background, he could hear Vicky saying she wanted to talk to him.

"If you hurt her—"

"You're in no position to make threats, cowboy," Claude snapped. "She's going with me back to Dallas. After that, I really don't care." He ended the call.

Ryder swore again and concentrated on his driving. He'd driven these backroads since he was a boy. He knew them by heart. Still, he feared he wouldn't get there in time.

UNABLE TO SIT, Charlotte was pacing the hotel suite when her phone rang. It startled her, even though she'd been expecting the call. She saw at once that it was the sheriff calling, yet she didn't pick up. Her heart had already told her that it was going to be bad news. She'd thought she'd been ready, but realized she would never be ready to hear that one of her children was dead.

"Stuart?" she said after the fourth ring, knowing she couldn't put it off any longer. The silence in answer made her fear that she'd waited too long to answer. But then she heard his sigh. That was when the tears rushed to her eyes, hot and blinding.

"It's CJ," the sheriff said. She heard nothing after that. She'd known because she'd done this as surely as she'd pulled the trigger. She used her son's insecurities against him, poisoned him with his own mistrust, and now he was dead.

"Treyton too," Stuart said as she regained focus.

"It appears they shot each other. I already called Holden." He'd called Holden first.

She could hear the anger in his voice. He knew that she was responsible for this, but he didn't know how. He also didn't think that Holden had anything to do with it, and he was right. Charlotte made a swipe at her eyes and straightened her back. "Thank you for letting me know. I'm on my way out to see Holden at the ranch now," she said before he hung up.

She didn't know how she was going to tell Holden. While she'd had months to accept who her son CJ was, he'd still surprised her at how much hatred he had for her and his siblings. Not to mention what lengths he would go to and how many people he would hurt to get what he wanted.

Pocketing her phone, she picked up her purse and headed for the McKenna Ranch, worried about Holden. He hadn't been ready for this. He'd known that Treyton and CJ had been working together and that Treyton was behind the recent supposed accidents with Brand and Oakley.

The man knew her so well. Would he know what she'd done? How could he not suspect the moment he saw her face? She'd killed them both.

THEY MET IN the middle of the county road. Charlotte saw Holden coming down the road first. Her heart lifted at the sight of his pickup coming toward her. She'd known he would come to her. He'd be worried about her. That was the man she loved. Holden had always been the generous one, the loving one, the forgiving one.

She hated to think of the person she'd been. The one she still was. Did he have any idea of the kind of woman he had asked to marry him? That was just it. He did. He knew her—yet he still loved her. She would always be grateful for that. Still, she worried that if he knew what she'd done that he would finally give up on her.

He pulled alongside her SUV and put his window down. She'd already had hers down, letting the summer breeze blow in with its familiar smells as if they could give her strength.

"Lottie," he said the moment their gazes met. She saw the heartbreak in his handsome face and felt it soul deep. He didn't ask. He didn't have to.

She nodded and burst into tears. The next thing she knew he was out of his pickup, opening her door and dragging her into his arms. "I'm so sorry, I'm so sorry." She couldn't seem to quit saying it.

He brushed away her tears, kissing her to make her stop. As he pulled back, he looked at her. "It's going to be all right. Everything is going to be all right now." His strong arms drew her in, and she knew it was true. This land, this life, their love had punished them for years, but it had also made them stronger.

They would get through this, just as they'd gotten through everything else.

CLAUDE DROVE THROUGH the largest city in Montana, fighting the traffic to climb the road up onto the rock rims to the airport. Victoria hadn't said anything since Ryder's call to her phone, but he'd seen her relief that the cowboy was alive. Now she seemed to be biding her time as if she thought somehow she would be reunited with her lover.

He gritted his teeth at how quickly she'd fallen for the rancher. What did Ryder have that he didn't? He hated to think. Right now he didn't seem to have much of a future. But that million dollars Wen would be putting in his offshore account would help him figure it out. Maybe he'd catch a slow boat to a tropical island to think about it.

Glancing over at Victoria, he wondered what she would do. The cowboy's ranch was gone. He figured she'd be gone as well. Love was one thing, but money was another. No one wanted to marry a homeless saddle tramp, especially the likes of Victoria Forester. She was her daddy's daughter.

Well, he thought, it wouldn't be the ending he'd thought he'd have when he flew to Montana to make Victoria his fiancée. But it would have to do. Between Wen and him, they'd done plenty of damage. His boss and his daughter would probably walk away, and their lives would go on just fine. If Wen had cut off her finances, Claude was sure he'd remedy that after this.

Not that he planned to worry about her, he thought with a silent chuckle. The woman could take care of herself. Ryder Stafford? Who knew about him. But something told Claude that the cowboy would come out smelling like roses, as his grandmother used to

say. The bad stuff didn't stick to some people, as if
they were Teflon, he thought as he pulled up to the
gate in the area reserved for private carriers.

Claude could see that the steps were down and
the door open on the Gulfstream G550. JJ would be
doing his preflight check. What Claude didn't see
was Wen as the guard at the gate nodded and let him
drive through. Only a man as rich and powerful as
Wendell Forester got this kind of service.

"We wait here for your father," Claude said as
he parked, surprised the cops weren't here. But of
course Wen wouldn't call them. His boss liked to
handle problems himself.

Victoria, he saw, had perked up considerably
since getting the call from the cowboy. Maybe she
really did have feelings for him.

"You should just let me out and you can make
a run for it," Victoria said. "Seriously, just take off
and don't look back."

He shook his head. "You and your father would
both like that, wouldn't you? You use people and
then walk away. Wasn't that what you were planning to do with Ryder when you tired of him?"

"Isn't it possible that I'm serious about him?"

Claude laughed and shook his head. "You're kidding yourself. I'm surprised you're not bored with
him yet—not to mention he no longer has a ranch."

"We'll get another one," she said.

"Seriously?" he said. "With what? I thought your
father cut you off?"

"He did. But I have the money my grandmother left me. It's more than enough to buy a small place, and Ryder isn't broke either."

He shook his head. "Of course, the two of you have money. I forget who I'm dealing with. So why did you buy that old pickup?"

"I've never touched my inheritance. Maybe I was waiting for the day I needed it for something important."

He sat fuming, hating his life, jealous of people who had options he'd never been provided, but mostly feeling sorry for himself. He finally couldn't help himself. "What was wrong with me?" he asked. "I could have made you a good husband if you had been just a little nice to me."

"You weren't in love with me. Also, you work for my father, and I wasn't in love with you," she said. "It would have never worked. I never planned to ever marry, if you want to know the truth. After meeting Ryder, I've changed my mind. But I would never have let my father force me into marriage with anyone I didn't love, with you or anyone else."

"Maybe if you'd given me a chance, you might have fallen in love with me," he said, hating how pathetic he sounded.

She smiled over at him. "It wouldn't have worked. You didn't want me. You wanted a little of my father's life." She shook her head. "Trust me, it wouldn't have made you happy. Look at my father. Does he seem happy to you?"

Claude had never thought about it. He just assumed rich people lied about money not making them happy because they felt guilty.

They sat for a moment of silence, then Victoria looked around nervously. "Claude, this is your chance to make a clean getaway. It's a mistake waiting for my father. He isn't going to go with you. He's going to stop you from getting on that plane."

He studied her for a moment, thinking that she might be right. Maybe taking her father at gunpoint wasn't the best plan. Leaving with Victoria in the jet to Dallas should show the man how serious he was. If Wen didn't send him proof that the million had been deposited in his account, Claude might just dump her out over the mountains. He hadn't bought any of her reasons for why she couldn't have married him—let alone loved him.

"Let's go," he said and climbed out to go around to the passenger-side door. "I'm going to untie you, but I have a gun. I will shoot you if you give me any trouble. We're just going to board the plane. I'll have the gun in your back the whole time. I no longer have anything to lose, so keep that in mind."

He cut the zip ties and dragged her from the vehicle as she reached back in for her phone.

CHAPTER TWENTY-ONE

VICTORIA KNEW SHE should stall. She had to do whatever was necessary because there was no way she was getting on that plane with Claude. Ryder would be coming for her. When she'd heard his voice, her heart had leaped. He was alive. He wouldn't hesitate to come after her because he felt the same way she did. She knew it.

With a start, though, she feared what would happen when he got here. Maybe it would be better if she was gone—even with Claude—on the plane to Dallas. She could always call him and let him know she'd be on the next flight back. She might be saving his life if she did.

She had no idea what her father would do—if he did anything. He might not show up at all. He might call Claude's bluff: that was how he usually worked. Then again, the way he dealt with trouble wasn't with guns but with lawyers. He had enough money to drag things out for years in the courts. It was why he always won. But he wouldn't win this if he did show up.

"We should get on the plane and go," she said to Claude. "Let's not wait for my father."

He turned her to face him. She felt his gaze surveying her expression. "What's going on? There's a reason you don't want to wait for him or your boyfriend."

"I don't want you to kill them," she snapped. "There's no reason for bloodshed. You don't want that any more than I do."

Claude seemed to consider that for a moment. "Give me a minute." He pulled out his phone. After a moment, he swore. "Your father hasn't moved any money into my account."

Victoria wanted to scream. Did he not know her father at all? Wendell Forester didn't pay off blackmailers or kidnappers.

As if on cue, her father drove up, parked and got out. While he must have broken speed records to get here so quickly, he moved slowly now, looking calm. Claude had driven under the speed limit the whole way as if this was exactly what he wanted—a confrontation that ended in spilled blood. He wanted this showdown.

As three security men from the airport and several cops came running toward them, Wendell waved them away as he calmly advanced on her and Claude. "Drop that gun and let go of my daughter," he said quietly. "You've made your point. I'm here."

"But you haven't put the money into my account," Claude said, pressing the barrel to her side.

"I haven't had a chance since you also wanted me here," her father said without raising his voice.

"I can transfer the money once you and I get on the plane. Victoria isn't going."

"Like hell," Claude said and started maneuvering her toward the jet. "The three of us are flying back to Dallas now. There is nothing you can say to change my mind. If you call those guards over, I will kill your daughter, then you. Your choice."

"Claude," her father said, measuring his tone, "listen to reason. Victoria doesn't want to leave yet. Let her go. You can take the plane. The deposit will be waiting for you when you get there, and before you land I will give you the million in severance pay."

"You're saying you'll tear up my contract?"

"Consider it done," Wendell said. "You're right. You probably deserve it after everything I've asked of you. Most men wouldn't have put up with me this long. How's that? Now, let her go, and let's get this plane to Dallas."

Victoria could tell Claude wanted to believe him, but he'd known the man long enough that he was skeptical. She didn't blame him.

"He thinks he can control me by saying he's going to throw money at me," Claude said after apparently giving it some thought. "He thinks I'm a fool. The minute I let you go, he'll call those guards over here and have me arrested for kidnapping you. Wouldn't matter that he paid me to go after you and use my good judgment as to how to handle you." He turned to his former boss. "The thing is, Wen, this time I got it all on my phone. I can prove it was your idea, not mine, and that you blackmailed me into doing it."

At the roar of a vehicle engine, they all looked up to see Ryder come to a skidding stop. The distraction was exactly what her father had apparently been waiting for. He grabbed her before Claude could react, shoving her out of the way as he went for the gun. She screamed as she fell to the tarmac, but in an instant Ryder was there helping her up and pulling her aside.

When she looked toward her father, she saw that Claude had the gun pressed against his side as he backed him toward the plane.

RYDER COULDN'T BELIEVE how close a call it had been getting here. If he'd been even a few minutes later . . .

"Don't try anything, cowboy," Claude warned as he maneuvered his boss over to the plane's steps.

"Don't worry, this is between you and the man who stole my ranch," Ryder said. "You work it out between yourselves."

"Ryder, no," Victoria cried and tried to get past him to help her father. He held on to her, not about to let her go. From the look in Claude's eyes, he feared the man would gladly kill both Victoria and her father, so he held her back.

Not that he was doing it for her father's sake. Wendell Forester had made this mess. Let him figure it out, he thought, though he feared Vicky would never forgive him if Claude shot her father. But he knew this woman. She would attack Claude if he let her go, and that would get everyone shot.

"He doesn't have the guts to kill me, don't worry," Forester said to Victoria. "We're just going to go for a plane ride. I'm sure Claude and I can work it out." The security guards had started to approach again, but Wendell waved them back. "Everything's fine!" he called to them. "Just a little disagreement. We'll be leaving now." Clearly, he thought he could talk Claude down.

Ryder wasn't so sure about that. Claude seemed to be at the end of his rope.

"Right, we'll work it out, unless I drop him off over the mountains," Claude said with a laugh as he pushed his boss up the first couple of steps. Forester tripped on the third one and teetered for a moment before taking a step back as if to catch himself.

At Forester's stumble, Ryder realized that he'd been waiting for an opportunity to present itself. He shoved past Vicky and rushed forward as Claude, too, was thrown off balance.

Knowing he was taking a hell of a chance for a man he despised, Ryder grabbed the weapon and wrestled it out of Claude's hand, hoping the man didn't pull the trigger and shoot Forester.

Claude stumbled into Forester, knocking him over the railing to the tarmac. Vicky cried out and rushed to her father as Ryder quickly pocketed the weapon so one of the security guards didn't get trigger happy and shoot him.

Claude, no longer armed, apparently saw his chance. He ran up the steps into the airplane, pulling the door closed quickly behind him. The security guards advanced as its engine revved and it began to pull away.

"You can still stop him," Ryder said as airport security and law enforcement officers reached them. "Security can keep him from taking off."

Forester shook his head. "No, let him go. He'll be dealt with when he reaches Texas." He was cradling his arm and limped over to talk to the guards. Ryder could hear him telling them to let him go. "No harm's been done. I'll take responsibility."

The guards and cops hesitated a moment, then must have remembered who they were talking to because they turned and headed toward the terminal. Ryder heard one of them on the radio telling the tower to let the jet take off. He was sure that money would change hands.

As he joined Vicky, Ryder said, "Sorry about your dad," although he wasn't that sorry when he thought about it.

"You saved him," Vicky said as she stepped into his arms. "I knew you couldn't let Claude take him."

Ryder shook his head. "You don't know how tempted I was to let them both fly away. He just wasn't taking you."

Her father walked back to them, looking confident that he'd handled things. "Thank you," Forester said as he cradled his left arm, looking in pain. "But

I would have been fine if I hadn't stumbled. I could have handled him."

"I didn't do it for you," Ryder snapped. "I did it for your daughter."

"Yes, of course," the man said. "My daughter."

At the sound of the plane taking off, they both turned to watch it soar into the air. "I wonder what's waiting for him in Texas," Ryder said.

"Knowing my father, I wouldn't want to be Claude."

CLAUDE MOVED UP into the cockpit once the jet was in the air. He dropped into the copilot's seat and looked out at the mountains looming ahead. He liked the view. He could get used to this.

"I suppose we could steal the plane and take it to South America," he said, only half-joking.

JJ laughed. "Why not? It's a nice plane. We could run drugs."

It wasn't the future Claude had envisioned for himself, but at this point it sounded good to him. "You're sure Wen wouldn't have us shot down before we could leave the States?"

"He'd have to find us first," JJ said.

"You're serious? We could pull something like that off?" Claude looked back as Billings began to disappear behind them.

The pilot shrugged as they continued to climb, the jet rising as he pointed it toward Dallas. "Planes disappear all the time. We'd have to make some changes to it, but it could be done." JJ glanced over at him. "You're really ready to burn the last of your bridges?"

Claude gave it only a moment's thought. "Damned straight. There's nothing for me in Montana or Texas anymore. Let's steal this sucker and make a new life for ourselves."

JJ nodded and grinned.

Below them, all Claude could see was mountains with jagged cliffs and dark green pines. Nowhere did he see even a road. "You know anyone in South America?" he asked.

"Not yet," JJ said, still grinning. "When we show up with this jet, we'll make friends fast."

Claude laughed, feeling better than he had in a very long time. He was finally free of Wendell Forester and his daughter. The cowboy could have her. He was now in charge of his own life. No looking back, he thought, pleased with himself.

THE PLANE HAD begun to swing toward the east away from the city and out across the mountains.

Wendell walked up to join them. "We should all leave before the cops show up. I'm sure they were called. I'll take care of Claude when I return to Dallas."

"You aren't going to give him any money, are you?" Vicky said.

Her father didn't answer. "Claude and I will work it out, don't worry. He's just disappointed about how things turned out."

"Aren't we all," Vicky said almost in unison with Ryder.

"It's just business," Forester said.

"Right. You want to get out of here?" Ryder asked her. Vicky nodded, and they started to turn away when they heard the explosion. It made them all start and turn toward the sound. As they watched, the Gulfstream turned into a fireball. All three of them stood stunned and horrified as flaming pieces of the craft began to fall from the sky in the distance. Vicky's hand went to her mouth, her eyes wide. All the color had drained from Forester's face. Ryder figured he was picturing himself on that flight as he now looked wordlessly at what was left of the plane disappear from view.

Weak with relief and revulsion, all Ryder could do was pull Vicky close. If he hadn't arrived when he did, she could have been on that plane—Forester as well.

CHAPTER TWENTY-TWO

WHEN HOLDEN MCKENNA had dreamed of bringing the family together, he'd never envisioned it being for a funeral. He looked around the family gathered here in the ranch cemetery, feeling the loss even as he saw how much his family had grown. Lottie stood next to him, holding his hand. Next to her was the girl he'd adopted. Holly Jo was growing into a young woman before his eyes. She'd never really known Treyton. Holden wondered if even he had ever known his son.

Treyton's funeral had brought home his son Duffy, who'd been working down in Wyoming. He couldn't believe how much his youngest son had grown into a man of his own. Cooper held his newborn daughter River, his wife Tilly beside him. Holden's daughter Bailey stood with her husband Sheriff Stuart Layton, both somber as the weather.

Pickett was there with his wife, Oakley, along with ranch manager Deacon Yates and Holden's friend and longtime housekeeper Elaine.

Lottie stood with him, their son Brand and his wife, Birdie, next to Ryder.

This was his family, he thought as he took in the

group, awed by the feelings they evoked in him. He was blessed more than he deserved by the strength they gave him.

Tomorrow they would lay Lottie's son to rest with all of them here again.

Then in a week he and Lottie would get married, bringing both families together.

He thought of that as the preacher droned on about a young man struck down in his prime who Holden had never met. But then, the truth got buried at funerals. He supposed it was best.

CHARLOTTE SHADED HER eyes from the last of the sun's rays, the preacher's voice a buzz in the background as she thought back to her infant son in her arms. She'd had so much hope that day for the man he would become. Her firstborn, CJ, had been destined to one day run the ranch. He'd been her hope for the future. She'd put so much of her love into that child—at the detriment of her other children.

And now she was burying him.

She'd been expecting the call from the sheriff when he'd gotten back to her, but in truth she'd been waiting for that call for years. She'd done her crying a long time ago. Now she stood here about to bury her son, dry-eyed. Not because her heart wasn't breaking. Or that she didn't want to curl up in ball with the pain of what she'd done. But for so many years she'd done what she'd had to in order to survive. All she knew was living with the pain. Nothing had changed.

She couldn't help but remember when she'd finally seen the monster she'd produced. It had been the night she found out he'd hired two men to kill his sister Oakley. That night after she'd called the sheriff and had her son arrested for attempted murder, she'd sobbed until there was nothing left. She'd washed her hands of CJ, blaming herself for him being the way he was.

He would have gone to prison possibly for the rest of his life had she not intervened and gotten him out. She'd wanted to give him another chance, but what she'd really done was gotten him out to die, she thought now as she realized the preacher had finished talking.

Swallowing the lump in her throat, she stepped forward to take up a handful of Powder River basin dirt to drop on the casket. She watched as his casket was lowered into the ground. She no longer had to worry about CJ or what he would do next or who he would hurt ever again.

Her daughters and sons stood silently nearby, their heads down. Tilly was the only one who'd cried when she dropped her handful of dirt on her brother's casket. "It's the pregnancy hormones still in her system," Oakley had whispered. Charlotte thought she was probably right. CJ had been terrible to his siblings growing up, almost taking both Oakley's and Tilly's lives. It was no secret that they all assumed CJ had also been behind Brand being shot and Oakley's house almost burning down.

Holden put his arm around her as the funeral

ended. Yesterday she'd stood by his side as he'd buried his oldest son. He'd come to her the moment he heard about their sons' deaths. He'd held her as she told him how sorry she was. He'd never know just how sorry. Then they called their other offspring to let them know, before planning their family-only funerals.

Together she and Holden now walked away, both she suspected feeling guilty at the relief they felt. It was a horrible feeling.

"Surely you are going to postpone the wedding," Tilly said after the private funerals. They'd all gathered back at the McKenna Ranch. "What will people think?"

Charlotte smiled. "Everyone who matters knew CJ and Treyton. They will think what they will. It was a horrible tragedy what happened to our sons, but Holden and I are getting married. We aren't putting it off any longer."

She'd told Wendell Forester that she wanted to bury CJ on the Stafford Ranch. "I'm sure you have your reasons," he'd said.

"My son blackmailed me to get it and then he sold it to escape his past," she said. "It's only fitting he spend eternity there."

"We can postpone the wedding," Holden said.

"No, we can't," Charlotte said. "We aren't waiting any longer."

He looked relieved. "You're sure? People are probably going to talk."

That made her laugh. It felt good since it had been a while. "You sound like Tilly. Everyone in three counties have talked about us our whole lives. Is there anyone who doesn't know about the Staffords and the McKennas?"

He smiled. "You're probably right. Have you read my daughter's book?"

"Cover to cover," Charlotte said. "I loved it! How about you?"

"I read it," he admitted. "Bailey was nice enough to give me an advanced copy. But I can't say I loved it. I'm worried about how everyone in it will react, since it is set to release next week—right before our wedding."

"Perfect timing," she said. "Isn't that what a wedding is for, hanging out all your dirty laundry for everyone to see?"

"Actually, I don't believe so."

She laughed again at the thought of what people would say about her laughing so soon after burying her oldest son. Not that she cared. It was freeing, just as dropping that handful of dirt on his casket had been. She desperately missed the CJ she'd loved with all her heart and her hopes and dreams for him. There would always be a terrible ache inside her, but now she had to move on. Marrying Holden was a start. She wanted her children to see that people could change—even their mother.

"I know Bailey changed the names in the book, but you did recognize the two of us, didn't you?" he asked.

Charlotte nodded. "I'm glad she didn't pull any punches. She didn't cut anyone else any slack either. I admire that about her, and I told her so in the note I sent her after I finished the book."

He studied her openly for a moment, then pulled her to him. "I love you so much."

"Warts and all?"

Holden chuckled. "Warts and all—just like our families."

WENDELL FORESTER DIDN'T like the way the federal agent was looking at him. For the past seventy-two hours he'd been answering questions, first by security at the airport, then local law enforcement. Now the feds were involved.

Agent Al Brooks was with what was called the Fly Team, investigating the explosion that destroyed his plane, he explained. Surely, the feds didn't think he would blow up his own plane? It had to have been an accident.

"Are you familiar with a man named Brice Schultz?" the agent asked.

"Of course I am. He was one of my security guards."

"But wasn't he also a pilot and mechanic who had done work on your plane?" Wendell nodded, wondering where this was going. "Was he in your employ at the time of the explosion on your plane?" the agent asked.

"No, I'd fired him a few days before, along with my other guard."

The agent considered his notes. "John Jacob Gibson?"

"Was it JJ piloting my plane when it blew up?"

The agent didn't respond. "Did you give him permission to be piloting your plane?"

"No. I assumed my assistant Claude Duvall put him up to it."

"You allowed Claude Duvall to leave in your plane, is that correct?"

"After he held a gun on both me and my daughter, yes, I let him go. He was upset. I didn't want to see him get arrested. I figured I'd deal with him when I returned to Dallas."

"You planned to have your plane sent back?"

"Yes," Wendell said, trying to keep his temper. "If you're asking if I knew it was going to blow up, how could I? Wasn't it a malfunction?"

Again, Agent Brooks checked his notes before looking up. "There was a bomb aboard the plane. We believe it was activated from Billings once the plane was in the air and away from the airport."

Wendell's jaw dropped at what the agent was telling him. "Someone purposely blew up my plane?"

"I can see that this comes as a shock, but you were obviously concerned, otherwise why did you hire two bodyguards before your trip to Montana?"

"You're saying this was an attempt on my life?"

"We believe so. I understand you've been getting threatening letters." The agent continued. "You were worried enough to contact local law enforcement, who in turn contacted us."

Wendell felt as if the earth under him was no longer solid. He gripped the edges of his chair as if hanging on. Someone had tried to kill him and would have if he'd been on that plane. He felt a shudder at the thought that Victoria could have been on it as well.

"Do you know a man by the name Arnold Schultz?"

He frowned, confused, and shook his head.

"He is the father of the man you employed as a bodyguard," the agent said. "I understand he also had access to your plane as he is a pilot and often worked on it."

Wendell felt sick to his stomach as he saw the direction this was headed. "I don't understand," he said.

"According to Brice, who we picked up in Florida and extradited to Dallas, you sent his father into bankruptcy after he sold you part of his business. You stripped the assets and, according to his son, told him to sue you. He tried, spending the last of his money, but you dragged it out in court until you knew he couldn't keep going without the kind of money you had. Arnold Schultz died by suicide six months ago." The agent held up his hand as if he thought Wen was about to object. Under other circumstances, he would have. But right now, he was too shocked at what he was hearing. "I'm only telling you why Brice Schultz said he wanted to kill you."

"I didn't know," he said, a weak response at best. He could have argued that it had only been business.

That he was only doing what wealthy men across the country did on a daily basis. The country had a history of tycoons who'd operated the same way. But he held his tongue.

"You might take this as a warning, Mr. Forester," the agent said. "You have a history of these types of business deals. Arnold Schultz wasn't the only one to take you to court but couldn't afford to keep fighting."

Wendell heard him loud and clear. *Watch your back. There are no doubt others out there who want you dead.*

Some as close as Powder Crossing.

CHAPTER TWENTY-THREE

WHEN THE HOTEL suite door opened, Wendell couldn't help but stare. Charlotte Stafford had always been a beautiful woman. The years hadn't diminished that beauty. Time had only accentuated it. She wore cowboy attire—jeans, a Western shirt and boots—but on her, it was all very feminine and sexy as hell.

But what had appealed to him the first time he met her was the spirit of fire that burned bright in her. She was the kind of woman who didn't love easily, but once she did she loved with all of her heart. She was the kind of woman every man dreamed of.

Unfortunately, she'd always been in love with Holden McKenna over on Powder River. He'd never been there until recently. Now he owned her ranch, so he wasn't expecting a warm welcome.

"Did I catch you at a bad time?" he asked.

She studied him with those beautiful green eyes of hers, her expression giving nothing away. She could invite him in—or pull a gun and shoot him. With Charlotte, one never knew.

"Wendell," she said as if she'd been expecting

him. "Thank you again for letting CJ be buried on Stafford Ranch."

"It was such a small thing to ask, especially given how everything went down." He studied her for a moment. "It's been a while, but I can say you haven't changed a bit?" He saw something in those green eyes that assured him she definitely hadn't changed, and he should be very careful. "I thought we should talk."

She stepped aside to let him enter. "I'd ask what you were doing here, but I heard you're now in possession of my ranch."

"I heard you'd left town and turned the ranch over to your sons. I thought maybe you'd lost interest in it since I also heard you're engaged to Holden McKenna." He cocked a brow at her. "Congratulations."

"You're supposed to say *Best wishes* to the bride."

He chuckled. "In your case, I think *congratulations* is more in order."

She gave him a small smile. "All that aside, what are you doing here? You got everything you wanted."

Wendell considered her. "You're wrong about that. But that isn't why I'm here. I wanted to discuss my daughter and your son Ryder."

"I guess I'd better make us a drink," she said and headed over to the bar. "Have a seat. You still drink bourbon neat, don't you?"

"You remembered." He heard her chuckle and suspected she remembered that one weekend down in Dallas all those years ago. She had been in town to buy a bull. Their paths had crossed. He knew he'd caught her at a vulnerable time, and he hadn't told her that he was married. After that weekend, she'd gone back to Montana, making it clear she wanted nothing to do with him—especially after a confrontation with his wife.

"Are you sure there is anything to discuss?" she asked now as she handed him his drink and took a seat on the couch next to him. "Ryder is homeless. We all are, thanks to you."

"That's what I want to talk to you about." He took a sip of his drink. Charlotte had a way of looking at him that made him think she could see right to his tarnished soul. "I regret the way it happened. I was sorry to hear about your son CJ."

She nodded. "Me too. But if it hadn't been you who bought my family ranch, it would have been someone else. CJ chose his path." Her gaze questioned why he'd chosen his.

"I suppose that Holden told you he tried to buy the ranch back for you?" He saw her surprise. "I told him it wasn't for sale. Later, when I heard that you found most of the money I paid CJ for the place, I thought that you'd contact me." She still said nothing as if determined to wait him out. "You're not helping me out here," he said with an edgy chuckle. He was never nervous when it came to business. But he usually didn't deal with hardened women like Charlotte Stafford.

He finished his drink and put down his glass on the coffee table. "Here's the thing. I wanted to

see you. That's why I'd hoped you would call."
He raised both hands. "I know you're engaged,
and Holden is the man you've always loved. I just
wanted to see you. I'm going to give the ranch to
Ryder and Victoria."

She actually looked surprised. He watched her
take a sip of her drink before she spoke. "You're
assuming they're getting married and that way you
still have a connection to the ranch?"

He laughed. "This probably won't surprise you,
but neither of them want anything to do with me.
Victoria's in love with your son, and I think he
might feel the same. I had planned to drill for methane on the property, but changed my mind. Once I
sign it over to them, I'm hands-off."

Charlotte nodded. "You're doing this for your
daughter. She's still mad at you. The things we do
for our children . . . But you'll lose a lot of money
and not on just what you gave CJ. It sounds like an
expensive way to get her to talk to you again."

"I just want her to be happy. Will my giving the
ranch to Victoria and Ryder be a problem for your
other children?"

She shook her head. "Like me, they are more
interested in having the ranch in the family. If this
works, will it mean we're going to be seeing more
of you in Montana?"

He chuckled at that. "Is that going to be a problem?"

"Not for me. There's a good chance you and I
will be sharing grandchildren."

He groaned. "I'm too young for grandchildren."

"Holden and I just had our first. I highly recommend it."

Wen couldn't help smiling at her. "Does Holden know about you and me?"

"He does, but that isn't why he has a problem with you," she said.

"The way I got the ranch." He nodded.

"Don't worry. I can see the McKenna and the Stafford ranches as one large ranch in the future. Brand and Birdie, I believe, have their own plans, but will eventually come back to the Powder River and home. At least I hope so. I would love for us all to be one big family."

Wendell couldn't imagine it. He'd only had Victoria. After his wife died, he'd thrown himself into making more money. Now he had a chance to be part of this large, boisterous and growing family.

"That sounds wonderful," he told Charlotte.

RYDER WAS STILL reeling from the explosion days later. He couldn't believe how close he had come to losing Vicky. They'd had to stay in Billings for a few days to answer questions first from airport security, then the cops and finally the FBI. In the middle of all of it, the last thing he'd expected was the call from his mother about CJ.

"I'm afraid we lost CJ," she said.

His first thought was that his brother had taken off on the lam. "We lost him a long time ago."

"He's dead."

"Dead?" Ryder hadn't expected that. He felt surprise but no shock. His brother had been heading for a violent end for a long time. And from his mother's tone of voice he didn't even consider he'd been in an accident. "Who killed him?"

"Treyton McKenna. Apparently, they quarreled, and they ended up shooting each other," she said.

He heard something in her voice. "Are you all right?"

"I'm sorry it had to end this way for him, but I'll be okay."

She was taking this much better than he would have suspected.

"We're going to have a funeral tomorrow, family only. I'm burying him on the ranch."

"It's not our ranch anymore."

"I'm aware of that," she said. "I got permission from Wendell." He didn't say what he was thinking, remembering what Vicky had told him about their parents possibly having an affair years ago. "I hope you'll be there, Ryder. Treyton's funeral will be first, then CJ's. Both families will be attending, only family."

He almost laughed. For years he'd wished that the rivalry between the families would end. Now they were coming together for funerals for their eldest sons. "I'm still in Billings but planning to head back this morning." He wanted to ask what the rush was on getting CJ buried but realized he didn't really care. Neither he nor his siblings had ever been close to CJ. If anything, they'd avoided him for years because he'd always been so awful with them.

He'd disconnected, still shaken from everything that had been going on, and turned to see Vicky watching him. They'd been staying at the Northern Hotel. But now they would be returning to Powder Crossing for not one but two funerals.

With their twenty-four hours up, Wendell Forester would be taking over the ranch. Ryder wasn't even sure he and his family would be able to get on the ranch to pack up their personal belongings. Now his mother was having a funeral for CJ on the ranch?

"That was my mother," he told Vicky. "CJ's been killed. The funeral is tomorrow on the ranch." She lifted a brow. "Apparently, your father gave her permission. I think it's my mother's way of getting back at CJ in death since he blackmailed her out of the ranch and then sold it. Now he'll be stuck there six feet under. There is so much irony there."

"I'm sorry about CJ," she said, stepping to him.

He took her in his arms just as he had every night since the explosion aboard the plane. They'd held each other, both no doubt lost in the horror of everything that had happened. Claude had been so determined to take his boss's jet back to Dallas, and now he was dead along with JJ Gibson. Thankfully, no one else had been onboard, Ryder had thought again and again. In a matter of minutes, Vicky and her father could have both been on that plane.

"We need to leave for the ranch. Holden left a

message that he has room for us at the McKenna Ranch," he said.

She nodded. "That's good, because my father called. He's staying at the hotel in Powder Crossing. He wants to see me. He sounds really upset."

Ryder wanted nothing to do with Wendell Forester right now or ever. But he was her father. "You should go meet him. I'm sure he's as upset as we are."

The man had been shaken at the airport, but Ryder figured it had worn off by now. Forester was back in Powder Crossing, probably busy making plans for the Stafford Ranch. Hadn't Ryder heard that he had already contacted the methane gas company to start drilling wells on the property? Vicky had been right about her father only wanting what he could get from the land. He'd never had a real interest in the ranch except for what money he could make from it.

Everything felt on hold now until his mother's wedding. He couldn't help but wonder if any of this had changed Vicky's mind about Montana, ranching or him.

Her smile said it hadn't.

VICTORIA WASN'T LOOKING forward to seeing her father. She hadn't seen or talked to him. In truth, she'd avoided him as much as he had her since the plane explosion. So much of this was his fault. She couldn't believe everything that had happened since she'd flown into Billings for the weekend.

She couldn't help but think about Claude as she went upstairs to her father's hotel room. He'd flown up here with her father with such high expectations, thanks to Wendell. He'd had no idea how it would end. Claude had wanted what he'd been offered from his boss—her included. He'd been a fool, yet her father had made him promises he couldn't keep.

Worse, her father had worked with CJ to steal the Stafford Ranch. And now CJ was dead. How could her father not share in the blame?

Walking down the hallway, she felt sick at the thought that she might never be able to forgive her father. They'd often disagreed, but had she ever believed that he would really force her into a loveless marriage?

Victoria tapped lightly at her father's door. She heard footfalls on the other side, and a moment later the door opened. Shock. It was the only emotion she felt at the sight of him. She'd thought he'd be upset about the plane blowing up, but this was so much more. His pale face was drawn, and there were bags under his eyes. It was as if he'd aged overnight.

"Are you all right?" she asked in alarm.

"Not really. Please, come in." He held the door open wide. "I had the café bring up coffee. I thought you might want some."

She nodded. "Thank you."

He motioned her into a chair as he set about pouring her a cup from the carafe sitting nearby. "How are you doing?" he asked as he handed it to her.

"I'm still shaken," she admitted as he took the other chair.

"A hell of a thing. I spent the past few days talking to the FBI again. They finally know what happened." He raked a hand through his hair, sounding breathless. "There was a bomb onboard. It was meant for me."

"A bomb?" She couldn't believe what she was hearing. She'd wanted to believe it was an accident. This made it all the more horrible.

"My former bodyguard, Brice Schultz, planted it and, believing I was on that plane, detonated it."

"Why would he do that?"

Her father looked contrite, almost hanging his head in shame. "He told the feds that I cheated his father out of some property, and the man took his own life."

She didn't know what to say. Hadn't she known how her father operated? He saw something he wanted, and he went after it, no matter who got hurt—just as he had with the Stafford Ranch.

"Victoria, you could have been on that plane with me. You would have been, if Claude had had his way."

"Claude," she said, knowing that she didn't have to say more.

"I know. It's all my fault, all of it." He shook his head. "When I saw Claude holding that gun on you and then later when the plane blew up, I knew I was responsible for all of it."

Seeing how hard he was taking this she couldn't help wanting to come to his defense. "You didn't put the bomb on the plane." But he didn't seem to hear her.

"I didn't mind the media and everyone else calling me names. But when I looked into your eyes and saw how disappointed you were in me, it was no longer a game I'd been playing."

"You knew how I felt about Ryder, yet you worked with CJ to take away the ranch."

"I didn't think you were that serious, and I saw a way to get the ranch. I'd told myself that I was building this dynasty for you. But in truth, it was all about me and what I wanted, what I thought I needed." He leaned toward her, his gaze imploring. "I kept thinking about how you looked at me when you were little. You used to think that there was nothing your father couldn't do. Maybe I was trying to prove that it was true. I'm so sorry."

"I know there are things from your childhood that put this kind of drive to excel in you, but—"

"I always took it too far. That kind of power is intoxicating and dangerous. That's why I wanted to see you before I left for Dallas. I wanted to apologize for the way I treated you and Ryder and so many other people. I'm going to try to make amends in the future."

She hoped he was serious and that once the shock of what had happened wore off, he wouldn't change his mind. "I need to go. Ryder is waiting for

me out at the McKenna Ranch where we're staying.
I would imagine you've already started drilling for
methane on his ranch."

"No, I canceled the drilling. You really care
about the ranch, don't you?"

"I fell in love with it. This lifestyle, Ryder and
his family."

"I can see that. I'm happy for you."

"Thank you. Will I see you before you leave for
Texas?"

"Count on it," he said.

CHAPTER TWENTY-FOUR

"People around the Powder River basin are calling it the wedding of the century," Bailey told her father when she stopped by and found him behind his desk doing ranch business. "Half of them bet it won't happen. The other half are convinced even if it does, it won't last. Holden McKenna and Charlotte Stafford are both too passionate and have spent too many years fighting each other."

"What do you think?" Holden smiled at his daughter as he pushed away his work and motioned her into his office.

"I think no one is about to miss the wedding," she said as she took a chair. "You do realize that there isn't enough room at the church."

He nodded. "I suggested the fairgrounds."

Bailey laughed. It was so good to see her happy. "I guess you heard we eloped."

"I'm not surprised." He didn't tell he was disappointed. He would have thrown her a big wedding if she'd wanted it. He would have at least liked to have seen her get married. "Marriage looks good on you." Did she actually blush, his daughter, a woman of the world? He chuckled. "I suggested we elope, but Lottie wouldn't hear of it. She thinks we owe the community a grand wedding after everything we've put them through."

"That's one way of looking at it," his daughter agreed and looked away. He was sure she didn't feel that she owed the community anything. She'd lost faith in anyone watching out for her after being attacked by a local rancher all those years ago. He couldn't blame her.

"How are book sales?" he asked.

She laughed and met his gaze. "Presales so far are surprisingly good—and not just here. I guess everyone has secrets so can relate to a community like this one. The book comes out just before the wedding."

"I know. Don't worry about it. I just want you to know that I'm so proud of you. What are you working on now?"

Bailey seemed surprised that he knew she was already working on another book. "Promise not to laugh? It's a romance novel."

He did laugh, but not for the reason she might think. "It's about you and the sheriff."

She shrugged. "I have to admit, he might have been my inspiration."

"I can't wait to read it."

"I should get going," she said, getting to her feet. "I'm sure you're busy with the wedding just days away."

"I'm glad you came by." She had no idea how happy her visit made him. They'd been estranged for years. He loved having his daughter back in his life, he thought as he got to his feet.

Bailey smiled. "Actually, my love story isn't the only one that inspired me to write this next book." She met his gaze. "You've always loved her, and even when she didn't want to, she's always loved you. Yours is a great story of two people who have finally found their way back together. It's epic."

He had to laugh. "It's been a lot of things, but *epic*?" He walked her out to her rig and gave her a hug. "What would you like for a wedding present?"

"I have everything I need, Dad. Just be happy." She hugged him back and left.

He watched her go, thinking how much he liked the sound of her calling him *Dad* again. Was it possible his marriage to Lottie would heal not just all the old wounds between the families, but the damage the two of them had done to their children?

OAKLEY HAD TO pee again. She hadn't had that much tea to drink at her mother's small engagement party. She'd barely made it home. As she sat down on the toilet, she noticed that her breasts seemed bigger and they kind of ached. Her eyes widened. Could she have been right? She'd been so sure that she'd felt it, and it really might be true. She was pregnant? She had been so afraid that she was just imagining it. She'd been disappointed too many times, not to mention the miscarriages.

She finished in the bathroom, but her mind was racing. She needed to find out if it was true, didn't she? Hadn't she waited long enough? With a start, she remembered that extra pregnancy test she'd hidden in the back of the cabinet. She'd hidden it because it was a constant reminder of her failures. She should have thrown it away, but that would have made her feel as if she'd given up all hope.

Locking the door in case Pickett came back too soon, she pulled out the test. Her hands were trembling, making her angry at herself. She'd been trying so hard not to get her hopes up, and here she was now afraid. She shouldn't have already peed. But to her relief, she had no problem getting the stick wet.

Now all she had to do was wait. She timed it on her phone and paced her new bathroom, thinking how much she loved the house Pickett had built her with all the extra bedrooms for the children they would have.

"You're going to jinx it," she'd cried when he'd showed her the design.

"We will fill those bedrooms, I promise." He'd kissed her then, and she forgot about it—until now.

The timer on her phone dinged, making her jump. She wished Tilly was here to look. Her hand shaking even worse, she finally got up the courage to look. Tears were already filling her eyes before she saw the results. She had to blink them away and do a double take. She was pregnant!

Her heart pounded, yet she warned herself of what had happened the two other times. She wouldn't tell

Pickett. She'd call the doctor and make an appointment. She wouldn't tell anyone until she was sure this one would take.

But she was *pregnant*. In the mirror, she saw the wide grin on her face. This one was going to take, she thought, and hugged her flat belly.

THE SUN ROSE over the mountains on the day of the wedding as if anxious to get the show on the road. Holden had been awake for hours. He felt as if he had to pinch himself. Was this really happening?

In town, Charlotte saw the sun rise from the hotel room. Her heart lifted at the thought of being Mrs. Holden McKenna before the day was out. She'd waited years for this and could hardly believe that it was finally happening. No matter what happened today, nothing was going to spoil this, she told herself. She was finally marrying the man she had loved since she was a girl.

Holden sat behind his desk as the sun rose, studying the plans for the cabin he was having built beside the creek where he and Lottie used to meet. Some of his best memories were of those sun-filled days lying naked in the tall grass at the water's edge. It would be their getaway, only accessible by horse or foot.

With a smile, he rose as Elaine called that breakfast was being served. It would just be the two of them like it had been for a long time now. His children were grown and on their own. Even Holly

Jo had gone to sleep over last night, but promised she'd be at the wedding. She was coming with her friend Gus, a nice boy from school.

He couldn't believe how quickly she was growing up and thought of that girl he'd gone to get after her mother had died. He'd had no idea what he was getting into, but he'd promised her mother if anything happened, he would take care of the girl.

Elaine was all smiles as he joined her at the huge dining room table. "I've dreamed of this day," she said, sounding close to tears.

"You and me both." He looked around at the empty chairs. Soon they would all be filled with family meals, he told himself. Sunday dinner would become an event. "We need to get a high chair," he said as they sat down.

"It will be a while before your granddaughter needs a high chair, but I'll put it on the list. That won't be all you'll need when you and Lottie baby-sit her."

He smiled at the thought and felt himself get emotional.

Elaine rose to put an arm around his shoulders. "I'm so happy for you."

Long before the sun rose, Tilly Stafford Mc-Kenna finished feeding her baby daughter and put her down again to sleep. She knew she wouldn't be able to go back to bed herself, not with the wedding today. She and Oakley were the attendants. She told herself that this was really happening.

So why was she worried? Because she'd grown

up worrying about what her mother might do. True, Charlotte seemed to have changed. She was a grandmother now, and she was getting married to the man she had always loved. So what was the problem?

Tilly shook her head. If CJ and Treyton were alive, there would be reason for concern. It would have been just like her brother to try to ruin the wedding. Maybe there wasn't anything to worry about, she thought as she climbed in beside Cooper just for a few minutes, she promised herself. He took her in his arms. His body was so warm with sleep and felt so good. She wouldn't fall back to sleep. She just needed this because it was the one place she felt everything would be all right.

Ryder lay studying the woman in the bed next to him and smiling. He told himself he had no reason to be this happy. The ranch was gone, he didn't know what he was going to do tomorrow, and all he knew was ranching.

But he was in love, so nothing seemed to matter except Vicky.

She looked so beautiful, so peaceful, so damned sexy lying there. He realized with a start that he trusted this woman not just with his heart, but his life and future. She opened her eyes as if feeling his gaze on her, smiled and closed them again.

"What are you doing?" he asked.

"Dreaming about you," she said.

"That's good. The wedding is today."

Her eyes opened. "I know. I'm excited," she said, no longer looking sleepy. "I finally get to meet your whole family." He groaned at the thought. "What?" she said, eyes widening. "You don't want me to meet them?"

"It's not that. It's my family." He leaned over to kiss her. "They're going to love you. But you might regret getting involved with me."

"Never," she said, closing her eyes as she reached for him. "Come back to bed."

Ryder hadn't asked Vicky how her meeting with her father had gone at his hotel. She'd been quiet ever since. He wondered if she could truly be happy living on a ranch in Montana with him. He was sure her father wondered the same thing.

"Want to talk about it?" he asked finally. "I never asked how things went with your father."

She blinked and sat up. "My father thinks he can change. He seems determined to do so. He says he's going to make amends for the things he's done. I think the plane blowing up and him finding out the bomb was meant for him has really shaken him. He did say he canceled the methane drilling on the ranch. He was surprised we were staying here on the McKenna Ranch since he has yet to take over yours."

Ryder couldn't help being skeptical. Once the shock of the jet blowing up passed, he figured Wendell Forester would go back to what he seemed to enjoy most: making money. But he held his tongue. "That's good. So it went okay."

She nodded. "It just felt sad. He looked so awful. This really did take a toll on him. I'm sure he'll snap back fast enough and probably change his mind about a lot of things . . . You're sure it's okay for you to bring me to the wedding as your date?"

"There is no way they would have let me come without you," he said as he leaned over and kissed her. Their relationship had happened so quickly that neither of them had really defined it, he realized. "Tomorrow, after this wedding is over, let's go for a horseback ride. Would you like that?"

"I would love that," she said, smiling, eyes bright. "Now, come back to bed."

CHAPTER TWENTY-FIVE

VICTORIA HAD BEEN to her share of huge, extravagant weddings. She'd thought that she'd seen it all, until the wedding of Charlotte Stafford and Holden McKenna. People, it appeared, had come from far and wide. She was shocked when Ryder told her that it was an open invitation. No actual invitations had been sent out. Everyone in the entire county and beyond was invited.

"That's ridiculous," she said as he tried to find a place to park within two miles of the church. "How would the caterer know how much food to prepare?"

He laughed. "Caterer? No, you forget we live on two huge ranches. Holden has had his ranch foreman Deacon Yates cooking enough barbecued beef to feed the entire county, and that doesn't even count how many hogs they have cooking in the pits. I hate to think how many gallons of baked beans and potato salad Elaine has made for the event. Trust me, there will be plenty of food. The only thing that was ordered, from what I heard, was the cake," he said as they got out and walked toward the church with the crowd headed that way. "There's a woman in town who makes wedding cakes. Jodee has probably been baking for a week. At least my mother had the good sense to move the reception out to the fairgrounds."

"The reception is at the fairgrounds?" she asked and laughed. No wonder most of the people attending the wedding were dressed in jeans and boots and fancier Western shirts.

"There are lights out there for the dance. Remember that band that played at the bar the night we went into town?"

"The Deacon Brown Blues Band," she said.

"They're coming up from Wyoming for this. But there will be a half-dozen different bands that will play before the night is over."

She shook her head. "You people really know how to throw a party."

"You'd best believe it." They'd reached the church. Ryder took her hand as he saw Brand at the door. The huge church was already full, standing-room only, but the doors were all open and chairs had been placed in the lawn next to the church clear out to the edge of the old town cemetery.

"Tilly saved you two seats at the front," Brand told them. "How did you get out of door duty?"

Ryder just smiled. "Now I'm Mother's favorite."

His brother slugged him in the arm. "Get in there. It's about to start."

"I hope they keep it short," he said under his breath, and they walked to the front where his sisters were waving impatiently for them. "And it begins."

RYDER HAD TO admit, his mother made a beautiful bride. He'd never seen her so happy, he realized because all his life she'd been struggling to run the ranch and work through her relationships— especially the one she battled almost daily with Holden McKenna. They had fought over water, land and methane wells. They had butted heads for years. No wonder so many people had turned out to see how this ended.

The wedding was both beautiful and blissfully short. Everyone cheered at the end and threw rice as the happy couple made their way out to the fairgrounds with everyone following in their vehicles.

"Why are they honking their horns?" Vicky asked, her eyes bright with excitement.

"They're happy, and it's a way to congratulate the happy couple."

"I thought maybe they'd already started drinking," she said jokingly.

"I'm sure there is some of that as well," he said with a laugh. He glanced over at her, surprised by how happy she looked. Weddings apparently did that to some people. Or maybe it was even the idea of love ever after.

"Well, what do you think of the families?" he asked. "You got to meet them all. Even Holden's youngest son Duffy drove up from the oil fields of Wyoming for the wedding. And Bailey and the sheriff were there. Her book full of the secrets of the people who live in the Powder River basin came out yesterday. I heard it's a bestseller." He shook his head.

"It was so fun to meet Tilly's husband Cooper and the baby. Did you know they named her River?" Vicky said. "It's cute and so appropriate for where they live."

Ryder wasn't so sure about that. He couldn't help but think about all the razzing he used to get because his name was different, but then again times had changed. Seemed all the kids had unique names. But River for a girl?

"Holly Jo is sweet, huh?" Vicky said. "And that boyfriend of hers, Gus? You can tell he loves her. It's so adorable."

"I adore you," he said and reached over for her hand. The traffic was backed up for miles on the way to the fairgrounds. He didn't mind. He liked sitting in the warm cab of his pickup with this woman.

She smiled at him. "And your sisters, I love them. Oakley was a lot quieter today than I expected. I asked her if she was all right, and I realize she was just busting at the seams to tell me something."

Ryder wanted to laugh at how quickly Vicky had picked up the local expressions.

"Oakley is pregnant with twins! *Twins!* Isn't that wonderful?"

"That is," he said, hoping the pregnancy went well. She'd always wanted kids, and he knew that she and Pickett had struggled some.

"Birdie might be pregnant too," she whispered. "I guess it's top secret. I'm not sure even Brand knows yet."

Ryder shook his head. "Love is certainly in the air." He'd also seen their ranch manager Deacon Yates with Elaine. They looked very close. He wouldn't be surprised to hear wedding bells in the near future and couldn't be happier for them.

Once at the fairgrounds, music echoed off the mountainside, the scent of barbecued beef and roasted pork filled the air, and lines began to form. Tables had been set up out in the arena and ranch hands tapped the kegs of beer and were filling cups.

There was a roar of excitement along with the music. He put his arm around Vicky. "We have a long night ahead. You ready for this?"

"I want to experience it all," she said, grinning at him.

"And we shall," he promised as they joined the crowd.

CHAPTER TWENTY-SIX

THE HORSEBACK RIDE was a little later than Ryder had planned. They'd stayed at the wedding reception until the sun came up—and they weren't alone. Everyone said it was the best party ever. He had to agree.

At some point his mother and Holden had sneaked away, but not before she'd sought him out and pulled him aside.

"I have something for you," she said and pressed a small velvet box into his hand.

"What is this?"

She gave him an impatient look. "It's your great-grandmother's wedding ring. I think it would be perfect for Victoria."

"Don't you think it's a little soon for this?" He had to ask since it was something he'd been asking himself.

She made a dismissive sound. "You're in love with her. Do both of you a favor, don't put it off. Get on with your life. It's the best advice I can give you."

He opened the box and saw the simple gold band and the tiny diamonds around it. "It's perfect for her." He looked up, surprised that his mother some-how would know that.

She smiled. "I promise you that your life is going to be blessed. Ask her to marry you. Don't worry about the future." Her smiled broadened. "It's already written in the stars," she said, glancing sky-ward at the blazing galaxy.

And then Holden was there, taking her away. Ryder pocketed the ring as he returned to Vicky.

"They're playing our song," she said, taking his hand and leading him toward the makeshift dance floor in the middle of the arena.

He laughed. "We have a song?" But the moment he pulled her into his arms, he remembered it. They'd heard it that night in town, which now seemed like so long ago. It was something about a storm coming. "You sure you want this to be our song?"

Nodding, she said, "I now love storms, and I love you."

Ryder could feel the small velvet box in his pocket as he smiled. "It's perfect, just like you." He pulled her close. It wasn't too soon to ask her. The timing was perfect.

IT WAS LATE afternoon before they saddled up for their ride. Once in the saddle, Victoria turned her face up to the low-hanging summer sun and knew this was exactly what she'd needed. The wedding had been amazing, meeting the family, partying with friendly people until the starlight.

Ryder's brother-in-law Cooper McKenna had taken care of the animals while they were tied up in Billings. She'd been worried about Vic, the new colt, but Brand had gotten out of the hospital and assured her that Vic was doing great.

She'd loved seeing the colt when they returned. "He's grown so much," she'd exclaimed. "He's so beautiful."

Ryder had smiled as they watched the colt run around the pasture for a moment before the two of them headed out.

As the sun lolled in the sky over the mountains to the west, they rode out toward the wide-open spaces. Victoria breathed in the afternoon as if she could tuck it into her heart and never forget it. She closed her eyes, letting the sun warm her face, enjoying being back in the saddle.

When she opened her eyes, Ryder was riding next to her, looking at her. She smiled, feeling his love in his gaze. She couldn't remember ever feeling this happy, yet she was going to have to go back to Dallas soon. She'd been debating if she should keep her apartment. If she didn't, she'd have to pack up her things and move them. She also needed to talk to the art center where she'd worked.

Ryder loved her, she knew that. She just didn't know about her future. It felt more tenuous than his. Where were they going to live? She and Ryder had fallen in love and talked about buying their own ranch, but they really hadn't talked about the immediate future. Everything had happened so quickly.

She was going to have to make some decisions pretty soon.

She pushed that thought away, determined to enjoy the rest of this day. Tomorrow she would tell him that she had to leave for a while. She wasn't sure how he would take it. His future was up in the air as well. How could either of them plan on tomorrow at this point?

As THEY RODE, Ryder was also thinking about the future. His mother was right. It was time to make plans for the future—their future. He loved her. He wanted to be with her always. He knew it was a huge step. Did he really know this woman? He looked over at her.

He knew Vicky, but he wasn't sure about Victoria. She hadn't mentioned going back to Dallas. He knew she had an apartment back there. Her old life and all her belongings were there. Not to mention the short time they'd even known each other. He could just imagine what Brand would say, let alone Tilly. Oakley would be all for him asking Vicky to marry him, but that was Oakley.

You can't seriously be thinking of asking her to marry you? That was Brand adding his two cents' worth in Ryder's head.

If Ryder wanted Vicky to stay, he had to make his feelings known. As they reached a rise, he reined in his horse, and Vicky did too. The view of the river bottom was beautiful from here. Soon summer would be over. The cottonwood leaves would begin to turn, and winter would come sweeping in with snow and cold.

He dismounted and ground-tied his horse as she climbed down as well.

"I think this is my favorite spot on the entire ranch," Vicky said as she moved to the edge to look down at the dark-leafed cottonwoods that marked the long trail the Powder River flowed to reach the Yellowstone River.

"This is my favorite spot as well," he said as he joined her. He hated to think that her father now owned it. He feared what the man would do with the ranch. But like his mother, he knew the land was lost and they had to move on.

He'd never been afraid of much, yet right now he felt terrified that Vicky might say no. He had nothing to offer her. No ranch and a questionable future, and they had spent only days together. She'd never seen a Montana winter, never mind come home to find a newborn calf in her bathtub because it would have frozen to death if he hadn't brought it inside.

For some reason, he recalled once overhearing his mother telling a friend that she'd fallen in love with Holden at first sight when they were kids. She'd said to herself that day, "I'm going to marry that man."

And look how that had turned out, he reminded himself. It had taken them years to finally be together. Ryder sure as the devil didn't want to make that mistake.

He took off his Stetson, raked a hand through his

hair and dropped to one knee. Vicky looked over at him, at first appearing alarmed, then surprised. "I know this is probably something you aren't ready for, might never be ready for, but dang it, Vicky, I have to do it. Nothing about our meeting or our falling in love has been typical. I never dreamed that you might come to enjoy this life, let alone want to stay. But I sure want you to. I love you. I can't see that ever changing. I want to marry you. You can take all the time you need to think about it. You don't have to say anything right now—"

"Yes."

Ryder thought he hadn't heard her correctly. "Yes?"

"Yes, Ryder Stafford, I would love to marry you. I thought you would never ask. It's been over a week since we've been together."

He laughed at that as he rose to his feet. "You sure?"

"Stop sounding so surprised. I'm sure. I've never been one for convention. Also, it doesn't take me long to make up my mind when I want something. You should know that." She grinned. "When something feels right—"

He grabbed her and kissed her. "Wait." He dropped back down on his knee, reached in his pocket and pulled out the small box.

She blinked. "I'm not that materialist girl you thought I was, remember. I would be happy with just a single gold band on my finger on my wedding day and I'm your woman."

Ryder laughed. "It belonged to my great-grandmother. I think it's perfect for you." He opened the box and saw her eyes light up.

"Oh, Ryder," she said. "It's beautiful. I love it. I want you to put it on my finger the day we get married."

WORD OF ANOTHER Stafford wedding spread through the community. Victoria wasn't surprised when she got the call from her father even before she could call him with the news. He wanted to meet in town.

"You're really going to marry a Montana rancher?" he said and chuckled once they were seated in a back table at the hotel bar. The place was empty this time of day. "I have to admit, I'm a little surprised. This change in you from the daughter I insisted meet me in Montana to the one you are now is kind of drastic. Are you sure about this?"

"I've never been surer of anything. All the party-ing, the clothes, the penthouse, it all just feels su-perficial after meeting Ryder and spending time at the ranch. This life energizes me. I'm going to be a ranchwoman, and I can't wait. I love his family. My future sister-in-law Tilly is going to teach me how to cook. Oakley has promised that I can help with the fraternal twins she's having. One boy, one girl. It will be good practice for when Ryder and I have our own babies."

"I'm just surprised," her father said. "Are you sure you're up for this life?"

"I have a lot to learn, but I'm ready. We're going

to pool our money and buy a ranch. It won't be as large as the Stafford Ranch, but we just need enough space for our kids to run around."

He chuckled again. "I've been waiting for this moment. All I've ever wanted was for you to be happy. I'd hoped marriage would do it. I was just wrong about what kind of man it would take. The Stafford Ranch is yours and Ryder's. It's my engagement present. I should never have taken it away from him and his family."

"Are you serious?" She sounded more astonished than he had about the engagement. "Why would you do that?"

"Because it's the right thing to do. And tell your fiancé that it comes with no strings at all. I'm signing it over to the two of you." He pulled the legal paperwork from his pocket. "I've already talked to Charlotte about it," he said. "She and I plan to be grandparents together."

"I see," she said, wondering if she should be worried.

"It isn't like that." Her father smiled at her. "Charlotte's always been in love with Holden. She's offered me a family to enjoy along with my daughter. I'd be a fool to miss out on it."

Victoria felt tears burn her eyes, and she jumped up to hug him. "Thank you. I can't tell you what this means to me, to Ryder."

Her father nodded. "Ryder is a good man. I approve."

She couldn't help being touched as well as both

shocked and impressed by his generosity and said as much.

"I told you I was going to make amends for some of the things I've done," he said. "You weren't sure I meant it, were you?"

She sighed and shook her head. "I'm proud of you. What will you do once you make all these amends?"

"Well, I'll probably be broke by then," he said, but smiled. "I might have to start again. I kind of like the idea. Only, this time it will be different."

She certainly hoped so. "Maybe you'll find someone to share your life with, and money won't be your only love."

He shook his head. "I can't imagine that."

"You might surprise yourself."

Her father smiled at that. "Who knows. I'm more open to a lot of things this time around. But you, my daughter, you're my greatest joy. I've always loved you more than making money."

She smiled at that as he handed her back the Stafford Ranch.

A MONTH LATER on a bright sunny day with fall in the air, Victoria and Ryder got married with both the McKennas and the Staffords in attendance, along with her father. The day was perfect—just as Victoria knew it would be when Ryder put that ring on her finger and they promised their love to each other.

She was now part of the people of the Powder

River basin. She had to swallow the lump in her throat as she was surrounded by family for the first time in her life. Ryder took her hand and she looked into his handsome face, seeing a future she'd dreamed of and couldn't wait to start.

The two of them would be writing their own history in this beautiful place where the river flowed true and steady—just like the people who made their lives here.

* * * * *